The Muse

Eliana Vazquez

Copyright

ALSO BY ELIANA VAZQUEZ

Fated Lovers Series

The Muse
The Vow

Poetry

The Evolution of Love

To JJ, my best friend, my pal, my homegirl, my rotten soldier, my sweet cheese, and most importantly my good time girl.

PLAYLIST

Cooks - Still Woozy

Bad Habit - Steve Lacey

Cruel Summer - Taylor Swift

Same To You - The Vamps

K. - Cigarettes After Sex

Toothbrush - DNCE

Wonder - Shawn Mendes

Animal - Neon Trees

Better - Khalid

Sex - EDEN

Sparks Fly - Taylor Swift

Fall in Love with You - Montell Fish

Electric Love - BØRNS

Chapter One

Jasmine

It's a waste of time to stop and think about the past. We're better off sticking the old memories in the back of our minds and refusing to look back at them. It's easier said than done when your mind keeps replaying intimate memories of someone that, after a while, only feels like some kind of dream. But reliving the heartbreak only reminds you of how real it all was.

They were so close within your arms, and then suddenly, they shattered into pieces, never to be contacted, seen, or loved again– or at least not by you.

But sometimes, life has a funny way of throwing it all back at your face even when you want nothing to do with it, like coincidentally coming across your ex-fiancé on Instagram once again engaged, but this time with a prestige heiress who seems to worry more about her photoshoots in front of her Ivy League school than about studying.

Well, maybe I'm just stretching it. I judge her only by her aesthetically pleasing social media profile. And I would be lying if I didn't say I was quite jealous that my ex moved on to someone younger and prettier than me.

Additionally, she's intelligent or well-off because the woman goes to Columbia. Here I am, working at a bookstore that pays me enough to get by with rent and groceries but too little to keep up with my social life. But somehow, I'm still stuck in the same place, rather than taking a chance and beginning to write my novel or owning the book café of my dreams.

Well, that had been a dream that was once ours, but he seemed to focus on another aspiration that didn't involve me. Regardless of my late-night Instagram searches, you can blame fate for having my ex-fiancé, Will, and his soon-to-be wife, Eloise, sitting across from me at a restaurant tonight.

"Can you stop hiding behind the menu?" my best friend Oren asks as he takes the menu out of my hands. I quickly pull it back, shielding myself from the enamors across our table.

"Oren, I am on a mission right now; I am trying my best not to be seen by my ex-fiancé and his fiancée. The last thing I need is for them to come over and pity me for still being in the same position I was in when he left me a year ago." I move the menu back up to cover my face, and though I can't see him, I can imagine Oren shaking his head as he chuckles.

"First of all, who the fuck cares? Second, how the fuck would he know if anything has changed in the last year? It's called lying. Tell him your book is about to be published and that he is currently looking at the new owner of "*Jaz's Book Café.*" I roll my eyes and bring the menu down again, making sure that Oren gets a look at me, cringing at the made-up name for my dream café.

"I would never call it that," I remark. Oren only smirked as he looked back down at his menu.

Oren's vernacular has always been vulgar for as long as I can remember. His parents and little sister Phoebe had moved next door from New York into my little suburban town in New Jersey.

His parents were Greek immigrants who spoke little English but always showed so much love through embraces and meals. Of course, our friendship was tested when our mothers decided they wanted to play Cupid and tried to get us to date. But it had never been that way between Oren and me.

We became great friends, and nothing would ever come between us—not even when he left for Boston to pursue his education in the arts.

"Oren, you know I am not going to lie. Lies only lead to more lies, and I can't keep up. I can barely keep up with my rent, let alone entertain Will and his lover." Oren doesn't hesitate to show his distaste on his face.

"I told you to move in with me; we could turn my office into your room. You don't even need to worry about rent; just focus on writing your novel and looking at different locations you'd be interested in having your book café instead of continuing to work for that dickhead, Marvin."

Marvin Scott was, in fact,t a dickhead, but he did pay me enough to be able to afford rent. Of course, that meant that there wasn't much money to spare. I didn't have any other close friends besides Oren, who I live with, but I wouldn't intrude in his personal space even if he asked. I knew he liked his office and wouldn't take that away from him.

"You could also always share the bed with me; you know I don't mind sharing, Jaz," Oren smirks as he arches his eyebrow up.

I blush in embarrassment, reaching across the table to slap his arm with the menu. "Shut up, you idiot. Don't even mention that again." Oren only laughs at my discomfort. You'd think that after years of meaningless flirting and teasing, I wouldn't get so flustered by his comments.

"Am I so disgusting that you can't even fathom sharing a bed with me? You know we used to cuddle all the time as kids, right?" Oren teases.

Truthfully, I wasn't disgusted at all. Oren was an attractive man. His beautiful Greek attributes would have landed him a role in any Hollywood film about a Greek god. He was tall with a dark head of curls and light green eyes that stood out against his olive-toned skin. What made him even more attractive was that he was an artist of many sorts. The man could draw, paint, and sculpt and was a god behind the camera.

But we had never seen each other as more than friends and wouldn't have wanted to, either.

"You know I don't," I say, sipping my water. "You're very handsome. But I would never want to intervene in your private life like that. Everyone needs their privacy, Oren. I know you love your office space; you keep all your work there. Where would you put all of that? You're a freelance artist; you need an office."

Oren shrugs and looks down at the menu. "Don't worry

about it, Jaz. You know I'd do anything for you. Plus, it gets lonely alone in my New York City apartment."

Living in Jersey could get expensive, and if you were like Oren, living in New York, you would pay an arm and a leg. But that wasn't a problem for Oren. Despite coming from a lower-income household, he had become very successful in his career, which allowed him to enjoy the perks of living luxuriously.

Often, he's hired as a freelance photographer or videographer in another state or country. Sometimes, paying for a couple of months a year becomes silly.

"Oren, I said no already. Just drop it and pick out what you want to order. I'm starving." I mutter.

"Ugh, fine, just promise me you'll at least think about it, Jaz. I could use a roommate, and I plan on getting a cat and some plants, so I would need someone to take care of both when I'm away for work. That would just be a great advantage of having you around."

I knew Oren was bluffing, or at least about getting a cat, not so much about the plants. He was trying to throw anything that would make me say yes.

I rolled my eyes and finally set the menu down, only to have my eyes land on a tall, well-dressed William hovering over our table with his fiancé.

"Jasmine, I can't believe it. I knew it was you. You have not changed one bit."

Ouch.

I mean, I cut my hair; he could at least notice that.

William and I had been together for four years, during which time I maintained my long bundle of curls. During our relationship, we dedicated our weekends solely to ourselves.

We'd lay in bed for hours after our intimate endeavors, and he'd brush his hands through my dark curls, which had made their way down my back. That was until I decided to chop them off after our breakup.

And as much as people liked to view it as some form of lashing out or trying something new after a breakup. I had just done it because he loved it. He would spend his weekends brushing his hands through my curls, and after he left, I wanted the length gone, too.

"Hello, Oren. It's good to see you, too. How's the art going?" William asks, facing Oren, who shows nothing but a blank expression, declaring his disinterest in my ex-fiancé.

William stood over Oren, but even if Oren had been standing up, William would still be a few inches taller than him. He was very well put together in his polo and black slacks, and his dark hair was slicked back, a strand falling over his face. But regardless of the loose strand, it didn't look out of place. But then again, William was never the type to look disheveled. It was one of the few reasons I felt we wouldn't work out right from the beginning.

William came from a wealthy family. His father owned a multi-millionaire tech company, and William was following in his footsteps. Meanwhile, I was just a girl still working at a bookstore, hoping to get by until I found the time to write my novel and hopefully get it picked up.

Even when I met his parents, they did very little to acknowledge me in William's life, even after he had proposed. I guess they had seen the breakup coming from a mile away.

"Great, as always, William," Oren states, setting down his menu, this time looking annoyed at William's presence.

By the whitening of her knuckles, I was guessing that

Eloise seemed to be tightening her grip around William's arm to get his attention. But despite her strong grip, William didn't seem to be aware until the clearing of her throat reminded him of her presence.

"Oh, sorry," William says, turning to face Eloise. "Jasmine, Oren, this is my fiancé, Eloise Richardson." William states, bringing his arm around her waist and pulling her closer. It would be a lie if I said that Eloise was all photoshopped on her social media, but the woman looked just as beautiful.

She was tall and slender, to the point where you could confuse her for a model with her sleek blonde hair and the blue eyes that matched William's so perfectly. The blue silk dress she was wearing complimented them even more.

"Hello, it's very nice to meet you—especially you, Jasmine. William has told me so much about you. It's finally nice to meet the first woman who had my Will ready to tie the knot before meeting me." Eloise giggles.

I wasn't sure if I should be ecstatic that Will had me on his mind enough to speak about me to his gorgeous fiancé or annoyed that her voice seemed to somewhat taunt my past with William.

There was never a doubt in my mind that William wouldn't have ended up with someone like Eloise. She had been the heiress his parents had wanted him with initially.

"What brings you here?" Will asks.

"We are famished, William; why else is anyone at a restaurant?" Oren responds with an aggressive tone, which only insinuates the desire to have him away from our table.

"I know that, Oren, but Jasmine isn't a big fan of Thai," William states.

"No, she isn't a fan of Pad Thai, but she loves everything else on the menu, especially pho." Oren remarks.

"Did I hear you say fiancé before, William? Congratulations to both of you. You must be excited." I cut in to diminish any argument between the two men.

Oren was never a big fan of William, but he tolerated him because I had asked him to. That was until he decided to break up with me a couple of months after our engagement. Since Oren made it his duty to be William's biggest hater, the fact that he hadn't thrown himself out of his chair to attack William showed a lot of self-restraint. "Yes, look at the ring; isn't it so precious?" Eloise asks, extending her hand towards my eyes to show the enormous rock sitting delicately on her finger. It was larger than my own, but not that size mattered at all; it was just enormous. I had seen them in the pictures, but I assumed Photoshop had made them stand out even more than usual. Obviously, I stood corrected.

"It's very gorgeous, Eloise. Again, congratulations." I say, looking down at my own finger, which William's engagement ring had once hugged. Oren brings his hand over to my own and grips it gently. I look up and see his little menacing smile, which means he has something up his sleeve.

"Honestly, where are my manners? Congratulations to both of you. It seems like both you two and Jaz and I have new doors opening up for us." Oren states, tightening his hold on my hand.

"You two are engaged as well?!" Eloise exclaims in excitement while William's face pales right before me.

"God, no, well, at least not yet, but we are currently moving in together. We want to test the waters before committing to living together for life." Oren says nonchalantly.

If there was ever a moment in which I wanted to strangle Oren, this would be that very moment. Oren always liked making up little white lies or pranks, but this was stupid and too big of a lie.

"Since when– how long, wait, you guys are dating?" William asked, a shocked expression on his face. As terrible as it might be to admit, it brought me some pleasure knowing that William seemed to care.

"William, you always knew that Jaz and I had a connection. I mean, we've been friends for sixteen years. I guess when you left, everything seemed to come together, and one thing led to another, and now, we are madly in love." Oren gives him a sly grin. I swear I could see William's jaw tighten at the smug look on Oren's face.

Oren was enjoying this too much, and it was time to end this conversation.

"Well, congratulations to both of you! Will you be having a housewarming party?" Eloise asks cheerfully. Now that Oren and I are madly in love, there is no need to be so nasty towards us anymore.

But the answer was going to be no. The last thing I needed was for this to become a theatrical play.

"We are. This upcoming Saturday. You two are welcome to come. William, you have the same number, don't you? We will just send you our address, and you two are welcome to come if you'd like." Oren says.

I kicked his shin from under the table, causing him to jolt slightly. He looked at me and rolled his eyes as if I were being dramatic. He was taking this lie out of hand and needed to stop.

William opens his mouth to respond, but Eloise quickly beats him to it.

"We would love to be there, right, William?" Eloise asks, focusing her gaze on William.

"Yeah, why not? Jasmine, you can send me the address and time, and we will definitely make it there," William says, but his jaw tightens, indicating his irritation with the whole situation.

Eloise squeals in excitement before clapping her hands. "Yay! This is so exciting. I cannot wait to see you guys this Saturday. It was so nice meeting you two. But we should be returning to our table and leaving you so you can enjoy your dinner."

"Yes, it was great meeting you, Eloise, and it was great seeing you, William." Oren murmurs before they both turn around and walk back to their table. I nudged Oren again from under the table to have him look back at me.

"What the fuck was that, Oren?" I yell in a whispered tone.

"Whatever do you mean, my love?" He teases.

"You know what the fuck I mean. Why would you even say that? Why would you let your lie go that far?" I fall back onto my seat, crossing my arms over my chest, glancing around the entire restaurant, too annoyed with Oren to look back over at him.

"Jaz, there isn't much of a lie. You were already going to move in with me. I only added in a little spice by saying we were lovers." I turn my head back towards Oren and glare at him.

"But that's the thing; I am not moving in with you. I already have an apartment." I reiterate.

It was always typical of Oren to try to help me however he could, but I didn't need his help. I am doing just fine on my own.

"Well, we'll have to let your landlord know as soon as possible that you are leaving, so we should also start inviting a couple more people to the housewarming party. If it's just us four, it'll be awkward." Oren rambles as he calls the waiter to take our order.

"Oren, I am not moving in with you," I utter, hoping that he will listen and stop this nonsense this time.

"Fine, then you can text William and tell him that it was all a lie and that we were just trying to make him jealous." Oren's stare battles my own from across the table, and even though there's chatter among us, I can only hear the silence between us. I clench my hands around the table's cloth before letting go and letting out a sigh of frustration.

Oren knew I would rather play this game with him than admit to William that I had only agreed to this lie. I enjoyed seeing William's blank expression when he discovered I was with Oren.

"Fine, but I am paying half the rent, and you're paying for the moving company." I snap.

"Yes, love, don't you worry about anything. I've got this under control."

I hope he did because something told me we would get into a bigger mess than we were already in.

Chapter Two

Jasmine

Oren was my best friend, and it was hard to stay angry with him, especially when his heart always seemed to be in the right place. At least, it seemed like it did when it came to me. Believe it or not, this isn't the first time Oren and I have pretended to be a couple.

In the seventh grade, this one boy, Gus Henderson, kept picking on me and making rude statements about my appearance. It wasn't until Oren, who was fed up with the teasing, came up to me and kissed me right in front of Gus and made sure to let him and everyone know that if any of them said anything to me again, he'd make sure to punch the teeth right out of their mouth.

Of course, that threat got Oren a week of detention, but it got me a peaceful rest of the year.

"Cherry dipped, right?" Oren asks, breaking me away from my memories.

"What was that?" I ask in confusion.

"You want the vanilla cherry-dipped ice cream cone, right?" He repeats, pointing towards the ice cream truck's menu.

"Oh, yeah, that's fine."

Oren nods, turns to the man, and begins ordering our dessert. Oren had asked, but he knew what my response would be. That was always my go-to, and he was chocolate with rainbow sprinkles. Our orders seemed to stay the same from childhood to adulthood. I think we're just people who enjoy consistency.

"Here you go, love. This should help simmer down the anger you have towards me." Oren says, handing over the ice cream cone. I roll my eyes and sigh before taking the cone from his hand.

"You can't buy your forgiveness through food." I take a lick of the ice cream. Its taste has remained consistent, so I have always chosen it. The moment this ice cream tastes even a tad bit different, I'll know the world must be coming to an end.

"Jaz, I am not trying to buy your forgiveness. I am only providing my best friend with dessert and a nice walk in the park. If I wanted to be forgiven for something, I would've just said,d 'I'm sorry,' but I'm not going to say it because I am not sorry about anything". Oren explains, putting his arm over my shoulder as we walk through the park.

This was typical of Oren; he never apologized unless he truly meant it. However, it could be frustrating because it meant he was too hard-headed to admit he was wrong about most things. At least it helped you know that he was sincere when he uttered those apologetic words.

"Jaz, I was thinking I'd go by your place tomorrow and help with the packing. We have to get all your stuff ready by Saturday if we want to host that housewarming party. Honestly, I am looking forward to this because I've never had one before." Oren continues with his banter, but the thought of having to see William again makes my stomach turn.

"It's fine. I can pack it on my own; there's not much to pack anyway." I reassure. I shrugged his arm off my shoulder and walk ahead of him to show that I was still annoyed with his lie. I can hear Oren stop in his tracks and sigh before jogging towards me.

"Jaz, come on now, don't be annoyed. An apology is what you're looking for, and you know I won't apologize for that. I did what I did to show that dickhead that you deserve much more than he was willing to give. He should be throwing the tantrum of his life right now for missing out on an opportunity to have called you his." I stop in my tracks to face him and hear him out. If I didn't get an apology, at least I would get some explanation for his lies.

"Jaz, I want you to show him that you are more than just a girl who works at a bookstore with dreams that she hopes to aspire to. I want to show that you are the girl who is currently having those dreams come true. So, come on, let's do this as a team. Let's show this dickhead what he missed out on." Oren grasps me by the waist and brings me closer to him.

If I were honest, or if any other man were holding me the way Oren was right now, I'd probably melt in their arms, but this was Oren, so this did nothing but frustrate me.

"I understand where you are coming from, Oren, but I

need you to let me fight my own battles. I don't need to prove anything to Will; I am doing great. I'm happy, and that's all that matters." I push Oren away and walk back toward my apartment, feeling like my bold statement might have gotten through his thick skull.

"Great! So, I will come by tomorrow morning and help with the packing!" Oren shouts.

I ROLL MY EYES AND JUST KEEP MY MOUTH SHUT. NOTHING was going to get Oren to back out from his stupid idea.

I hated restless nights, but not as much as I hated waking up to Oren knocking on my door at seven in the morning. "Well, hello there, my love. How can you still look so beautiful after just waking up?" Oren walks into my apartment and lands a kiss on my cheek. I wipe my cheek and slam the door shut before walking to my couch and letting my body fall onto it.

"Come on, Jaz, you can't start the big move if you're sleeping all day," Oren states, lifting my legs to sit on the couch and lay my legs over his lap.

"I don't want to move. I want to stay here and sleep." I mumble, my eyelids still glued shut.

"Come on, Jaz. We don't have too much to do. We just have to compile the things you want into a pile, and any other things you no longer want will be put in a separate pile for donations." Oren rubs his hand gently up and down my legs, making me want to sink deeper into the couch and sleep.

"I'm too tired," I manage to say between yawns.

Besides, how the hell do I get stuck with having to do all this work when it wasn't even my idea?

"Fine, you can stay and slouch all weekend long." Oren removes my legs from over his lap and gets up. "But I, on the other hand, am going to start packing everything in your underwear drawer." He says, making a run towards my bedroom.

I quickly bolt up and follow him to stop his perverted antics from continuing. I reach my bedroom door only for it to be locked. "Oren, don't you dare go in my underwear drawer."

The problem wasn't necessarily the underwear within the drawer. It wouldn't be something that Oren hadn't seen before. It was just us for a long time before I had settled down with William, and I never thought I would shy away from changing myself in front of Oren. Of course, he's never seen me fully naked; that would've been a little too intimate for my liking. Speaking of intimacy, that would be the same reason why I'm banging on my bedroom door, calling out Oren's name in hopes that he will stop looking through my drawers before he finds my vibrator.

"Jaz, I'm seeing a lot of granny panties in here. You know you should try to remember that you're a twenty-five-year-old woman. Finally, a thong, and it's red. That's a sexy color, Jasmine."

"Oren!" I scream, banging on the door once again. "Stop it, you perv!"

"Perv? Well, I'm not the one hiding a vibrator within my drawers, Jaz." Oren opens the door wide and presses the button on the vibrator, making it buzz loudly. I drag my hand across my face, mortified. I know it's completely normal for a woman to need and want some sort of release, but some things should just be kept private, and this was one of those things. I try to snatch the vibrator away from his hands, but he brings it up high, making me jump. I reach over to his shoulders, my hands holding on tightly to them as I jump and wrap my legs around his waist.

"C'mon, Oren, give it back." I reach up, trying to grab it without making us fall to the ground.

"Give what back?" Oren teases.

"You know what!"

"Oh, come on, Jaz, I know you can say it. If you can use it, you can say it." Oren teases. I unwrap myself from him and cross my hands in front of my chest.

"Now, since we're a couple, you won't need this, so we can donate it to a lonesome lady." Oren leans against the wall, a sly smirk playing on his lips.

"Stop it!" I say, slapping him repeatedly on his arm.

"Jaz, you better stop before I use it on you."

I stop and look up at him, flustered, surprised by the words that just came out of his mouth. His grin turns into a smirk, knowing that his commentary is riling me up. Oren hands me my vibrator before giving me a wink and walking over to my unmade bed, tossing himself onto it. I quickly put it back into its box and shove it back into my drawer. I stand in front of the bed, looking down at Oren, who has his hands behind his head and eyes closed.

"That was way out of line, Oren."

"Me finding your vibrator is out of line? It's not a big deal, love. We all need to release some stress from time to time. What better help than a vibrator?" Oren says with a cheeky grin.

"No, your teasing was out of hand, and I told you I didn't want you to look through my things. Despite that, you still looked through them. It's an invasion of privacy." I say, making Oren open his eyes and adjust himself to look up at me.

"Jaz, let me tell you something. We have undressed in front of each other and have told each other every little secret. I don't think there's anything called privacy within our relationship. Besides, we'll be living together now. I'm surely going to hear your moans in the middle of the night, along with your vibrating friend buzzing from within your bedroom. And you'll probably find some cum stains on the tile wall of the shower."

I scream out in aggravation before grabbing a pillow and hitting him repeatedly with it.

Why was he like this?

"Okay! Okay! I'll stop, I promise!"

Those are the only words I need to hear out of Oren's mouth to stop the pillow abuse.

"Jesus, Jaz, you're a feisty one in the mornings. I'll make sure to remember that. But we should get back on schedule and start by making two separate piles. One to keep and the other one to throw out. Like your granny panties, for instance, we should burn those." Oren says, nodding his head towards the drawer he opened.

"Those are my comfy period panties." I defend, knowing very well those are just my everyday comfy panties.

"Well, according to your drawer, you're on your period every day of the month because there's nothing but granny panties in there." Oren teases.

"Can you leave my underwear alone? I like what I like."

"And I know what men like, and it's definitely something like that red thong," Oren says, opening his eyes to look back at me.

"I know what men like. I just don't want to be liked by men right now, and so my underwear is not something that needs to be a priority."

Oren gets up from the bed and reaches over to place a hand on my cheek, moving strands of hair away from my face and behind my ear. "Well, just let me know when it becomes a priority, love." I groan, slapping him gently on the arm before moving past him to begin packing for a new life in Oren's apartment. I am living out a lie he started, and who knows when it will end.

Chapter Three

Jasmine

Oren's apartment was bigger than my own and much more expensive. Living in New York was never cheap, but Oren had made a name for himself, enough to afford his luxury apartment here in New York. He made enough money off his freelance work to be able to buy a house all on his own, but it made sense for him to continue to prefer to live in an apartment. He was constantly out on trips; his apartment wasn't a home; it was more of a rest stop.

For the most part, Oren had turned his apartment into his work of art. From the paintings hung on the wall to the sculptures placed around the apartment, the well-thought-out interior design screamed Oren's name. The walls of his apartment were all white, but the décor made the apartment stand out.

Oren walks over, setting a box of my stuff onto the ugly orange couch that was placed against the living room wall. Just looking at it was an eyesore. "Now that I'm living here, do I have a say in the home's interior design?" I ask, settling myself down on the couch and opening the box. Oren snorts as if my question is an absurdity. But the only absurd thing was that a man like him, an artist, bought this couch.

"The couch stays, love."

I scrunched my face in disgust before peeking into the box to see what was in it, only to find office supplies from my desk. I pick up the box and bring it to my bedroom which had been Oren's office. I had to admit I felt quite guilty, having taken away Oren's space. But I wouldn't have taken it if he hadn't decided to pull out this charade of his.

Oren passes by me and lays himself comfortably on my bed before facing me as I begin to put everything in its place. "You know, you can always have a bigger office space if you just share a bed with me, Jaz."

"Then what would've been the point of moving your workspace? Speaking of which, where did you put all the stuff that was in here?" I question, turning to face him.

My breath hitched as I looked down at Oren; his arms were behind his head, his shirt riding up to show his defined abdomen, and those flexed arms were sending me into a multitude of scenarios that my best friend shouldn't be in. This couldn't be happening. My year of abstinence was getting to my head, and it was making me delusional. I couldn't be getting turned on by him.

"Jaz, you can take a picture, or you can just come and enjoy me now. I have a few minutes to spare." Oren smirks at me, shifting himself to pat the space right next to him.

"Oh, shut up," I say, walking over and falling beside him. "Now tell me, where is all the stuff that was in this room?"

Oren shrugs before lying back down to look up at the ceiling. "It's in my new office space." I sit back up to peer down at him.

"You're renting a whole other space?" I ask.

"Yeah, I need a bigger space. I have a gallery coming up at the end of the summer, and all the art is piling up. This space just wasn't going to do it for me anymore. So, I bought myself a loft, which'll be my designated workspace."

"You bought it?" I knew Oren had the money, but I was shocked he hadn't mentioned anything before. This was his business. This was where he would continue his career. It seemed like a big deal to me.

"Yeah, I figured since freelance work is piling up and I'm fully booked with clients and my own personal work, I feel as if I need to establish a more professional environment that isn't just my apartment." Oren shrugs as if it was nothing.

I reach over to hug him and press my lips against his cheek. "You know, I was thinking that we would be getting a little bit friskier, but I can take it slow, just for you, love." Oren teases, earning him a slap on the chest, leading him into a fit of laughter.

"It's a joke, woman. There is no need to overreact. Besides, don't pretend like you weren't just standing over there picturing me in one of your little sexual fantasies. Tell me, Jaz, what were you picturing? Were you tying me up, or were you enjoying being tied?" Oren's teeth graze his lips as he bites down on them, looking at my own.

Heat rises to my cheeks, but I don't try to escape his stare. This was just Oren's way of changing the subject and making me shy away. Oren was always a big flirt, which is why my relationships never lasted much longer than a month. Oren crossed boundaries that made past boyfriends uncomfortable and jealous. Though I should've distanced myself, I could never choose a man I barely knew over Oren, who had always been there for me.

The only reason I think I had lasted so long with William was because when we met, Oren was away finishing up his education and pursuing his career. By the time he was able to meet William, we were already engaged after two years of dating.

At that point, Oren stopped flirting with me and began to respect our relationship. My parents liked Will, and Oren's mother tolerated him, still holding a bit of resentment that I was with a man who wasn't her son. And when Will had broken my heart, I was expecting Oren to brag to my face about how he was right about Will all along. But Oren only brought me into his arms and held me all night while I cried into his chest for a man who had thrown me away and moved on as if our commitment was just an act.

Oren's hand caresses my cheek, wiping away a tear I hadn't realized was there. "Hey, what's wrong?" He asks. This time, there's no joke or stupid rebuttal. It was just Oren being my friend.

I wiped away my tears before settling back onto the bed and letting him hold me while I pressed my face against his chest. With my ear pressed firmly against him, I listen to his heartbeat pick up.

"Nothing's wrong, I'm just exhausted," I murmur, even though I knew Oren wasn't dumb enough to believe an excuse like that.

Bᴜᴛ Oʀᴇɴ ꜱᴀɪᴅ ɴᴏᴛʜɪɴɢ ᴡʜɪʟᴇ ʜᴇ ʀᴀɴ ʜɪꜱ ꜰɪɴɢᴇʀꜱ through my curls. It wasn't until minutes later that my body relaxed in Oren's embrace, and right before I fell asleep, I heard Oren whisper, "he never deserved you."

I wouldn't recommend walking around a city with a blindfold on, but when Oren is the one leading the way, you can't help but follow his orders, even if that means walking blindly around the busy streets. "Oren, can I please just take this off already? This is absurd." I mutter as I tighten my grip around his arm, fearing tripping and landing right on my face.

"Stop complaining; we are almost there. Plus, I want you to be surprised when you see it." Oren says.

"I will be surprised; it's my first time seeing it. I was even surprised when you told me." After my brief nap, Oren brought me to his new workspace. I think it was just his way of distracting me from my thoughts. But regardless of his reasoning, I was ecstatic to be able to see Oren's loft.

Oren didn't become a well-known artist with the help of family or friends. He spent hours of his days working to make a name for himself. He believed in himself, and his work ethic only pushed him toward his dreams—unlike my own, where I sit at a computer with a multitude of ideas for a novel but never get anything onto the page.

"Okay, Jaz, are you ready, my love?" Oren whispers from behind me, his hot breath sending shivers down my body.

"I've been ready. Can I take the blindfold off?"

I anxiously await his cue to remove the blindfold and look at his new workplace.

"Hmm, it depends."

"On what?" I ask, exasperated by the back and forth of this conversation. I probably look absurd to the pedestrians walking past Oren and me. But then again, this was New York, and they'd seen weirder things happen.

"Well, my love, it all depends on whether you'll be a good girl when we get up to the loft," Oren whispers again, allowing his index finger to slip under the string of my tank top. Before I can respond, Oren snaps the string onto my shoulder and pulls my blindfold off with his other hand.

"Surprise!"

My eyes squint at the sun's brightness only to be met with *Marvelous Books*. Which just so happened to be the bookstore I was in a committed work relationship with. I had tried quitting a couple of times, but each time I did, I somehow always got sucked back into staying longer than I should.

"No offense, Oren, but some people aren't so in love with their job that they want to come see it on their day off." Oren chuckles, wrapping his arm around me to bring me closer to him.

"Well, the thing is, Jaz, we aren't here to see your job. We are here to see what lies right above it. In other words, we are not only roommates but also work neighbors now."

My head shoots up to take a look at the giant windows that are right above the bookstore. "No way! Let me see! You know I've always wanted to take a look upstairs. Those windows must bring so much light into your studio. Let's go!" I pull on Oren's arm and drag him towards the door. He fumbles with the keys to get the door open.

Once Oren unlocks the door, I shoot upstairs to take a look at his studio. I reach the top of the steps to be met with a large open space. Linen cloths cover what can only be paintings and sculptures Oren has made.

I bring my hands under one of the sheets and begin to raise it before Oren slaps my hands away. "No peeking, not until the gallery. I want you to be surprised." Oren states, adjusting the sheet once again over the bust.

I didn't argue, though. As much as I wanted to take a look at Oren's art, I wanted to respect his timing in showing it. I knew I wouldn't want him reading my work until I felt it was ready to be viewed by the world. Then again, I wanted to be a romance writer, and I don't think I'm entirely ready to have Oren read smut written by me.

"I'm sorry, I should've asked. I just haven't seen any of the art that you're going to be putting up at the gallery. You only show me your freelance work. And though it's nice, I'd like to see what goes on in Oren's head when he's focused on his own imagery and not someone else's."

A smile plays on Oren's lips before he grabs my hand, leading me to the window. "Thank you. As much as I want to show you what I've dedicated so much of my time and years to, there will be a time and place to showcase it. And when I reveal my years-long work to an audience, my eyes will find yours through the crowd because regardless of all the critics, your opinion is the only one I'll ever care about."

My cheeks heat up at his words, and in that moment, I give thanks to my darker complexion for hiding any redness from appearing.

"So, what do you think of the view?" Oren asks, breaking the silence.

I gaze towards the window and admire the view of the busy streets and the crowd of people enjoying their evening throughout the area. "It looks beautiful," I say. My eyes are mesmerized by the city's lights, which must look even more beautiful at night.

"Yes, it does," Oren responds, but his eyes are not once looking at the city but at me. For some reason, I can't help but like the possibility that his response may be towards me rather than the view.

"Come on, let's go out and get something to eat. I have to wake up early to meet with a client tomorrow." Oren says, breaking his stare and walking towards the stairs.

I take one last look around before heading down the steps, curious about what Oren has worked so hard on throughout the years and excited about their unveiling at the end of the summer.

"Don't worry, my love. I think you'll be a big fan of what's underneath the sheets. Especially if you're a big fan of me underneath yours." Oren blows me a kiss before moving down the steps.

"I'm going to put an electric collar on you," I state as I roll my eyes and move past him.

"Jaz, I think you may be kinkier than me. But that's not a problem; I like trying new things." I step out of the building and look over at Oren as he follows right behind me, turning around to lock the door.

"This is exactly the moment in which I'd zap you."

"Then right after, that would be the exact moment I'd get on my knees and beg for more," Oren says, removing the key and pulling on the door to ensure it's locked.

"You wish," I remark, unable to come up with anything better.

Oren stops and takes a look at me up and down before giving his head a nod for me to follow and turning around to walk. And though that wasn't a verbal response, I think Oren's silence said more than any words could say.

Chapter Four

Jasmine

There are very few moments in which I blame myself for William and I's break up. But this is one of those times I feel I may have been part of the reason. My boss, Marvin, is currently standing right in front of me, a little too close than I'd like him to be, pestering me about going on a date with him.

"Marvin, I've said no three times already. You're my boss and nothing else." I grit my teeth, walking past him to restock the shelves.

"Come on, Jasmine. I heard about Will moving on with that blonde. He probably met her in this bookstore while waiting for you to finish your shift. Complete dickhead move if you ask me." He states, running a hand over his slicked-back hair.

Don't get me wrong, Marvin wasn't bad-looking per se,

but I would never be with a man like him. Not that Will had been a good man in the end, but I had learned my lesson, and being with someone right now was not what I wanted or needed.

"You know, Marvin, by the looks of it, you're no better harassing me. So, I'd highly appreciate you leaving me alone and staying out of my business."

I shove myself past him and hide between one of the aisles, organizing the books while repeating the same words of encouragement, "He pays you well, and you need the money."

Could Marvin have been right? Did Will meet Eloise here? If someone would know, it would be Marvin, who's constantly peering at the cameras from the back as if he has nothing better to do. But maybe he had seen them talking once. Maybe it was all happening for a while, even before the engagement. Maybe I just pushed him away. William disliked but tolerated my friendship with Oren, but he hated Marvin most of all. This is usually why he would come and stay for a while before my shift ended, to make sure Marvin didn't cross a line, which he had been doing more of ever since my breakup with Will.

Maybe if I had found another job, things wouldn't have ended between us. All he had to do was communicate it to me. But even if Marvin wasn't the issue and instead it was Oren, I would always choose Oren. Oren would always be there for me when William wasn't, and it was a good thing I was on Oren's side because William seemed to be thinking of having Eloise on his.

"I knew you'd be here."

I freeze at the sound of that voice. There was no way this man had the audacity to show up at my workplace.

I turned to face the voice that belonged to William, and as mad as I wanted to be, my heart still skipped a beat, knowing that he had come to see me. Our run-in at the restaurant had irked him enough to come and speak with me.

"What do you want?" I ask, turning back around to continue stocking the books onto the shelves. It was easier to just focus on the task rather than look at him and fall for one of his lies.

"I wanted to talk; you haven't answered my messages or calls."

William had tried calling me occasionally and left a few messages. Especially after I had sent over the new address. I had been ignoring him, and I had every right to. His questions pertained to my relationship with Oren, which was none of his business. If anything, this showed me how he didn't care about me but rather my relationship with Oren. He wanted to know if what Oren and I have is real.

"What do you mean? I sent you Oren and I's address." I say, playing dumb.

"I don't care about the address, Jasmine. I want you to tell me the truth." He rasps, coming closer to me. I look over and bring my focus to him. If either of us moved any closer, the tips of our noses would be touching, and I don't think I would hold myself back from being able to kiss him one more time. It had been a while since we were this close to one another, and feeling his breath so close to my skin felt right.

"What are you talking about?" I curse Oren in my head. I was never a good liar, and now, he has me participating in his lies.

"Jaz, you know what I'm talking about. You and Oren, please tell me it isn't true that you guys are still just friends. That the whole time we were in a relationship, you didn't lie to me about you guys just being friends." Looking at Will's eyes, I almost felt sorry for him, but I was quick to remember that we were in this situation because of his new fiancé.

"How dare you come to my workplace to try and gaslight me into thinking that I was unfaithful and that I wronged you in the relationship." I poke my finger at his chest, and William continues to walk back even more as I invade his personal space.

"You broke up with me just to want to tie the knot with your heiress, so don't you ever come to my job to interrupt my tasks to make me feel guilty for realizing that the man I was wasting my time on is nothing but a coward who can't admit his wrongs, and had me realize that the only man I could ever trust was the one who had always been there from the start."

I turn around and walk over to my cart, walking into a different aisle hoping William would get the hint and leave me alone. But instead, I'm pulled back towards him just to be face to face with him again. "That wasn't my intention, I'm sorry. I wish I could tell you why I had to do what I did, but it wouldn't change anything."

"But it would've given me closure." I snap.

William inclines his head lower, towering over me. He smelt of aftershave and mint. Despite our closeness, I don't push back instantly.

"Why would you need closure? You're happy in his arms now, aren't you?" William whispers.

His blue eyes were pleading for me to say no. And no

matter what he did, I couldn't continue Oren's lies. They were hurting William, and even though he deserved it, I think this was just enough to get back at him.

"William —"

"What's going on here, Jasmine?" I hear Marvin utter from behind me.

William looks towards Marvin and rolls his eyes before letting me go. "Hello Marvin, nice to see you're still as bothersome as ever."

"Bothersome? Listen, buddy, I'm taking care of my staff. The last thing I want is for Jasmine to get hurt."

God, I think I just vomited in my mouth.

"Marvin, please, everyone knows you're just trying to get into her pants, so why don't you mind your own business." William towers over Marvin, but Marvin doesn't even bat an eye. Instead, he takes a step closer to William and looks up at him.

"News flash, this is my business. You're in my store, so it's best that you leave, and if you need to speak to her so badly, you can do it on your own time. But just make sure your new girl doesn't know a thing. Wouldn't want to break off two engagements in a row." Marvin says before stepping away and walking to the back.

"He wants to fuck you," William murmurs, his eyes fixated on the back door where Marvin walked back to.

"I know," I say, walking away to check out some customers in the front. As I scan the books given to me by the customer, I can't help but look up to see William looking at me before stepping out of the store. I watch him walk away until he's out of my visual perception.

"You should stay away from him." I hear Marvin say from behind me as he munches on his apple obnoxiously.

"AND YOU SHOULD, ONCE AGAIN, STAY OUT OF MY BUSINESS," I say before continuing my tasks.

"What do you mean you want to break up?" Oren asks dramatically as he removes the cork from the expensive bottle of wine.

"I just feel like this shouldn't continue. Let's just cancel the party tomorrow; we can use the excuse of our apartment being under fumigation." I explain, pondering whether anyone would truly believe a luxury apartment was under fumigation.

"I like that," Oren says, looking at me with puppy eyes. I look away and make my way to the fridge to stop myself from feeling anything but friendly towards my best friend.

"What exactly do you like?" I ask him as I rummage through the fridge's drawer, trying to find something to snack on before dinner.

"I like that you called it ours."

I froze for a minute, taking in what he had just said, before rummaging through the fridge again. "Her,e let me help you; what are you looking for, Love?" Oren asks, placing his hands on my waist and moving me to the side. I look up at him, and suddenly, I'm in the same position as I was with Will not too long ago.

"I saw Will today," I say, grabbing a string cheese, and walking right back to the counter to take a seat. The aroma of the kitchen was making my stomach rumble with hunger. Oren was good at cooking. He had learned from his mother, and every time that man cooked, it made my mouth water.

"Where?" Oren asks, stirring his homemade tomato sauce.

"My job. he stopped by to ask about us– I mean about you and me, not me and him." I clarify.

"Did you tell him the truth?" Oren asks, not once looking up from his task in the kitchen.

"I was going to, but Marvin stepped in before I could rat myself out."

"You know I hate that dickhead, but thank God he interrupted your contact with the enemy."

"The enemy." I let out a chuckle at his exaggeration.

Oren turns around and makes his way between my legs, leaving little room for me to even breathe. His hands pressed against the counter, confining me to the area. "Yes, Jasmine, the enemy. The man who hurt you. The man who dared to walk into your job and corner you even though he knew you were taken."

It took a while for me to process Oren's words when he remained so close to me. His biceps flexed, and his jaw tightened as he held my stare. "Oren, I'm not taken." My hands wrap around his arms, trying to pull him away, only for Oren to put more weight onto the counter, refusing to move. Oren lowers his head towards the side of my face, his hot breath on my neck sending shivers throughout my body.

"He doesn't know that Jaz. He thinks you're with me; he thinks we go on dates, cuddle, and *fuck*." Oren slightly pauses to move a strand of my hair behind my ear before bringing his lips to it. Oren's lips graze my ear before he takes my earlobe in between his teeth and sucks on it. My body hitches at his action, my nipples becoming more prominent beneath the tank top I was wearing. Oren releases my ear before bringing himself to face me once again.

"And he still decided to go looking for you. That man has no respect for you, me, or himself. And if he comes into our apartment with that type of bullshit, he pulled today. I'll give him a nice little show like this one to watch." Oren says before stepping back and continuing his cooking as if he hadn't just made my body react in a way; it's only ever done to men I have dated.

"I think this sauce could use a little bit more salt. Do you want to taste it and tell me what you think?" Oren asks, his eyes remaining on the stove. I hop off the counter and walk over to him, grabbing him by the elbow to face me.

"You can't just do that, Oren," I state angrily. He had no right to cross boundaries I didn't even think I needed to set for him. Oren only sighs before putting the lid back on the saucepan and turning off the stove before facing me.

"I don't understand what the issue is," Oren says, crossing his hands over his chest before leaning back on the counter. I wasn't surprised by Oren's nonchalance. This is the same man who sleeps with multiple women and acts as if they never even met the next day. His little scene in the kitchen was like a hug in his eyes. But meanwhile, it was sending my body into a frenzy. Especially after having lacked a man's touch for over a year.

"It's not like I just ate your pussy out on the counter; it was just a little nibble," Oren states, a smirk appearing on his lips.

I can feel my cheeks heat up at his statement; I cover my

face, which is currently beaming red from embarrassment, before letting out a groan of exhaustion.

"Oren! Stop being so… dirty."

"Fine, love, but just so you know. Many women would kill to be in your position right now." I roll my eyes before moving away and finally pouring a glass of wine.

"True, but most women don't know you sleep with a night light."

Oren steps over to me grabs the glass of wine I had poured out for him, and takes a sip before leaning in closer. "What can I say? I like there to be a little light in the room when I'm fucking a woman. There's no satisfaction if I can't see her tits bounce while she's riding my cock."

My mouth drops at his perverse response, only for Oren to reach out and close it. "Don't leave your mouth open for me, love. I might think you're inviting me in." And with that, Oren Samaras walked away confidently, knowing that his words affected me more than I would've liked to admit.

Chapter Five

Jasmine

To say I was nervous wouldn't be enough to describe the waves of anxiety that were flooding my chest. I had begged Oren to put a stop to the housewarming party, but like everything in our friendship, Oren always had to have his way. Though I was aware of this party for days, it didn't make things any easier. I was currently pacing the living room while Oren was in the bedroom getting ready before this shit show began.

"I've invited Kora over for the evening," Oren says as he walks into the living room, adding one of his many golden rings to his fingers. I freeze in place and watch him walk in. My eyes can't help staring a little longer than they should, admiring the veins within his hands that rise up his arms, only leading to fantasies of his hands wrapping around my neck.

"Jaz, are you listening?" Oren asks, stepping closer and reaching over to have his hands cup my face.

"Huh? Yes, of course. Kora is coming over. I'm excited I haven't been able to talk to her much." I ramble.

Kora was Oren's— well, I guess- and also my neighbor now. She was sweet, and we always said hello when we saw each other, but we never shared more than a casual greeting.

Oren and she seem to always hit it off. From what Oren had told me, Kora was a phenomenal pianist. She spent her days going from rich home to rich home, making piano prodigies out of the children of wealthy families within the area.

"Hmm, you seem distracted and ill." Oren brings his palm to my forehead to check for fever like our mothers would do when we were children since we always got sick at the same time. We'd spend our days sick in bed, cuddled up together. One of our moms always checked in and made sure we were all right. And if they had tried to tear us apart, one of us would eventually begin to riot against the separation.

"I'm just anxious," I state while grabbing ahold of his hand to push it away from my face. But I don't let it go. Instead, I begin to trace the outline of his veins as I calm the anxiety that continues to brew within my chest.

Oren leaves my hand within his while the other continues to caress my face, his thumb rubbing circles on my cheek. "Don't worry, Jaz. I'll be right here the whole time. I'll worry about the lies. After today, I promise we won't have to deal with them again. Besides, I want you to get to know Kora. I would like for you to have someone you can speak and confide with while I'm away on trips for work."

I lean into his hand and shut my eyes before muttering an "okay." Oren brings his lips to my forehead, helping to calm down my nerves. I look up, our eyes meeting. His green hues made my breath hitch. There was no way I could let this little infatuation of Oren carry on anymore. It would only lead to more problems than I could already handle.

Oren's eyes move down, now staring intensely at my lips. I lick them in response, not because they're dry but because, for the first time in our friendship, I think I wouldn't push away if Oren decided to make a move.

Oren closes in on the little space that's left between us. The only thing separating our lips from touching is the one centimeter of space that seems to be diminishing from the magnetic pull between Oren and me.

My eyes lock with Oren's once again, his eyes filled with tension and, if I'm not mistaken, lust. "Jaz—" Oren begins to whisper before getting cut off by the repetitive knocks on the door. "Fuck me," Oren mutters, dropping his hands away and taking a step back. I tuck my arms awkwardly behind my back, unsure how to proceed after our interaction. Oren looks back down at me, making me feel a bit vulnerable.

I SEARCH FOR ANY SIGN OF REGRET ON HIS FACE, BUT ALL I can see is his own curiosity, as if he's trying to figure out if I regret our almost kiss. Oren sighs before leaning back down to me, "Well, Jaz, the show must go on. But I will be looking forward to your encore when everyone leaves."

William had yet to arrive, not that I focused solely on him walking through the apartment door. But the need to prove to him that I was much happier and doing better without him was something I wouldn't mind rubbing in his face.

"Are you expecting someone important?" A delicate voice breaks me away from the intense stare I gave the door.

Kora Young was breathtaking, and that beauty had nothing to do with her immaculate clothing taste and exquisite makeup artistry. She was taller than me, but only by a few inches, but her heels did help her look much taller. Her hair always seemed to stay at the length of her shoulders, never any longer or shorter.

In fact, I don't think I'd ever seen Kora without makeup or on a bad hair day. She always seemed to be pristine. The thought of that could seem intimidating, but Kora never seemed to stop to stare or judge anyone who wasn't so put together like her.

I would know, being that most of the time I was ever at Oren's apartment, my curls always seemed to be in a frizzy mess, matching my chaotic fashion style of a hoodie, shorts, and slippers.

"No, I'm just not the best at socializing," I state.

"I completely understand, though I'm actually good at socializing due to my parent's strictness when it came to being out in public with them during important events. But that doesn't mean I like it one bit. In fact, I'd much rather be at home running my head around various notes until I compose a piece that actually satisfies me."

I nod my head, not quite sure how to respond to her rant. Kora lets out a laugh before setting her hand on my arm. "I'm sorry, I tend to get carried away at times. I'm kind of an open book of sorts. Again, I guess you could say I'm somewhat of a social butterfly."

"No, I understand. I'm sorry, I'm just a very awkward person when it comes to getting to know new people." Hence why Oren was my only friend.

Kora moves her hand between us, holding it out for me to shake. "Well, then, let's just start over. Hi, my name is Kora Youn,g and I am your amazing, beautiful, intelligent next-door neighbor."

A giggle escapes my lips as I extend my hand over to hers and give it a playful shake. "Hi, Kora, my name is Jasmine. Your new awkward, anti-social, writer-wannabe next-door neighbor."

Kora smiles as we let go of each other's hands before reaching over to the counter to grab her drink.

"Well, I do have to say Oren has amazing taste when it comes to his girlfriends," Kora says, bringing the cup to her lips but not before giving me a playful smile.

"Oh, yeah — I mean, y-you know we've—"

"We've been friends for the longest time. Of course, she kept denying our love. But as you know, Kora, no straight woman could ever keep denying a man as eloquent as myself." Oren cuts in, wrapping his arm around my waist and taking over for me. I ease into him, laying my head back onto his broad chest.

Kora rolls her eyes before giving me a face that can only be saying, *can you believe this guy?*

"Something tells me she took pity on you when you kept chasing after her like a dog wanting attention from its owner."

Oren shrugs, taking the drink I had been holding in my hand since the party had started, still waiting to be sipped from. I turn my body over to see him bring the cup to his lips but right before he takes a sip he makes sure to give me a smirk, "what can I say, Kora? I don't mind being pulled around on a leash as long as I'm crawling towards my treat."

My eyes bulged out of my head before lifting my hand and smacking him right in the chest.

"Behave yourself!" I shout in a whisper.

Kora bursts out in a fit of laughter, which only has the other guests turning to face us. However, none of them seem to be fazed by the outbursts. Everyone here was practically friends with Oren, so they could more or less assume that Koras's outburst was due to Oren's unfiltered commentary.

"I like you, Jasmine. I love a woman who takes charge. Plus, someone needs to hold Oren back. He doesn't seem to have any self-control."

"Tell me about it; I grew up with him. All the trouble I got into was because of his lack of self-control."

"Hey, hey, hey. There will be no Oren shaming in this apartment. You girls should be showering me with praises." Oren says, handing me back my drink.

"You know, I first thought it was all some facade. Now, I am actually worried that you may be delusional." Kora says. Before Oren can respond, a knock on the door has us turning our heads over to it. I stiffen at the sound and look around to see who else besides Will and Eloise is not yet here. "That must be the last of our guests," Oren states, answering my question.

Oren presses a kiss to my head before walking towards the door, leaving me frozen in place next to Kora.

"Hey, is everything okay? You've gotten a little pale." Her observation is enough to tell me that having Will come here was a mistake.

"Yeah, I'm fine."

"Is that who I think it is?" Kora asks, peering over my shoulder. I can only imagine that she recognizes William and Eloise.

"If it's two wealthy individuals on their way to a marriage license, then yes, it is." Kora's eyes peer back at me with a questioning look.

"Two wealthy individuals?"

"Well, yeah. You're speaking about Will and Eloise, right?" I ask, turning around and spotting Eloise looking stunning in her blue jeans and white blazer. Her hair combed back in a sleek hair tie. That woman radiated elegance and old money. My eyes wander over to William, whose eyes seem to be glued to me from across the room. Though he was well dressed in his beige polo shirt and white dress pants, I wouldn't go as far as to say he was better dressed than Oren.

Oren stood out more than any man in the room with his loose-fitted white linen shirt and green slacks.

"You're down bad, aren't you?" I looked over in confusion, unaware of what she was referring to.

"What? Do you mean for Will?"

"William? God no, the way you were just staring at Oren as if no other man could ever compare."

I blush, not having realized that at some moment while Will was staring right at me, I was solely focused on Oren, and nothing or no one else seemed to matter.

"What's up with you and Will anyway?" Kora asks, shifting her body so that she is suddenly in front of me, obstructing Will's view from me.

"What do you mean?" I question, but I'm not entirely sure how much information I should be giving out, especially when the goal of today is to keep this lie that Oren has culti-vated as simple as possible.

"He's been looking at you since he stepped into this apart-ment. And though you look outrageously gorgeous, especially in that black dress, the way he's looking at you seems to show that there is definitely some history." I sigh, unsure of what exactly to tell Kora. It wasn't a story I wanted to tell, espe-cially not when Will and Eloise were only a few feet away.

"It's nothing; we were once a thing, but now we aren't. That's it." Kora lifted her brow in curiosity before turning back to face the couple that were now walking around the apartment. Observing the art pieces that Oren had around.

"Well, you're lucky you got out of that one. His family only brings drama."

"You know them?" I ask curiously.

William never mentioned having a friend named Kora, and Kora seemed to know much more about William's family than I ever did.

"Our families know each other; you know how wealthy people are. They stick with their own. We aren't friends by any means, but we all know one another from the multiple events we were forced to attend, thanks to our parents." I only nod my head in response.

When it came to Will's family matters, there wasn't much that was ever said. I had met his parents a few times, but they never really tried to get to know me, and William never tried to tell me about his family. All I knew was that his father was the CEO of Wren Technology. And from what Will had told me, everything seemed to be going well. But Kora's statement stuck with me from before, "Kora?"

"Yes?"

"Why did you question me when I stated they were both wealthy?" Kora opened her mouth, but the minute she looked behind me, her mouth shut. I immediately turn around, only to be faced with William's chest.

"Oh, hey," I say, stepping back until I feel Kora behind me.

"Hey," William whispers before peering over to look at Kora.

"Kora, it's always nice to see you. I didn't know you were such good friends with Oren and *Jaz*."

"Yeah, *Jaz* and I are quite close," Kora replies as she intertwines her arm with my own.

William's eyes trail over from Kora to me. I can't help but feel naked under his stare. It's as if he could see right through the lies. But that might be the guilt trying to trick me into spilling out the truth.

"So, how has it been?" William asks.

"How has what been?" I ask, unsure of what he was trying to get at.

"Life with your new roommate." He states knowingly. William had made it known at the café that he did not believe Oren and I's little spectacle. But being so upfront about it right in front of Kora made my face redden in embarrassment.

"You mean her boyfriend?"

Oren comes from behind me and snakes his arm over my chest. I relax before setting my chin on his arm. This has been the second time tonight that Oren has saved my ass from an awkward interaction. But in my defense, he said he would take care of the lying.

"You two look so adorable together, don't they, William?" Eloise asks, coming over to stand right next to William.

"Extremely."

Though William's response was dry, his death stare toward Oren was not. But it didn't seem to bother Oren a bit. His lips press against the top of my head as his fingers play with the ends of my curls. My eyes focus on Kora, whose eyes keep jumping from Oren and William. This can only tell me that even though Oren is doing everything to make me feel comfortable, his eyes are fixed on William in a way that declares his possessiveness over me.

"If you don't mind me asking, when did you two realize you wanted to be more than just friends?" Eloise asks.

Her questions and statements seemed innocent, but I knew she had to be playing dumb. The real reason behind all these questions had to be a way for her to make sure that William and I were completely over. And even though Oren and I aren't a couple, I could guarantee to her that William and I are forever done.

"Well, the best thing I can say is that it just happened. Love has always been there, but time has never been on our side. And we came to a moment in our life where everything seemed to line up, and I'd be a complete idiot not to take my chance to have her be mine. Especially when fate was giving a helping hand."

My breath hitches at Oren's words.

He's only acting, Jasmine; control yourself.

Even though he had made everything up, my heart still swells at the sappiness that just came out of Oren's mouth.

"That is so cute; I think I might throw up," Kora says, giving Oren a slight shove with her hand.

"Me too," William states before heading across the room towards the hall.

An awkward ambiance settles in the kitchen before Eloise dismisses herself to go after William.

"Well, that was awkward," Kora states.

"Whatever do you mean?" Oren jokes, unwrapping his arm from my body.

"Only you, Oren, would think it's a good idea to invite your girlfriend's ex-boyfriend." Kora retorts.

"I never said nor thought it was a good idea, just a messy one. And I can't help but love a little drama. Plus, I like him realizing how much of an idiot he is for letting go of something so beautiful and valuable." Oren's eyes remain focused on my own.

"You two could get a room, you know?"

"Well, what do you say, Jaz?" Oren asks, stepping closer to me and lowering himself so our noses are close enough to touch. "Why don't we unlock our little sex dungeon of a room and let our guests find themselves out."

My face reddens, knowing his reference is about my bedroom, which we decided to lock so that no one would question my belongings within the room. Of course, Oren would go around telling people that he used the room for his perverse activities.

"Oren!" I shout, making Kora burst out in laughter. Before I can reprimand him for his misbehavior, he quickly exits out of the kitchen and goes towards the living room to converse with the others. I roll my eyes in irritation before facing Kora once again.

"I'm so sorry about that."

"Don't be. I know how Oren is, and it's nice to see someone put him in his place." Kora reassures.

I give her a shrug in response and take the first sip of my drink of the night.

"Well, regardless, Oren is a much better choice than William. I can guarantee that. And by the looks of it, I think Oren is very much aware that you are a much better choice than any woman who could come his way." Kora says before walking away towards the living room, leaving me in the kitchen, consumed by my thoughts.

Chapter Six

Jasmine

Laughter erupts throughout the living room as Oren continues to capture the attention of our guests with his stories of doing any type of job for a client at the beginning of his career for the money. "I was still in college at the time, so it was literally the first time I had a client. And because he was my first client, I wanted to make a good impression, so when he asked me what exactly I painted, I told him anything." I hold back my laughter, already aware of where this story was heading, having already heard it before.

In fact, the minute Oren finished his first day of painting the client, he called me in hopes of me becoming some sort of savior who could remove any memories of what he had just experienced.

"The minute he questioned my response, I should've known something was wrong. But I was just so desperate for a job that I didn't realize what I had gotten into until I showed up and this 5 '6, heavy set man got undressed in front of me and proceeded to tell me to slim him down a bit when I get to painting him."

Laughter erupts through the crowd of guests. There was never a dull moment with Oren's stories. He always had something unbelievable going on. Though Oren had been horrified by the incident at that moment, he had stuck through it in hopes of being able to network in the future and obtain more clients. Nevertheless, Oren did just that and has become quite successful. As Oren's friends begin to question his stories and ask for more details, I take a look around and count the heads within the room. My eyes land on a head full of blonde hair. However, though Eloise is standing by the window and is focused on Oren's story, Will is nowhere to be seen.

Had he left her here?

There was no way William would have left Eloise here alone. Though Eloise has no problem socializing and defending herself, just like Kora had said, when you're born in that society, you're forced to socialize whether you like it or not. Regardless of how social Eloise was, it would still be out of the ordinary for Will to leave her here alone.

I turn around, walking towards the hall to see where he could've gone. Maybe he had gone outside for some fresh air, or maybe the man just needed to use the bathroom in peace, and here I was searching for him.

Why was I even looking for him?

If Eloise wasn't worried about her fiancé being gone, then he had to be fine. Regardless, he was no one I should be worried about. If he wasn't with all the guests, that was his problem.

I turn to head back toward the living room, but the sound of something falling onto the floor makes me pivot back to Oren's bedroom door. I open the door and peer my head inside, not expecting to see William holding the perfume I had displayed in Oren's bedroom to make the room look like both Oren and I inhabited the area.

"It rolled off and fell," William mutters before setting the perfume bottle back onto the dresser.

"I didn't ask, and even if I were to ask a question, it'd be connected to the reason as to why you're in my room."

I step into the room, leaving the door ajar, not wanting to get any closer but also not wanting to have him or anyone who may come in get the wrong idea.

"I don't know." William drags his hands over his face, letting out a frustrated groan. The look of annoyance plastered on his face the minute he drops his hands to stare back at me. The room fills with silence, but amongst the silence, I know there are questions from both of us circling the air.

"Why did you do it?" Will asks, and though I'm not close enough to see by the sound of his voice and the redness in his eyes, it almost sounds as if tears are threatening to appear.

"Why did I do what?"

Why he's asking such vague questions?

"Why did you cut your hair?" I open my mouth to respond, but nothing seems to come out. That wasn't the question I was expecting because, until this very moment, I hadn't realized that William had even noticed the change in my hair.

I bite my lips to keep myself from muttering the truth.

Because you liked it.

William takes a step closer, but I take a step back to let him know that we won't be getting any closer than we are. There are boundaries that he needs to follow. Though Oren's way of stating his annoyance towards William's actions at the bookstore was a bit over the top, he was right. In his eyes, Oren and I were committed to one another, and his only goal was to break us up while he stayed committed to Eloise.

"I don't understand any of this, J," William says, waving his hands around the room.

"And I do? William, you left me. You practically pushed me into Oren's arms, and now that I'm happy, you feel the need to stampede into my life demanding answers? It was you who left me. And when you left, there was no answer as to why. I spent months trying to understand where I went wrong, and now that I realize that the problem wasn't me at all, you want to come back and make me feel like shit for being with someone that values me." William flinches at my words.

I don't bother with a response as I turn towards the door to leave. Lying seemed to become easier, but Will's victim mentality made it easy; it made it feel valid.

"I know it's not real," William states, my body freezing in place before turning back around. I was probably better off walking away from the problem, but I couldn't help myself. I didn't get this far with Oren's plan for him to disregard it as a lie. He would come out of this party with the idea of Oren and I as a real couple engraved in his brain.

"You don't know a thing, Will."

"I know that you still have my ring. You keep our engagement ring with the rest of your jewelry." My eyes widened at his reveal. He had been snooping around through my jewelry box. It shouldn't come as much of a surprise, being that I found him in Oren's room with my perfume in his hand, but to open my jewelry box and search for our engagement ring is absurd.

"I'm sorry I haven't gone around to pawning it yet. I'll make sure to put that next on my agenda for the week, or if you'd like, you are more than welcome to take it back." Despite my encouragement for him to take it, the tightness in my chest was hoping he'd just leave it in the jewelry box and that he instead walk out with Eloise in hand, leaving me and the ring alone.

The idea of pawning the ring had never really occurred to me until now. At the beginning of the breakup, I had thought about contacting him to give it back, but the longer I kept it with me, the harder it got to get rid of it.

It became the only thing that connected me to Will, and even though I was heartbroken by the abrupt end of our relationship, there was some good within. I wouldn't have agreed to his proposal if there hadn't been a reason.

"God, Jasmine, I don't want the fucking ring. I want you to tell me the truth!"

"What truth?" Oren's voice sounds from behind me,

I turn back to face Oren, his eyes darkening as he stares at Will, his hands clenched to his sides.

"Stay out of this, Oren; this is between Jasmine and me. And though you're fond of playing house with her, I know it's all fake, so you have no right to be in this conversation, so stay out of it."

Oren takes a step forward, and I quickly put my hand on his chest, stopping him from getting into any altercations that would cause a show for the guests.

"I don't know what makes you think that we aren't

together, but we haven't given you a reason to believe otherwise. You interrupted us on our date, and your fiancé practically wiggled her way into our housewarming party. And you still have the balls to corner my girl in our bedroom and question her about our relationship?" Oren growls, his arm circling my waist, pressing me against his body.

"Jaz, please say something, anything." William pleads.

I sigh, turning to face him, Oren's arms still clinging to my waist.

"William, I don't know what else you could possibly want from me. I've said all I could say. The ring is just a ring; Oren and I are real. He was there when you weren't. I don't understand how suddenly it's me offering you closure when I was the one who should've received it, but if it gets you to stop, then have all the closure you need; just please leave."

Silence fills the room as William shakes his head in denial. Of course, this man isn't letting go that easily. If he had held onto our relationship the way he did, with his stubbornness, we wouldn't have to have this discussion.

"I don't believe it," William mutters; Oren scoffs at William's thickheadedness. I had been with William enough to know he was a man of facts. He wouldn't believe something until he'd seen it with his own eyes. Seeing that ring gave him the answer to his question about Oren and me being fake.

I closed my eyes, pondering the next decision I was about to make. I face Oren as he looks down at me with confusion, obviously confused by the questionable look on my face.

Was I really going to do this?

My eyes find Oren's lips, and I think he gets the gesture by the way his tongue peeks out to wet his lips.

Fuck it.

Before I can overthink my next move, I bring my hand to Oren's neck and push him down, bringing his lips down onto my own. Oren's arm snakes around my waist while his other hand grazes my cheek slightly. His tongue grazes my bottom lip, asking for entrance, and instead of pulling apart and ending our show of proof, I open my lips, allowing his tongue to enter.

My hands remain frozen around his neck as he lowers his hand from my waist, bringing it down to my ass, giving it a firm squeeze. I pull away, distraught from the heat that's ablaze between us. My eyes flutter open to meet his green ones, peering down at me with lust. And with the reaction that his one kiss gave my body, I would bet that my eyes held lust in them, too.

"William, you may go now. But before you go, please pass your engagement ring over. I like to see it on her while I'm fucking her," Oren says, his eyes shifting away from my own to look back at Will. "Because it truly feels so fucking good to know that I fuck her so good that it makes her want to take it off," Oren says with a wink.

My eyes practically bulge out of my eyes at Oren's unnecessary commentary. The kiss had been enough for William to get the point. My eyes wander over to Will, whose eyes are filled with hurt. But, I guess that made us even, in some sick way.

William's jaw clenches before he walks past us towards the door, and before he makes it out onto the hall, he looks back to face me.

"No," he whispers.

"No, what?" I ask, feeling Oren's hand clench around my own in annoyance.

"No, I don't love her." He says before making his way down the hall, responding as if he had heard my thoughts through that brief moment of silence we shared in the room earlier.

I turn to face Oren, and though I want to reprimand him for his comments, I can't help but let the tears brimming in my eyes out.

Oren stretches over and shuts the door before bringing me into his arms.

"I know, my love; I'm sorry I've caused you this much hurt and anxiety. This was the last time. I promise, no more pretending." Oren whispers before bringing me towards the bed to lay with him as his fingers brush through my curls; I press my head against his chest as I fall asleep, listening to the steady beating of his heart.

Chapter Seven

Oren

It wasn't often that I thought about murder, well, unless it involved that shit face William being anywhere near Jaz. Then, in that case, murder was the only thing on my mind. For some reason, that man had Jaz's heartstrings tied in a knot that I couldn't fucking untangle, and that shit was pissing me off. I reach over and tuck Jaz in while I make my way back to my living room.

I'd put on her bonnet later, but the silk sheets would do for now. That's the only reason I always ensured that the sheets I bought were silk.

I shut the bedroom door quietly, not wanting to disrupt her sleep.

I walk out into the living area, where everyone seems to be enjoying themselves. I look around, trying to spot William and Eloise, but they're nowhere to be seen, so they must have left already.

"Trouble in paradise?" I look over my shoulder where Kora is leaning against the wall, a drink in hand.

"I'd have to be in paradise before any trouble appears."

My lies had been known to go a little too far occasionally. Maybe this had been one of them. But seeing the smugness be wiped away from Will's face the moment Jasmine kissed me made it worth it.

Jaz had kissed me.

She had initiated something I was too much of a coward to do myself.

"I don't know. Fake or not. You guys played a believable part. And I think that if you continue this little game of yours, it will start confusing her." Kora says, pushing herself off the wall and walking up to me.

"Just tell her how you feel."

"I will, at some point. Kora, it's not that easy. She's got a lot of things happening right now. She wants to grow, and I won't stop her growth because I want her." I say as I move over towards the kitchen, beginning to put things away and in the trash.

"That's the dumbest crap I've ever heard. Why can't you just grow with her?" She questions, throwing her empty cup into the trash as well.

I ignored her question, walking to the center of the room and letting everyone know that Jaz wasn't feeling too good, so the party had to be cut short.

No one complained, and no one would complain unless they had a death wish. The only person who stayed behind was Kora, who was not done grilling me on my relationship or lack thereof with Jasmine.

"Come on, Oren, you know this is stupid."

God, some people needed a muzzle, and not in the kinky way.

"Kora, I shared my feelings with you because I thought I could trust you and that you'd respect my decisions on how I wanted this to go." I sigh, laying down on the couch, Kora falling into the spot right next to me.

"No, you told me how you felt because the moment you knew that they were engaged, I found you blabbering drunk on the floor of our hallway. Lying right in front of my door, which you had mistaken for yours. Which didn't make the situation any better." She taunts.

But she was right. I hadn't expected that when Jaz said she needed to tell me something, she would be announcing her engagement to the pile of shit that is William.

So when I threw back more tequila shots than recommended, I ended up in front of my neighbor's door, who, before that moment, I had never even said hello to.

"You know, there is no reason for you to bring that up, and in fact, I remember the next day you had sworn that you wouldn't bring that shit back up," I say, removing the blanket that Kora had put over her as if she was planning on staying long.

Kora reaches over, pulling the blanket from my grasp. "You're wrong; I told you I would take our little interaction to my grave. Which means I won't be letting anyone else in on our little secret. But that doesn't mean I can't bring it up to you every chance I get."

Kora begins fluffing her pillow before laying back on the couch and tucking herself in.

"Alright, that's enough. I think you're getting a little too comfortable here." I mutter, not actually caring about how comfortable she's getting but just wanting to switch the subject.

"I just don't understand, Oren." Kora sighs, shoving my shoulder to get my attention. "What are you waiting for? And don't say some dumb shit like growth or stability. That's just called stalling."

As annoying as Kora is, she was always right, and that shit pissed me off the most. But she just didn't understand that even though a year had passed since Jaz and Will's break up, she had yet to heal. I didn't want to be her rebound. I didn't want to ruin what we already had just because I decided to speed things up in hopes of her falling for me.

And even now, I wasn't doing my best to separate our lies from real life.

Damn it, Oren, have some self-control.

"Kora, she just needs some time to figure things out. She needs to accomplish her goals first. You're a musician; I'm an artist; let her be a writer. Let her start accomplishing her dreams before my greediness gets in the way of any of that."

I lay my head back, ignoring Kora's glare. The last thing I needed was to get in the way of Jasmine finally getting what she wanted in life. I couldn't allow that. I would help her in any way I could to make her succeed, but I wouldn't be a distraction in her healing process.

"Oren, you are possibly the dumbest and sweetest man I have ever met," Kora responds, wrapping her arms around me in a firm hug. I wrap an arm, taking in her loving gesture before groaning at the sudden sound of my phone ringing, knowing exactly who it was.

I pick up the phone, not bothering to check the caller ID.

"What is it, Garrett?"

"I need you in Alaska." He mutters, obviously annoyed at something that must have happened on set.

"No," I responded, not bothering to give it a second thought. If Garrett was working on something for his magazine, he was going to be meticulous, and that meant he was going to keep me in Alaska until he was satisfied with every fucking image I took.

"Come on, man, you know I wouldn't ask unless I really needed you. My photographer's wife went into labor earlier than expected, and now I'm down a photographer, and you're the only person I trust to get the job done."

Garrett and I met in college and have always been very good friends. Especially when he began taking his traveling blog much more seriously, leading him to create and publish his own magazine; this year, he was determined to finish up his visits to every state in the United States. I had worked on a few of his projects before, but flying to Alaska to help a friend versus staying home with Jaz didn't make the decision difficult.

"I'll pay you well; the flight is on me." Garrett bargains.

This man was not going to take no for an answer. But I couldn't just up and leave Jasmine. I look over at Kora, who's currently distracted by her Instagram feed.

"Fine, I'll do you this favor. But you owe me."

"Fuck, man! You're the best; I definitely owe you one. I'm going to need you down here ASAP. I'll send you all your flight information soon. See you." Garrett rambles before hanging up. His job was done, and now I had to wait for my tickets, but not before giving Kora her job.

"I'm leaving for a few days," I say, facing Kora again.

"I love this game!" Kora exclaims sarcastically.

"What game?"

"The game where you say shit randomly without giving actual context. Where are you leaving to?" She questions, the annoyance clear on her face.

"I'm going to Alaska for a project. Knowing the guy running it, I'll be gone for two weeks. I need you to do me a favor."

"Two weeks?!" Kora's eyes practically jumped out of her eye socket as if I'd just told her I'd be gone for a whole year.

"Keep it down; Jaz is sleeping. Will you do me the favor or not?" I reiterate.

Kora sighs before nodding her head. "

What is it?" She asks, knowing it'll already pertain to Jaz.

"Just look out for her and make sure she's writing. Don't let her diminish her work; she's very good at self-sabotaging."

Kora nods in agreement, getting up from the couch and grabbing her things to get ready to leave.

"I got it, don't worry. I like Jasmine. I would've been there for her regardless of you asking me to be."

"I know you would."

No one could resist Jasmine after meeting her. She was the type of person you'd want to move mountains for. And for Jasmine, I'd move the entire continent, planet, or universe to make her happy.

"Are you still going to give her the gift?" Kora asks.

"Yes, I'm going to give it to her."

I open the door for Kora, hoping it urges her to leave and stop asking so many questions.

"You have to tell her, you know? Even if she's allowing you to help, I don't know how well she'll take the news of you overstepping." She says, referring to another secret I made her keep.

"Kora, zip it. It'll be okay; I've got this." I assure her, even though, in reality, I'm hoping shit won't hit the fan when Jaz realizes that my decision was only a way for me to help her.

Chapter Eight

Jasmine

I'm startled awake by the breath of someone hitting the back of my neck and their arms wrapped tightly around my waist. It takes me a while to realize that the room I'm in belongs to Oren. I reach over to the nightstand to see my phone charging. Oren must've brought it over and put it to charge before falling asleep. I grab the phone and take a look at the time. It's only three in the morning. So, the guests must've gone home about two hours ago.

I can't believe I fell asleep during a party I was meant to host. They probably thought it was so rude of me not to stick around. I can't believe he didn't wake me up in the first place. It seemed to be a coping mechanism of some sort every time I got overly stressed or anxious for my body to go into a deep sleep. Throughout high school, my life consisted of naps and over-studying. Oren would have to practically pull me out of the house to do anything other than sleep and study.

Despite my annoying coping mechanism, Oren always knew how to take care of me. He brought me to the bed without me having to say a word, already knowing that our little event had given me more anxiety than I could handle.

I stretch out my arms and untangle Oren's hold from my waist. Uncovering myself and lifting myself up, I feel a slight breeze on my legs, sending shivers throughout my body. I looked down to realize I was no longer in the dress I wore at the party. Instead, I was wearing one of Oren's linen dress shirts and underwear. The bra I was wearing was no longer attached to my body. I bring my hands up to my head, where Oren hadn't done such a terrible job securing my bonnet, being that I was in a deep sleep. Normally, I wouldn't have cared about Oren changing me so that I was comfortable in bed. But after our kiss, I didn't know what to think about it.

I mean, the kiss felt real. The way Oren kissed me back and held me in his arms. There was no real reason as to why he would add tongue and an ass squeeze. Especially when a regular firm kiss would be enough to make William back off. But knowing Oren, it was probably just to take a jab at William himself.

Though William had crossed a line, Oren didn't have to say those things to him. He was just adding salt to the wound. The look of hurt on his face broke my heart, but not as much as his revelations about his feelings towards Eloise. How did I go from being jealous of the woman to wanting to bring her into my arms?

She was going to marry a man who didn't love her. But it didn't make sense. None of this made sense. William had left me for her; they're engaged to be married. William must've said that to get to me; there was no reasoning behind his admittance.

I peer down to look at Oren, sleeping soundly on his bed, the moon's light reflecting onto his skin, illuminating his defined muscles. The covers laid over his waist; if he hadn't been spooning me, I would've thought he was completely naked under the covers. And I wouldn't put it past Oren to sleep completely naked.

I get up from the bed, but before I can go anywhere, a hand wraps around my wrist, pulling me back down.

"Where are you going?" Oren whispers as he pulls me back into his arms.

"I'm going to my room," I say as I try to unravel his arms from my waist, but Oren's grip tightens around me.

"Why would you do that? Just stay; I'm comfortable here with you."

"I bet you are, but I just want to be alone for a bit."

I didn't know how else to tell Oren that I needed a break from him right now. The day— no, the week had been exhausting, and I needed to be alone. How did a person go about asking their friend for a break? Was that even a thing?

"Just stay, love. I leave tomorrow, and then you'll have all the time that you need for yourself." I bring my body around to face him, confused about his groggy mumble.

"What do you mean you're leaving?" I ask, fully awake at this point.

Oren opens his eyes to look back at me, becoming aware that I'm not going back to sleep anytime soon.

"I have to work on a photojournalism project in Alaska for

about two weeks. So, that should be enough time for you to relax your precious mind and begin writing your novel."

I turn over and turn on the lamp light atop the nightstand before facing Oren again. He begins covering his eyes from the light, but I pull them down, forcing him to look at me.

"When were you planning on telling me this?"

Oren's eyes continue to squint, trying to accustom to the room's brightness.

"It's something that's just come up. You were asleep at the moment, and I wasn't going to wake you up just to inform you about a stupid work trip."

I let out a sigh, lying back down on the pillow and facing him, our eyes looking back at one another. "It's not a stupid work trip; I like knowing about your upcoming projects. Plus, as much as I would like to start writing, I don't think I'll be able to do so with the hours I'm picking up this week."

Oren lets out a hiss as he turns his body away from me.

"Oren, what did you do?" I ask, reaching my hand over to his chin so that he's looking at me once again. Whatever he had done must've been something terrible or something that would frustrate me because he was trying his best not to have to look me in the eyes.

"Well, you see, I kind of told Marvin that you would be working part-time until further notice."

"Oren! You did what?" I shriek.

"Why can't you just say thank you and go back to cuddling with me?" I let go of Oren's chin, lifting myself to hover over him.

"I wasn't cuddling you; I was being suffocated by your embrace. And I wouldn't have to argue if you just stopped doing things behind my back. This is also my job, and it has nothing to do with you. When did you even find the time to talk to Marvin?"

Oren brings his hand up to my cheek and brushes it delicately. He continues to look at every feature of my face besides my eyes.

"Jaz, I did it because I know you. I know you would just keep working overtime for that jerk rather than taking the time off to be able to focus on your aspirations. Now, in regards to when I spoke to him, it was obviously at a time in which you weren't there." I remain still on the bed, unsure what to say to him.

"Please don't take it the wrong way. I know I overstepped, but I don't regret it. I think this will be very beneficial to you. All I am asking is that you give it a try, and if it doesn't work out, Marvin can just add you back to your full-time schedule."

Oren's eyes finally meet mine, and I let out a groan, letting myself fall right onto his chest. Oren knew me better than anyone; I knew he was right in making that decision for me. But I hated that he went behind my back to do it, and most of all, it bothered me that he hadn't just talked to me about it rather than doing it himself. The whole point of my moving in wasn't to trick Will; it was all meant to be for me to focus on my writing without worrying about bigger obstacles in my life, such as rent and food.

"Fine, I'll give it a try," I mumble into his chest as Oren's hand down my back, trying to soothe me. A contentful moan escapes my lips, and Oren stops his motion. His hand lays still on my head.

"Do you want to speak about it?" He doesn't need to specify what he's referring to. It's the giant elephant in the room that I wish I could keep ignoring for all eternity.

"No." There was nothing more to say. Oren and I could just pretend that nothing had ever happened. After today, we will be taking a long break from one another, and when he comes back in two weeks, everything will be back to normal.

"You don't want to speak about the make-out session we gave your ex in the middle of this room?" Oren taunts.

I let out a grunt as I lift my head back up to look right at him.

"Oren, I don't want to speak about it. We did it to get back at him, but it didn't feel as good as I thought it would. We don't have to bring it up ever again. It happened, and now we can pretend it never did."

"Why would I pretend it didn't happen?" Oren asks, pushing himself up to face me. "Jasmine, I would have to be a complete lunatic to want to pretend like that kiss was nothing."

My breath hitches at Oren's words; his eyes stare into mine, and as much as I want to look away, my eyes stay connected to his.

"Oren, it was just a kiss. You've kissed plenty of women before. I'm no different."

Oren's eyes averted my own as if my words had physically hurt him.

"Jaz, you can't even begin to compare yourself to them." Oren's hands reach out to my own. He tightens his grip in intervals, which he has only ever done when he gets nervous, and it is something he hasn't done since we were children.

"Ore—"

"No, Jaz, I need to tell you something. You can't compare yourself to those girls. They have never been anything more than hook-ups. They weren't my girlfriends, they weren't my friends, and they weren't my love." Oren holds my hand tightly as if he's afraid I'd turn and run.

"Oren, I understand." It had been a stupid idea for me to kiss Oren, completely out of character. Having Will there taunting me made me do it, and now it's made things awkward between us.

"No, I don't think–" Before he could say anything that would only make me feel worse for overthinking our little scenario, I begin to rant in hopes of getting him to let things go and move on from the conversation.

"I do; I promise you that I understand. The kiss shouldn't have happened. We are best friends, and it's just made things awkward. I don't want to be awkward. I want to be us. I want to continue to be your roommate and help you with your daily routines. I want to help pay what I can. It's the least I can do for all that you're doing to push me into my dream career. Basically, what I am trying to say to you, Oren, is that I want to remain just us as we are. Just Oren and Jaz."

I take a deep breath and let out a big sigh. Oren's eyes stayed on me the whole time. His Adam's apple bobbles as if he were about to say something, but no words escape his lips. Instead, Oren lets go of my wrists and stretches over to turn off the lights before laying back down under the covers.

"Oren?" I whisper, bringing myself closer to him, concerned about having said something to offend him.

"It's late; let's go to sleep, Jasmine."

"But you said—"

"You said exactly what I was thinking. Now, come and lay back down. We can cuddle, just like the old days. Just Oren and Jaz." A smile tugs at my lips; I scoot in closer and place my head on his chest.

Oren's toned arms wrap around my body, holding me close. And though I just agreed that our relationship would be nothing more than a friendship, my mind couldn't do anything else but run around with the idea of what it would be like to be more than friends with Oren.

A thought that should've never crossed my mind to begin with. But Oren's two-week absence would be enough to get me over this stupid crush I had been developing.

Oren's lips press against my forehead, "goodnight, my love," he whispers.

"Goodnight, Oren," I whisper back before shutting my eyes and falling asleep on his chest.

A loud buzzing noise stirs me awake from my sleep. Disoriented, I lift my head and let out a groan to look around the room. I stretch towards the nightstand to snatch my phone, which is currently bombarded with calls. I look down at the caller ID just to have my stomach churn at the sight of Will's name on the screen. After last night, I was sure he had gotten the message loud and clear. William held no embarrassment or shame; if he had, he wouldn't continue to bombard my phone with his persistent calls.

I deny the call before tossing it on the empty side of the bed that no longer holds Oren's frame.

Had he left without saying goodbye?

I untangle myself from the sheets and walk out towards the kitchen. Despite the silence within the apartment, I called out for Oren. I walk over to the kitchen, and a plate of blueberry waffles is laid out on the counter; next to it is a bright blue bag with a note.

Was there some sort of anniversary or birthday that I was unaware of? I grab Oren's handwritten note and peer down to read it.

I'm sorry I had to leave early, love. I wasn't supposed to be called in for this project, but I couldn't say no. Regardless, you should start your day off with the most important meal. But since I'm not there, the blueberry waffles will just have to do.

If you haven't noticed, there should be a blue bag on the table. Though I wanted to be there to see you unwrap your gift, I couldn't have you wait two weeks to be able to use it. Please enjoy your breakfast and begin using that gift as soon as you scarf down those waffles. No ands, ifs, or buts. I want to see you get started on that manuscript so I have something steamy to read when I return.

Love, the sexiest man on the planet... Oren.

I drop the letter onto the counter and grab a hold of the bag. There was no way Oren had wasted that much money on me. I grab the item from the bag and pull it out to reveal a brand-new laptop. My grip tightens around the wrapped box. He had gotten me a brand new computer. And as nice as it looked, it wasn't something I could accept. This wasn't something I needed; I could continue to use my old computer until I could afford a new one. I rushed back to the room to grab my phone, which continued to vibrate, this time inconsistently. I grab it from the bed and look at the texts William has bombarded me with.

WILLIAM

Jaz, please call me back.

I'm sorry; I know that I was completely out of line.

Please, just call me.

I need to explain everything to you. I should've told you all this before.

I'm sorry.

My brain ponders the idea of giving him a callback, but that would mean that the kiss with Oren proved nothing. I couldn't feel bad for a man who only realized what he had lost after he saw me with someone else. I would just be crawling back, and he'd be more than content to see me do so. Whether he loved Eloise or not was not my problem. I delete the messages and press on Oren's contact to write to him.

JASMINE

Thank you for the gift and breakfast; you really shouldn't have done that. I promise I'll pay you back.

OREN

Funny, I don't recall asking for money in return. In fact, I don't think I asked for anything but the start of a manuscript in return. So get on it.

I'll make sure to get right on it.

When you're done, let me know because I
have something else you can get right on,
and it'll be much more fun.

Oren!

I shut off my phone before returning to the kitchen. Today, I was going to make sure that I got started on my dreams. There were no more excuses. Oren had made sure of that for me. No more self-sabotaging by working overtime, dealing with computer troubleshoots, or running behind on house-work. If a manuscript was what Oren wanted, I would make sure that when he returned from his trip, he had something to read.

Chapter Nine

Jasmine

This wasn't working out. Maybe this idea of becoming an author was just that, an idea. The only thing I had started on my manuscript was *chapter one*.

The words, not the actual chapter.

I had been ranting about my aspirations of becoming a writer for years, and now that I could become an actual author, it was proving itself to be harder than I had thought.

I had ideas, but I had never thought of them fully. They were just characters, tropes, and a world I could escape to. How the hell did I go about bringing it all to life?

Oren had gifted me the laptop in hopes that I would get something done that he could read, but regardless of whatever I wrote, I wouldn't want him reading any of the vomit that I had been writing and right after deleting because of how terrible it was.

If Oren had been here, he would've reprimanded me already for being too in my head about all these things. And he'd be right. I can't keep trying to find ways to deteriorate my motivation to stop myself from writing.

Come on, Jasmine, just write something.

My fingers find the keys again and begin typing; of course, it all looks and will probably sound like a vomit of words when I re-read it. But I had to start somewhere. And if working at a bookstore ever did anything for me, it was the ability to give me access to a multitude of romance novels that gave me nothing but more knowledge on what I and other readers were looking for when sitting down to read a book filled with pure smut.

The clacking sound of the keys, as I write begins to relax my mind, and my brain takes over, building a world and introducing a character that has been held within my mind for what feels like ages. The sound of a knock on the door is the only thing that tears me away from my screen, which now holds a page and a half, which is already a great start compared to nothing at all.

I push my desk chair and walk over to the entrance to take a look at the peephole. I hadn't been expecting anyone and the last thing I needed was for Will to be at my door. Now that he knew my place, there was no stopping him from trying to come and talk to me like he did when I was at work. I stretch out onto my tippy toes to look through the peephole and see Kora getting ready to knock on the door again. I unlock and swing the door open. Kora's standing there with a reusable Target bag filled with snacks.

"Hey, I'm sorry I took a while to open the door. I wasn't expecting anyone." I say, gesturing to my appearance. I had on some sweatpants and one of Oren's graphic t-shirts, which I never saw on him, but he had his drawer filled with them regardless. My hair was wrapped up in a messy bun on the top of my head; I couldn't be bothered to deal with the curls this morning.

On the other hand, Kora looked as presentable as any other time I had seen her, from her hair to her washed-out jeans paired with heels and a white shirt. The woman was always ready for a photoshoot.

"Please, you look beautiful in anything. Besides, I'm the one knocking on your door unannounced. I wasn't expecting you to be in a little black dress and heels like yesterday."

I moved out of the way, nudging my head for her to enter. As I close the door, I feel immediately guilty for not having said goodbye to her yesterday. The other guests didn't really matter to me. Kora was my neighbor, though; she was also good friends with Oren. I wanted to do my best to make a good first impression.

"Crap, Kora, I completely forgot that I hadn't said goodbye to you yesterday. I'm so sorry."

Kora turns around to face me with a confused look.

"Jaz, you don't have to apologize to me for not feeling well. I didn't take it to heart when I saw Will storm out, with Eloise running right after him. And then I saw Oren coming right out of the same room. I knew that nothing good had conspired. That and Will had stormed out of here looking pissed, so I think that everyone knew that it was time to go by then."

I groan and cover my face in humiliation, "I'm so embarrassed. Now everyone knows that something must've happened or that I did something wrong."

"Jaz, I don't think anyone believes you did something wrong. God, all throughout the party, Oren was just non-stop talking about how perfect you are, and when Will came acting like a goddamn Neanderthal, we could all see it." A sigh of relief escapes my mouth, and I walk over to the couch to sit; Kora follows right behind as if this were a casual thing in her daily routine.

Maybe Oren and her were used to this type of interaction more often than I thought. Guess while Oren was gone, I'd have to step in.

"Poor Eloise looked so out of place and alone." Kora begins saying while simultaneously removing the snacks from the bag and laying them on the coffee table. "Do you mind if I remove my shoes? They make my outfit look cute, but they're not really feet-friendly." I shake my head, and Kora reaches down to unlatch her heals from her ankle

"Not that we were ever close or anything," Kora begins to speak again, referring to someone I can only assume is Eloise since that's where our conversation had been prior to her removing her shoes. "But she just never seemed like the type of person you'd want to revolve yourself around. Don't get me wrong, it may seem fun being rich, but not when you have to allow yourself to be molded by your parents. You end up becoming some sort of puppet for them." Kora continues opening the bag of chips and offering some to me. I reached my hand, grabbing a few to keep in my palm as we spoke.

"But you don't seem like a puppet."

And she didn't.

Kora might dress phenomenally and know how to work

a crowd, but she had a mind of her own, or at least it always appeared as if she did. As little as I knew about Eloise, she didn't seem like the type of girl who would sit on your couch and eat chips with you on a Sunday afternoon.

"That's because I'm not," Kora shrugs. "My parents always had this view of what my life would be like. Like many children that grow up around wealth, you're forced to play an instrument, take classes on mannerisms, go to prestigious schools that you could give less of a fuck about, and you're forced to hang around and socialize with all of your parent's rich friend's children. It kind of fucking sucks."

"But, I thought you liked making music."

"I do, but that was always meant to be a hobby in my parents' mind, so when I told them that I would be continuing my education in music, they got extremely upset. It was either pursuing a career in anything business to work in the business or doing it all on my own."

"They kicked you out?" I question mid-chew.

"Not necessarily; they talk a lot of crap. Yeah, I had to move out and pay for school myself, but my trust fund was all from my grandfather, and once I had turned eighteen, it was all mine. So, I had more than enough to pay for my education. After college, I started teaching piano lessons, and I continue to do so because I like it, and it's mainly just my side gig while I'm not composing music or working with other musicians on their songs."

Kora seemed nonchalant when it came to speaking about her family, but they seemed like a nightmare. I knew William came from wealth, but he never really spoke about that part of his life. He never spoke about having to be a puppet for his family, and he never seemed more than real when he was around me.

Oren and I grew up entirely differently. We were surrounded by love from both his parents and mine. Despite whatever decisions Oren and I had made as individuals regarding our career paths, they were supportive. Even when I moved out, my parents told me I always had them to fall back on if I needed help.

For the most part, there had never been a day when my parents didn't send me a message regarding their support. I couldn't even begin to understand what it must be like for Kora to live alone and not have anyone else.

"Do you have any siblings?" I ask, hoping that maybe if she did have siblings, it would mean she wasn't entirely alone.

"Yeah, but we don't talk much; we never really got along anyway. Raya is ten years older than me and is my parent's favorite. She, unlike me, chose to become a puppet." Kora shrugs as if the lack of relationship with her sister didn't affect her.

"What about you? Do you have any siblings? I've met Oren's sister briefly once before. But, even when he's told me stories of you guys, he's never mentioned other people besides you and Phoebe."

I reach over, grabbing a few more chips from the bag, before shaking my head. "No, it's only ever been my parents and I. Then, later on, Oren and Phoebe became my neighbors, so they were the closest thing I ever got to siblings."

"Well, it seems you see Oren as more than just a sibling, maybe an *actual* boyfriend?" Kora asks.

I freeze at her choice of words; I inch my head upward to

look back at her. "What do you mean actual?" I ask, unsure of whether she knows the truth or not.

"Oh, I thought Oren had told you already. He let me know that the whole dating thing is a facade to get back at Will for being such a douche."

"Oren told you?" Oren wasn't someone who trusted many people; for him to have trusted Kora with our little secret meant that he saw her as a close friend, and so I could, too.

I let out a sigh of relief.

"Thank God, I'm sorry for lying. I hate lying; I promise Kora, I wouldn't have done that in other circumstances. But once Oren has a stupid idea in his mind, it becomes quite difficult to remove it." The air had suddenly become more breathable, or maybe that was the weight of guilt of having to lie and finally being released.

Kora moves the snacks she had in her hand and lays them back on the coffee table.

"Jaz, you do not have to apologize. Trust me, I completely understand the circumstance." Kora says, giving a subtle shrug before looking around the quiet apartment. Her eyes looked as if they were in search of something in particular.

"What were you doing before I came?" She asks.

"Oh, I was writing, but something tells me you already knew that."

Kora shrugs her shoulders before giving me a sly smirk.

"A little birdy might have told me that another artist in the building was starting off their career, and it was important that I come in to check on them. Just to ensure she wasn't burning herself out on the first day."

There it was, the real reason behind Kora's visit. I wasn't shocked; I knew Oren had something to do with Kora being here. Whether that was just to make sure I hadn't burned down the apartment or to check my progress. Despite Kora being here because of Oren, she seemed to be the type of person who would come because she truly wanted to be here, not because someone asked them to be.

"I came here because I wanted to be here, Jaz. Oren asked me to stop by here and there just to see if you needed anything. But it's Sunday,

and I thought we could hang out. Besides, I want to hear more about this book of yours."

"I mean, there's not much to it yet." I begin pulling at the strings of my sweatpants, hoping Kora would see this off behavior as a sign to switch the subject.

"That's okay, what's it about?"

I guess not.

"It's a contemporary romance. I'm kind of a hopeless romantic. I find gratification in building a world where two individuals just click, and even though it takes some time, they figure out that the person they're with is worth more than anything else in life."

I look over to see Kora staring at me with puppy dog eyes. "That is the cutest thing I've ever heard. I was just expecting you to say that you like writing smut, and there is no shame in that at all. When you write a sapphic romance, you should send it my way so I can review it. Just to make sure that it's accurate, you know?"

I let out a giggle, surprised by Kora's interest in romance. "Kora, I promise you that you will be the first person to get the chance to read any of my sapphic romances. But I'm treading the water with what I know for my first book, and even that seems to be rough."

Kora returns to the snacks, opens the packet of gummy bears, removes only the red ones, and begins to eat them. She extends her hand and offers me the bag: " The red ones are mine. I don't like sharing them, but the rest are all yours." I reach over and grab a couple, making sure to avoid any red gummy bears.

"Why do you say it's a little rough?" Kora asks as she pulls off the head of the gummy bear like a crazed gummy bear sadist.

"Well, I've read thousands of romance novels. Even ones I wish I hadn't. But I don't know how to start it exactly. And how do I write about love when I haven't been so great at it myself?"

"Hmm," Kora stretches onto the couch, the gummy bears still in her hand as she chews and looks straight at me in deep thought. "Then don't write about love; write about lust."

"Huh, isn't that basically the same thing? You can't really have a romance book without love and some sort of insinuation of lust in it."

"Yeah, but maybe instead of a contemporary romance, you can focus on just the lust aspect of the relationship and then work your way around the love later on."

"An erotica?" I question, pondering over the idea of basing a novel fully on a sexual relationship.

"Yes, Jaz, an erotica," Kora says, lifting herself up from the couch as if she's just hit a major breakthrough. Yeah, your characters can find love. But maybe it doesn't start out that way. Maybe it starts off as a man wanting a woman to fuck and a woman wanting to get fucked."

I had to admit that Kora's idea wasn't terrible. Maybe it was just a great way to view my story from another perspective. And despite the disappointment that is my love life, sex has always been easier and much better, even with Will.

"You might be right, Kora."

"Oh, I know I'm right. Just like I know that I definitely have a cavity." Kora says, setting the gummy bears back down as she sucks her teeth to relieve the toothache.

"I'll leave you to it, Jaz, but just so you know. I'll stop by later this week to see where you've gotten with this book. And hopefully, you'll let me read a few pages, just so I can rub it into Oren's face that I got to read it before him."

Kora gets up and stuffs all the snacks back into the bag before handing them to me and walking back to the front door with me right behind. "You can keep these for next time." She says as she opens the front door to leave.

"Oh, and just so you know, Jaz. What is said between you and me stays between us. Oren is my friend, and you are too. And even though Oren will call to ensure you're okay, nothing you say to me will be reported back to him. What's said between us stays between us."

"Thank you, Kora; I could use another friend other than Oren.".

"Me too," Kora says as she stands still for a moment as if contemplating what to say next before ultimately saying goodbye and heading over to her apartment.

I shut the door and put the snacks away before returning to my desk. I sit back down, regressing into the chapter and highlighting all I had written before Kora's visit before pressing delete. I was going to take a different approach to this book than I had first started with. For some reason, I felt that I was on the right path.

Chapter Ten

Jasmine

I've been enjoying my time off to write these past few days, but I have to admit that I missed not coming to work as often. Something about the smell of books and being surrounded by a multitude of them in the first place brought me peace. I've always liked bookstores. The first few memories I had of my childhood were with my dad. He'd bring me to some of his favorite bookstores around Jersey and New York on weekends. It was just a him and I thing, and later on, it became a him, I, and Oren thing. But Dad never seemed upset about sharing our time with Oren. It had always felt right for Oren to be a part of everything.

The only time Oren and I had ever been a part was when he had gone off to college in Massachusetts, and I had stayed here. Granted, I had met William at that time in my life, which made the process of being away from my best friend much more durable. And though I had wished at the time that Oren had been around to meet William much sooner, fate had decided against it. But in the end, it didn't matter.

"I have to tell you, Jasmine, that having you as a part-time employee now has opened my eyes to how much you do around here," Marvin says, passing by the aisle I'm currently stocking and taking a seat on the couch that's stationed by the windows for our customers to sit and enjoy.

"I'm glad you've come to see my diligence, Marvin," I say, letting the sarcasm roll right off my tongue as I stock the shelves that seem emptier than usual.

"Are these the only books we have in stock? The shelves look a bit empty. Do you need me to make a few more orders?"

I didn't tend to make the orders for Marvin, but sometimes, when he was *too busy* to do it himself, he would assign the task to me.

"Um, no. These will be the last books we put on the shelves." Marvin shifts on the couch, looking uncomfortable, which is out of character for him.

"What do you mean by that?" I didn't understand what exactly had brought on Marvin's vague comment. But if he had to inform me of something, he had better spit it out.

"Well, you see, I got an offer."

"Like to sell the place?"

"Well, obviously, what other kind of offer would it be?"

I roll my eyes at his sarcasm, which I would agree I deserve after having asked that question. But Marvin had never mentioned wanting to sell the place, so it took me a bit by surprise. His bookstore had been passed down from his family for generations. Sure he wasn't a book fanatic, but he loved the income that it brought him.

"So, you're selling the bookstore?"

"For a woman who reads many books, you ask some dumb questions. I thought we went over that when I had to specify what kind of offer."

I lower my gaze, ignoring Marvin's snarky response. He was not worth arguing with. While he got a fat check for his business, I would be sitting at home in front of my laptop, navigating through job applications, hoping to get a similar job soon.

"You don't have to worry," Marvin's voice breaks me away from my anxiety-induced thoughts. "The owner said that they plan to keep this place as a bookstore, and I made sure to put in a good word regarding you as an employee. They said they would highly appreciate you continuing to work for them the minute they begin setting up for their grand opening."

Marvin gets back up from his couch, grabs the empty cart that I was using to stock the shelves, and leaves.

"I'm not entirely sure if they'll be expecting an interview process, but I will let them know that you are more than qualified," Marvin says as he walks away with the cart in tow.

I know this seemed like the perfect decision in Marvin's eyes, but I just couldn't wrap my head around how he could have so easily sold away his business. A business I would've killed to have myself. Buzzing from my right back pocket takes my mind off the upsetting news. And seeing Oren's name pop up on my phone made me feel better.

OREN

Hello, my love. I have to say being this far
from you is killing me.

I roll my eyes at Oren's cheesiness. However, it lifted my
mood.

JASMINE

We've been away from each other longer;
how's Alaska?

OREN

Yes, but that was before I knew I'd be
coming back home to you.

Alaska is fine. It would be much better with
you.

Heat rises to my cheeks at his response; I knew Oren
was just being a tease. But it felt good to pretend it was
real.

JASMINE

You'll just have to bring me with you next
time.

OREN

Jasmine, are you flirting with me???

You wish.

God, was I actually flirting with Oren?
No.
This was normal, friendly banter. We always talked this
way, right? There was nothing flirtatious about my response. I
had just been sitting on his bed a few days ago, practically
trying to pretend that kiss had never happened. There was no

way I would add to this flirtatious game that Oren had begun with me.

OREN

My love, at this point, you have me praying for it to be true.

How's the book coming along?

JASMINE

…it's coming.

And just like that, I shut off my phone and put it back into my pocket, ignoring the buzzing that was coming from my phone.

I HAD GOTTEN A FEW CHAPTERS INTO THE BEGINNING OF MY book, but I didn't want to jinx anything by telling Oren it was going well. I wanted to surprise him with my first few chapters when he returns home. I hadn't encountered writer's block, and I was hoping it would stay that way. For the first time in a while, I had faith that I could accomplish something I had set my mind to. And I wasn't going to let my anxiety take over to self-sabotage.

I never responded back to Oren's text after that last message, despite knowing it was rude of me. He didn't say much after, except remind me not to feel pressured to have much done. I knew that Oren wouldn't have been upset if I didn't have much written down, but I would. I wouldn't have the face to show a blank Word document. I wanted him to be proud of me, but I also wanted to be proud of myself. This self-loathing needed to be removed from my body, and the only way I was going to remove that little shit from my body was by pushing through until I accomplished writing my book.

My novel had become my biggest priority at the moment, but I was also focused on developing other friendships and relationships that weren't just Oren. A huge part of Oren's success had been because of his social personality, which had him networking with anyone who came his way. I didn't have much of a life outside of the bookstore and my apartment. I had only met Will because fate had brought him right into the bookstore. But I didn't need fate's help anymore. Not that they had been doing a good job at helping. But I had made it a point to try to reach out to Kora and make plans.

I was currently late for my plans; lucky for me, Kora texted me and said that she was running late herself, which eased my anxiety a bit. The last thing I wanted to do was continue to make myself more of a fool in front of Kora despite her saying otherwise.

"Jaz! Hey, wait up!" I turned my body around to the sound of the voice that had called out my name from behind me. Kora's long legs carried her over to me swiftly. Her appearance is, like always, intact. And here I was in mom jeans and an overused band tee that I hoped no one would question me on.

"Hey, I thought you would get there before me," I say as Kora interlocks her arm with my own as we await for the crosswalk to change for our right of way.

"Oh, please. I'm usually late to anything and everything.

The only reason I made it on time to your little housewarming party was because I live right next door."

I can't help but laugh at Kora's honesty. It was something that I was beginning to admire. She was confident in who she was, with her flaws and all.

"Did you look at the restaurant's menu? You'll love it; I swear they have the best sushi here. I would risk mercury poisoning any day to come here and stuff my face every day of the week."

"If you're risking mercury poisoning, it must be phenomenal."

Kora leads me to an entrance with two tall wooden doors. Pulling one open and stepping inside, I immediately feel right out of place. When Kora tells me about this place, she doesn't mention how elaborate it is. Everyone in the restaurant looks as if they have just gotten out of their daily corporate meeting.

Maybe I was just in my head. This was just a regular place like any other restaurant. Every decent restaurant had hungry clients who came straight in from work. Turning my head over to the other side of the restaurant, my eyes landed on a man who took a seat by the piano before beginning to play an unknown symphony.

Kora turns to me with a giant smile on her face. Of course, she loved coming here. Not only did it have a great menu, but it also had live music, and that for Kora must've been like hitting the jackpot. "Isn't this place amazing?" Kora asks me before following the hostess to our reserved table.

"Yeah… It's amazing." I can't help but lose myself in thought as I peer around the restaurant, taking in everything once again. I felt the stares of some of the guests but turned away before I got any more self-conscious. I couldn't ask Kora why she hadn't warned me about the dress code, but in her defense, she had sent me the link to the restaurant. I just didn't feel that there was a need to observe much when Kora had already spoken so highly of the place. But that was a lesson learned for next time.

"You don't like it?" Kora asks, dropping the menu that held no price, which didn't mean free.

"No, no, no! Of course, I like it. It's just different from what I'm used to. I'm sure I'll love anything that's on the menu. Speaking of which… is there something equivalent to a four for four on here?"

Kora shoots up her eyebrow in question, remaining silent for a few seconds before bursting into a fit of giggles. Eyes turn our way, and I quickly bring my hand up to cover my face as I continue to look at the menu hoping it would shield me from anyone being able to take a good look at me.

Why did I even care?

It's not as if anyone here knew me and if they knew Kora. She obviously didn't care.

"Jaz, you are funny," Kora says, wiping away a single tear from her right eye. "But the answer is no, but you shouldn't worry about that. It's on me. But that doesn't mean I won't be expecting a four for four from you in return in the near future." Kora says, bringing the menu back up to her face to review the options.

"That I can do," I state, replicating her same action.

Kora and I ended up picking two rolls each to share along with some appetizers that Kora insisted I have to try. Her insisting was for a good reason, everything that had been brought out to the table was delicious.

"So, how's the book coming along?" Kora asks, bringing a roll into her mouth.

I take a sip of my water before giving her a shrug, "It's going well."

"Just well?" She questions, looking down at the plate and wondering what her next pick would be, no doubt.

"No, I mean, it's going good so far. No *real* writer's block."

"What do you mean *real* writer's block? Is there a fake one I should know about?"

"No, well, I just meant that I haven't had much trouble writing the book just yet, but regardless of the number of books I've read, I'm kind of nervous when it comes to writing out certain scenes."

When Kora gave me the idea to write an erotica, I hadn't really thought it through. The idea of a book solely based on a sexual relationship that built up to intimacy was exceptional at the moment. But when it came to thinking about how I would go about writing a scene that involved any form of BDSM, it became incomprehensible in my mind.

William and I weren't saints, but I wouldn't say we tested out the waters much when it came to our sex life.

"Hm, what kind of scenes exactly?" Kora smirks over at me before picking up another roll, but this time setting it onto my plate. "Eat; I'm practically stuffing my face alone over here."

I eat the roll just for it to give me enough time to think about how I would tell Kora that I— a wannabe romance author— was having trouble even comprehending how I would write the book's actual romance part.

"I don't know how to say this because I'll sound stupid."

"Has anyone told you how annoying your self-deprecation is?"

My eyes widen at Kora's hurtful but honest question.

"Just Oren."

Kora sets her chopsticks down before flipping her silky hair to the side and crossing her arms over her chest.

"Well, now you can include me on that list too. Have some confidence, woman. Not every struggle in your life has to define you, and you especially don't have to put yourself down because of it. So now tell me, is it sex?"

Leave it to Kora to make something as simple as writing porn simple and easy to talk about in public.

"Listen, if you're going to be an author, especially one that writes about smut, you need to be comfortable discussing these things. Plus, it's normal. Every adult has sex, and if they haven't, they're thinking, watching, reading, or, in your case, writing about it."

Kora was right; it's completely normal. I just felt embarrassed to say that I felt like I didn't know how to write a sex scene, and a big part of that was because my own sex life was lacking.

"I just don't think I know how to write, um, erotic scenes," I whisper from across the table.

"Oh, I get it. It's been a while since your last rodeo."

I held myself back from spitting out the water I was drinking, sending me into a coughing fit. If I hadn't gotten people's attention the minute I'd entered the restaurant, I had definitely caught it now. "I mean, I guess you could put it that way." I put my cup right back down and continue to clear my throat as quietly as possible to avoid any more stares.

"That's an easy solution; we'll just have to put you back

out there. There are plenty of apps we can look into, or if you prefer, I have a few bachelors I can set you up with." Kora reaches for her phone as if she's got these bachelors waiting for her call. I reach over to stop her before she gets ahead of herself.

"I'm not sure that's exactly what I need or if I'm even ready for that."

I hadn't thought about dating. It just wasn't a priority. The last thing I needed was to get distracted from my goals and find myself falling for a mediocre man.

"You don't have to pursue anything serious. It would just be something casual."

"Yeah, I don't think I'd be any good at the whole casual thing."

Kora looks me up and down and gives me a sly smile.

"There's always a first time for everything Jaz. And I think you'll definitely be seeing one of my available bachelors sooner than later. Trust me, you'll have fun. See it as networking, except you might just allow them to shove their tongue down your throat by the end of the night. Who knows?"

I burst into laughter with Kora, knowing she was insane but telling the truth. This woman was going to make it her mission to have me go out on a date to get my creative juices flowing, and despite my nervousness about the matter, maybe it wouldn't be such a bad thing.

Chapter Eleven

Jasmine

It's been a week, and I would be lying if I said I wasn't missing Oren a bit. We had texted here and there these past few days, but it wasn't the same as having him near me so that we could talk or just enjoy our time together. Despite his denial of not wanting to be in Alaska, his Instagram story said the opposite. Last night, he posted several videos and photos of his night out. And though I had no right to be angry with him for enjoying his free time with his friends, my mind couldn't help but wonder who the blonde glued to his arm was.

Oren had never mentioned any co-workers or any blonde woman who seemed to have had difficulty understanding what *keeping your hands to yourself* in kindergarten meant. It was outlandish of me to even care, even more outlandish for me to be scrolling through his list of followers in order to find out who she was. It didn't take much time for me to find her.

There she was, with her outstanding media presence.

I know I shouldn't waste my time on little things like these, because it's not any of my business. In pictures, Oren and I always looked like we were something more than just friends. People used to ask us if we were dating all the time. This is probably just a close friend of his. If it were anything more, he would've let me know.

But regardless of all the sensible thoughts trailing through my head, I still had to figure out who she was. And the last thing I wanted to see was a bunch of pictures of her marketing lingerie and bikinis. She was an influencer and seemed great at it because many of her posts were brand deal after brand deal. If she wasn't talking about clothing, it was about some sort of bloat-free tea or her favorite coffee. *Renee James* was gorgeous, and Oren probably thought so too.

I had never seen Oren with anyone, so it was quite difficult to distinguish his type. But I guessed that it had to be her. But I wasn't going to sit here and be upset about something that had no meaning. If Oren had something to tell me, he would. It's not like I had told him about the date Kora had set me up with tomorrow evening.

Kora hadn't given me much but his name and occupation. Which also seemed to be a work set up when she told me Terrence Brown was a literary agent. He had sent me a text here and there and let me know he'd be picking me up tomorrow to bring me to dinner. For a man who knew nothing about me, he didn't seem like getting to know me was important before agreeing to go on this date. But then again, I was making little effort to send him any message to get to know him.

FROM THE PICTURES KORA SHOWED ME, TERRENCE WAS A very good-looking man. He was an avid reader and athletic. From his Instagram, it seemed he was always on hikes or bike rides. And in his posts, he always wore a shirt his muscles were just asking to break free from. Though it was a bit out of my comfort zone, it seemed worth it to give it a try. It was time to move on and feel inspired again.

I wouldn't say I regret my decision, but overheating in the shower as I try to shave things that haven't seen the light of day in centuries makes you rethink decisions. I drag my body out of the shower and open up the bathroom door to make it easier to breathe again. I peer down at my legs, acknowledging the cut-free smooth skin that replaced the stubble that had been growing out. Nothing was going to happen tonight, but that didn't mean I wouldn't be prepared. I had made sure to pick out my red underwear, the same one Oren had been so in awe of when he was looking through my drawer and the matching bra I had bought with it.

Terrence had told me he was taking me out to a nice restaurant in the city, and I wasn't going to mistake that for the casual wear I had worn the other night with Kora. I rummaged through my closet, trying to find anything that would look nice for tonight. Why couldn't these people be normal and take me out to cafés or a Barcade? My wardrobe was not made for posh dinners overlooking the city or for live music while eating sushi.

A knock at the door breaks me away from the stare-down I'm currently giving my closet.

There's no way that's him. I walk over to the door and look into the peephole to find Kora standing there knocking a second time on the door. I swing the door open, having forgotten that I am currently only wearing a bra and underwear.

"Wow, I was no— wow— can I come in?" Kora stutters; I grab her arm and pull her into the apartment before shutting the door. I walk over to my bedroom and grab the robe that's lying on top of the bed before covering myself.

"I'm so sorry. I forgot I was practically naked. I wasn't expecting you to be here."

"Oh, I get it. You're getting into character." Kora says, laying down on my bed as I go back to looking at the mess of a closet I have.

"Getting into character?"

"Yeah, you know. You're trying to understand what your character would do and how she would act. I can definitely say that Terrence would be shocked, but I'm not sure he would deny the invite." Kora says nonchalantly.

My cheeks redden at Kora's insinuation of me wanting to seduce Terrence. I hadn't even thought of kissing the man, let alone trying to get him into my bed the minute I saw him.

"Kora, I was not planning on seducing the man. I literally just forgot that I was half-naked as I opened the door for you. And as I am saying this, I realize how stupid I sound." I pulled out a dark green dress from the closet and the black one I had worn for the housewarming party and lay them on the bed.

"Hey, even if you were, nothing would be wrong with that."

"Okay, quit the teasing and tell me more about this guy. He's barely said a word to me these past few days. I'm surprised he even agreed to this." I press the green dress onto my body, and Kora scrunches up her nose in disapproval.

Black dress it is.

"Yeah, Terrence isn't much for texting. But he can keep a conversation in person. Trust me, I knew I had him salivating when I told him you were an avid reader and working on your own material." Kora walks over to me as I bring up my dress, struggling once again to zip it up on my own. Kora walks over and zips it up, saving me the arm spasm.

"And the minute I showed him your picture, he was on board for the blind date. The fact that he wants to see you so soon means he's interested in getting to know you." I look over at the mirror as my curls drop loosely around my face after being unwashed and tied in a bun for the past few days because I had been solely focused on advancing in my book. Well, advancing as much as I could without writing smut. And when your book revolved around the smut, that meant there was very little advancement.

"You look beautiful, Jaz. Don't get too inside that head of yours. Enjoy your night. I promise you'll have fun. Nothing needs to be rushed. Get to know him and see how things go. Remember, this is supposed to inspire you to write about lust and longing to be with that person intimately. And by the looks of what's under that dress, I'd say you are yearning for something alright."

I turned around, bringing her into a hug. Kora barely knew me, and she was my biggest supporter. And though friendships with girls were still new to me, Kora made it a little easier.

"Now let's get you all fixed up; your hair looks beautiful. All you need is some mascara and some lipgloss, and you'll blow this man away." Kora reaches over to her purse and pulls out her makeup bag. "Figuratively, that is, unless you want it to be literal."

"Kora."

"Okay, okay, enough is enough. I get it." She says as she passes over some mascara and lip gloss.

My phone rings from across the room simultaneously as a knock is heard. "He must be here," Kora says as she runs towards the door. I walk over to my phone and pick it up, not bothering to look at the caller ID.

"Hello?" I answer as I continue to put on the mascara.

"All I get is a hello?" Oren's voice sends a tingling sensation throughout my body. I hadn't heard his voice in a while and was beginning to miss it.

"I'm sorry; how would you like me to greet your Highness?" I joke, peering down the hall from my bedroom to see if I can get a peek at Terrence, who is currently catching up with Kora.

"How about, how is my lovely Oren doing this fine evening?" I scoff at his cockiness but play along anyway.

"Hello, how is my lovely Oren doing this fine evening?" I repeat back to him in a teasing tone.

"I'm so glad you asked, love, because I'm having a rough time out here without you. I can't wait to come back home soon."

Oren lets out a big yawn at the end of the phone, which is very odd coming from Oren. He's always been the type to fall asleep when you have to wake up for work in three hours. So, work really must be getting to him. That or he's having the time of his life at these late-night parties with influencers.

"Jaz, your date is here!" Kora shouts.

"Date?" Oren questions.

"Yeah, Oren, I'm sorry I have to go. I kind of had some plans tonight. Can I call you after or tomorrow instead?" I suggest not wanting him to stay up when I didn't really know what time I'd be back tonight.

"Who's your date?" Oren asks, ignoring my question entirely.

"I'll call you tomorrow, Oren; love you."

"Jasmine, wait—"

I HANG UP, SILENCING MY PHONE, AND LEAVE THE BEDROOM to meet Terrence. But that doesn't stop the spam of vibrations from my phone due to Oren's consecutive calls. This time, I wouldn't let Oren take control of things. Kora was right; I deserved to have fun, and I was going to make tonight worth my time.

Terrence was probably any woman's dream date. Kora had been right; he could definitely hold up a conversation. He told me all about how he grew up in Connecticut and recently moved to New York to start fresh. Though he missed his hometown, he enjoyed the chaos of the city. And he obviously knew good places around the city because the rooftop restaurant we were currently at was outstanding. The hostess sat us outside, and the city lights were mesmerizing.

"This place is beautiful," I say, admiring the table's decor.

"Well, I can name something even more beautiful than this, and just if I'm not being clear enough, she's sitting right in front of me."

I raise my brows in astonishment; this had been his first move all night to show some sort of interest in me other than a casual conversation about who we were and where we were from.

"Thank you," I say, scrunching up my nose, unsure how to respond to his compliment. Terrence had been way more attractive in person than in his pictures. And the way his dark skin glowed against the city's lights only helped his image even more.

"Kora told me you're an avid reader. I would have to say that I am, too. But, I'm more of a non-fiction literary fiend."

"Well, as much as I do appreciate a non-fiction book here and there. I need fiction to find some form of escapism. I love reading them as much as I enjoy writing them."

"That's right, I have a future author sitting right before me. Come on, pitch me your idea." Terrence leans back in his chair, his arms settled on the table, awaiting my synopsis.

"I thought this was a date, and now suddenly, I'm in a one-on-one meeting pitching out my romance novel to you?" I tease, taking a sip of water to calm me down from his intense stare.

Where the hell did Kora find this man?

"Oh, this is a date. And what better way to spice up the date than to talk about your upcoming romance novel? Is it contemporary?"

I shake my head, not entirely sure if I should admit to working on writing an erotic novel.

"It's not a fantasy romance, is it?" He asks with a distasteful look.

"What's wrong with romantasy?"

Terrence laughs and points right at me.

"That right there is what's wrong with it. The word just makes me cringe. But to each their own. But truthfully, I'm just not big on fantasy. I mean, I read non-fiction, so fantasy is completely on the other side of the spectrum, but I'm willing to push through a book if you write it."

Damn, this man was smooth.

No, Jasmine, you cannot fall for the bare minimum.

It would be an honor for this man to read any book you've written, whether it's fantasy, fiction, non-fiction, or erotica.

"Well, lucky for you, it's not fantasy either."

Terrence opens his mouth to give another guess but gets cut off by our waiter, who's ready to take our order. Terrence places our order before going back to guessing what I could be writing.

"I think that at this point, I should just tell you, or we will be here all night."

"Well, that's not necessarily bad, is it?" Terrence's smile widens, and I can't help but admire it.

"I guess not." I reach over to take a sip of my water, and as my hand meets the glass, he reaches over to grasp it.

"Is it an erotica?"

I pull my hand away, but Terrence grips it, stopping me from moving away.

"Bingo." He says before letting my hand go. I bring the glass to my lips and take a sip before setting it back down.

"You've guessed it."

"Now, unlike fantasy, I am all for a sexual reawakening story. I can't wait to read it."

"And who says I'm going to let you read it?" I tease.

There was no way I was letting this man anywhere near my writing. Literary agent or not, he did not need to see any of my fantasies on paper, especially when I had no clue where this would end up.

"Oh, I'll be reading it. If not before it's published, then afterward."

ONCE AGAIN, THIS MAN WAS QUICK WITH HIS RESPONSE, AND I was left speechless.

The night had been amazing. The dinner, the stroll around the city, and the ice cream we had gotten afterward. Everything was amazing, except we were currently parked in front of my apartment building, and Terrence had yet to make a move all night.

All the flirting and not even a kiss?

"Thank you for driving me back to my place. I enjoyed the night a lot." I unbuckle my seatbelt, not entirely sure what to do next.

Do I open the car door and leave?

Should I give him some time to make a move?

Should I make the move?

Before my mind can overthink anymore, Terrence grabs my face and brings me over to him. His lips overpowering my own. His kiss is gentle but firm, nothing like what I had expected. Nothing like what I yearned for.

I push away from the kiss, laying my hand on his chest.

"I'm sorry, did I misinterpret the signs? Were there no signs at all?" Terrence's face shows actual concern about him having crossed the line. My chest aches a bit as I try to come up with a good enough excuse as to why I don't want to continue kissing him.

"No, you interpreted everything correctly. It's just getting super late, and I don't want to start something I wouldn't get to finish." I give myself an internal facepalm, knowing that flirting with this man isn't any better than telling him the truth.

"Yeah, of course, I'll text you sometime later this week. Maybe we can meet during my lunch break or go out for coffee."

Great, now he wants to go out for coffee.

"I'd love that," I respond before giving him a quick peck on the cheek and making my way out of his car and into the apartment building.

There was no way out of this; how would I go about telling Kora that my date with Terrence had been amazing, except his kiss hadn't been what I expected? It hadn't been what I needed.

His kiss hadn't been like Oren's.

Fuck.

Chapter Twelve

Oren

She was on a date, and though she had obviously agreed to the date, I knew this was all because of Kora. This is what I got for trusting her to look after Jaz. This she-devil was starting some unnecessary shit. To make it all worse, both Kora and Jaz were ignoring my calls, and I was in fucking Alaska. But I was getting on the next plane out of this state and hunting Kora down, and after I got the name of the guy who was out with Jaz, I was going to hunt him down.

I grab my clothes and items, stuffing them all in my suitcase. I grab my phone and give Garrett a call to let him know I'm leaving this goddamn state, and he's going to have to deal with it. Besides, I had given him more than enough material to work with. But of course, it seemed like everyone was playing the game of *let's ignore Oren*.

Fuck me.

I pick up my things and exit the hotel room, walking over to the elevator to head over to the top fucking floor rather than the lobby because Garrett only seemed to know how to use his phone when it was convenient for him.

Walking over to his door, I knock repeatedly until it swings open.

"Jesus, what's up your ass?" Garrett asks as he opens the door, his ginger hair in a mess, his glasses tilted, and the hotel's robe tied chaotically around his body. Meaning that the only reason Garrett failed to pick up my phone call was that he was enjoying his afternoon in between someone's legs.

"I'm leaving," I say, grabbing my things to turn back.

Garrett's hand grasps my arm, holding me back. "Hold up, wait a minute. The week isn't even over yet. Where are you going?" He asks while readjusting his glasses to not look like an idiot.

"I have an emergency back home, so I'm leaving. You have more than enough material to work with. Plus, if you really need something else that I couldn't capture, I'm pretty sure Renee can help."

"Sure, I won't mind." Renee's blonde head pops from behind Garrett. A robe was tied around her body but more put together than Garrett's.

My eyes trail over from Garrett to Renee, not knowing exactly what to say because it was none of my fucking business. And it was not something I cared about in the first place. Renee was Garrett's videographer and was pretty good at it, too. She also had a huge fan base as an influencer. Renee not only helped him create the content for his work, but she promoted it as well. This obviously made Garrett happy enough to want to break his strict rule of no fraternizing with co-workers.

"Um, this isn't—" Garret begins.

"I don't care, Garrett. I have somewhere to be right now. But if you need anything, try to contact anyone but me."

With that, I grab my things and make it down to the lobby, already placing an order for an Uber to get to the airport as soon as possible.

I place my key card at the front desk and head outside to wait for my ride. My phone buzzes in my pocket, and I pull it out to see the she-devil calling herself.

"What the fuck did you do?" I question through gritted teeth, placing the phone near my ear.

"Good evening to you, too, sunshine." Kora teases over the phone. There was no way this woman thought this was the right time to joke around. She had just sent my best friend out on a date with some random man, and she was trying to make small talk.

"Kora, who the fuck is he?"

Kora sighs on the other end of the line, taking her sweet time to answer knowing she's playing with my patience at this point.

"He's a friend."

No fucking shit.

I look over at the car, pulling up and opening the trunk for me.

"Give me a moment; do not hang up, Kora," I demand as I walk over to the trunk and shove my suitcase inside it before getting into the backseat of the car.

"Kora, who is he?" I ask, but instead of a response, I'm met with silence.

She hung up on me.

I dial her number and wait as she takes her sweet time answering the phone that I know is right beside her.

"Hello?" She answers as if I wasn't already on a call with her.

"Thank God you don't work for a hotline; you'd be pretty shit at it." Kora laughs, obviously enjoying my misery.

"Kora, just tell me who he is and why they're on a date together," I demand, holding back any temperament wanting to come out. I was willing to play nice with Kora to get the answers that I needed.

"I told you, he's a friend. Besides, you told me to help her out, especially when it came to her writing, and she needed some inspiration to get the creative juices flowing. You know how that goes." Kora replies nonchalantly as if she hadn't just admitted to setting my best friend up with some guy in hopes of having him fuck her for inspiration. I was really hoping her book had a plot twist that ended up as a murder mystery. If that were the case, I'd be down for this date.

But since I knew Jaz's passion was being a romance author, there was no way this date or book would end with a dead man.

"I'm coming home, Kora."

"Finally, you're welcome."

And just like that, I had fallen for Kora's stupid setup, but I wasn't upset about it because I would find this guy and make sure he knew that Jaz was mine.

Chapter Thirteen

Jasmine

I was making it a full-time job, ignoring Kora's calls the following day. I eventually sent her a message letting her know that the date went well and that I was trying to work on my book. On the other hand, while I was trying my best to ignore Kora's calls, Oren was doing the same with my calls. It's unlike him to ignore my calls even when he's upset. But, then again, last night, I had ended up turning off my phone because his calls wouldn't stop.

The way things had ended last night with Terrence made me feel guilty. Kora had said I just needed to focus on having fun. But as terrible as it was to admit, fun was not worth it if it didn't help me escape my writer's block.

How did someone even get writer's block when writing the juiciest part of the book?

Maybe I wasn't meant to be a writer, just a reader with

unattainable dreams. If Oren would stop ignoring me, this would be the perfect time when a friend would need some motivation and advice. One that doesn't have me going on another date.

Maybe it had all been too soon. I had been committed to sharing the rest of my life with William, and regardless of his feelings not being real, they had felt real to me. It was expected that I hadn't felt any real connection with Terrence.

And with Oren… it had just been a fluke. We've been friends for years, which obviously sparked those fireworks when we kissed. Then again, I wouldn't have expected anything else from Oren. From what I had heard, he knew his way around the bedroom, so that kiss was probably nothing compared to everything else he'd ever done.

I rummage through my nightstand drawer, looking for my pink vibrating friend, the same one Oren had teased me about. If dating didn't work, I would have to find some inspiration within myself. That and nothing cleared my mind like an orgasm, and maybe all I needed in order to find some creativity to write was to clear my mind in the best and most pleasurable way.

I pressed my head against the pillows, and even though this was something I had done a million times before, for some reason, I was getting nervous as my mind began running through fantasies I had set up for my characters but never for myself.

I remove my pants and underwear, spreading my legs on my bed. I grab the vibrator turning it on to my preferred mode before bringing it to my clit. Closing my eyes, I let my fantasy continue, the ropes tightening around my wrist. My legs open up wider as I fantasize about begging for Oren's hand—.

Oren?

No, Jasmine. The last thing you need is to involve your best friend in your sexy fantasies. Think of any other man you want inside your bed besides your friend.

"What are you fantasizing about, love?"

I open my eyes, and Oren is at the entrance of my bedroom, his body against the door frame. His eyes are on the toy in my hand that's currently vibrating on my clit. I close my legs and jump up, gathering my thoughts together.

What the fuck was he doing here? He wasn't supposed to be back for a couple of days, and now he had caught me masturbating.

"Oren— this isn't— what are you— "

Oren steps into the bedroom, walking towards the foot of my bed.

"Open them."

"What?"

Oren looks down, his green eyes darker than usual, and for some fucking reason, it was making me hornier.

"Jasmine, say the word, and I'll leave. But if not, open your legs."

Oren's eyes don't leave my own. This was so wrong; I couldn't possibly be thinking of having Oren in between my thighs. He was my best friend; this was going to complicate everything. But despite reasoning, my legs opened at his command. And Oren gave me a devilish smirk that made me aware there would be no turning back from this moment.

I'm suddenly dragged onto the foot of the bed by my ankle. Oren's bulge pressed up against my bare pussy, his hand around my throat.

"Show me how you were playing with yourself, love. No need to get shy on me now."

My hand reaches down back to my clit, rubbing the vibrator in circles. My eyes closing, picking back up on the fantasy I had been thinking of before getting caught.

I can feel Oren's breath by my ear as he begins sucking on my earlobe, "Tell me what you're fantasizing about, my love." His whisper sends shivers around my body, my nipples pebbling under my shirt. Oren leaves a trail of kisses down my neck, licking and sucking all the right sweet spots that have me moaning for more.

"Bondage," I whisper as he begins to play with the hem of my shirt. My eyes open to see Oren staring intently at my breasts. His thumb brushes against my nipples, my back arching in response. His eyes meet my own, his devious smile indicating he's having a good time teasing me.

"Listen to me, Jaz; I'm going to tell you what I want to do to you. And if you don't agree with something or don't want to do it at all, you tell me no, am I clear?" Oren asks me, his thumb continuing to play with my nipple. When I delay in answering him, he gives it a squeeze, my pussy clenching with need.

"Jasmine, answer me."

"Yes, I understand."

Oren grabs ahold of my hand and presses the vibrator harder against my clit. "Good, love. This is what's going to happen. I'm going to start with getting you completely naked. Then I'm going to take this shirt of yours and tie it around your wrists." Oren rubs the vibrator in circles, a moan escaping my lips.

"Oren, please, just do it. Do anything you want to me."

"Fuck me," Oren growls, tossing the vibrator to the side and pulling my shirt off. His hands capture my wrists, and as he promised, he ties them together. Tightening them enough for me to have a hard time trying to escape. Not that I was even thinking of a way to escape his hold.

Oren's lips find my ear once again, his thumb teasing my nipple.

"I can't wait to make you shake with pleasure, my love." His lips and tongue trail down my neck towards my breasts, stopping directly at my nipples, which are practically begging to be played with.

"Oren, please," I beg. I need his mouth on them. Licking, sucking, and biting them. I needed to feel his mouth on me.

"I love hearing you beg for me, Jasmine; beg for me again, my love." He says, flicking his tongue over my nipple, knowing it's not going to be enough to satisfy my need.

"Oren, please just suck on them."

Oren's breathy chuckle hits my skin before his lips wrap around my nipple. His teeth graze it slightly, pulling it into his mouth, sucking and flicking it with his tongue.

My pussy throbs, begging for his touch.

Begging for more.

Oren reciprocates his teasing onto the next nipple. My back arches in response, yearning for him to go lower and satisfy my pussy.

"Tell me what you want, love. Tell me what you need." Oren whispers, his hot breath caressing my skin.

"Oren, I need you." I moan.

Oren lifts himself up in response. Peering down at my naked body on display for him.

"Need me to what? Come on, love, use your words." Oren

asks, his fingertips dancing along every curve of my body but stopping right at my pussy.

"Fuck— I need you to make me come." I groan out in frustration.

Oren reaches over for the vibrator, placing it on my clit in a circular motion. His other hand teases my opening as he inserts two fingers in my pussy, pulling in and out achingly slow.

"Oren, stop fucking around and make me come."

Oren's pace remains the same as he looks up at me.

"Is this not enough,h Jasmine? Do you want me to go harder? Maybe faster?" Oren begins picking up his pace. His fingers slam into me as the vibrator continues to tease my clit. Oren adjusts his fingers in an upward motion; a moan escapes my lips as my hands clench down onto the shirt that's tying them down.

"Or maybe you just want me to change the angle."

"Oh fuck, yes, Oren. Please keep going."

Oren's pace doesn't halt. Instead, he continues to fuck me with his fingers. My cunt tightens around them, wishing it were more than just his fingers. Pressure begins to build up as Oren pushes the vibrator harder onto my clit.

"What's his name?" Oren asks.

"What?" I ask, confused, my orgasm building up and clouding my mind.

Oren removes the vibrator, his pace slowing down. I groan at Oren's denial of finishing what he started.

"What the fuck, Oren."

Oren brings the vibrator back to my clit; my body jolts back from the sensitivity.

"I can make you come, love. But, first, you have to tell me

the name of the guy you went out on a date with." He teases as he begins increasing his pace once again.

There was no way that Oren was serious. Why would he even care about Terrence? I had been on dates with men before. Why did he care all of a sudden?

Then again, I wasn't living with him before, let alone kissing him, and I definitely wasn't letting him anywhere near my pussy before.

Oren repeats his movements from before. The vibrator pressed against my clit in a circular motion, his fingers pumping in and out of me.

"Tell me who he is, love. Be a good girl, tell me, and I'll let you come."

Oh fuck. This was wrong, but it felt so good.

"Oren don't—"

"His name, love. I want his name, or I'll stop again."

The pressure was building up again, and I needed to release it. Fuck me, I had to tell him.

"Terrence." I moan out his name, not able to handle the sensitivity of my clit. Oren's hands lift and grasp my neck while the other one remains on my clit, building the pressure inside of me.

"Don't you dare moan out his name while I'm pleasing you."

The pressure of his hand around my throat sends off a wave of pleasure throughout my body.

"Fuck, Oren, I'm going to come."

"Come for me, love. Scream out my name for me."

I release my orgasm, letting the euphoria wrap itself around me. My eyes never leave Oren's.

"Fuck." We say in unison.

Oren drops the vibrator onto the bed and untangles the shirt from my wrist, and I quickly grasp my bedsheets, pulling them towards my body as if it would somehow erase my naked body being sprawled out right in front of him from Oren's memories.

Words begin to escape from my lips, but no clear sentence seems to form.

What would I even say to him?

Thanks for making me come?

Fuck.

What had we done?

"Jasmine, I'm sorry I shouldn't have overstepped. I got carried away." Oren's eyes looked away from my own as if it were too hard to look at me after knowing what we had just done.

"No, it's okay. I allowed it, too. This was all consensual, Oren. The good thing is that we didn't get too carried away." I grab ahold of his hand to have him look back at me.

"This doesn't change a thing. We're still friends, right?" I ask, and I swear Oren's eyes almost look hurt by the question.

"Always." He says, leaning down and pressing a kiss onto my forehead, his hand caressing my cheek.

"Why don't you get ready? I'm going to head out for a second, and the minute I come back, we can go and get something to eat. Then we can discuss how boring your life has been without me around." He teases, his hand falling from my face before stepping out of my bedroom and leaving the apartment.

I get up and put my clothes back on, heading to my closet to grab something to wear. Closing the closet door, I head out towards the bathroom, my eyes meeting my laptop, which I had left on the desk.

I can't help but sit down and begin writing the scenes I had struggled to write for the past few days. My mind spaces out, and my fingers type away, breaking down the wall that had restricted me from continuing my novel.

Suddenly, I was hit with clarity. I was finally able to write after feeling inspired.

Oren had inspired me.

Oren was my muse.

Chapter Fourteen

Oren

Friends? I make her come, but I still get friend-zoned. There's no escaping this hell. My fist meets Kora's door in a repeated motion.

Terrence.

She set Jaz up on a date with Terrence Brown.

"Do you have to bang on my door like that? A normal person would just knock twice and wait patiently." Kora opens the door, gesturing for me to come inside. She closes the door once I enter and heads back to her piano stationed in the center of her living room. I was still not aware of how they got that thing in here. She sits at the bench, continuing to play her notes as if I hadn't just come to speak with her.

"Terrence Brown? Kora? You set her up on a date with that dickhead?" I raise my voice over the sound of her piano. Kora was a great pianist. I had listened to her play many times, which is how I knew that, at this moment, she was only playing random keys to ignore this conversation.

"Kora, I'm speaking to you."

Kora rolls her eyes and sighs in frustration, her hands smacking down on the keys of her piano.

"God, Oren, it was just a date. Obviously, it didn't turn out well because she hasn't responded to any of my calls or texts. Unless she's busy with him right now. I never pictured Jaz as sex on the first date kind of girl, but she's full of surprises."

I groan in annoyance, "Kora, please just stop talking." This woman needed an off button. Jasmine had obviously not slept with him because she was still in our apartment this morning, and there was no sign of this man having been there, especially since I found her sprawled on her bed, pleasing herself.

God, she looked so fucking beautiful, and I didn't even tell her that she looked beautiful because I was so caught up in finding out who Kora had sent her out on a date with. I had come back home expecting to be able to talk to her, and I let my horniness get the best of me. The only reason my dick wasn't still hard was because an annoying, uncooperative Kora was standing right in front of me now.

"It doesn't matter whether the date went well or not. What matters is that I trusted you to take care of her while I was gone, and you sent her out on a date." I argue, trying to get her to understand.

"I'm sorry. Betrayal wasn't my intention, and I didn't see it that way because even though you're too blind to see it, Jaz does care about you more than a friend should. And I just wanted to prove that even though you think she's not ready to move on, she thinks otherwise because she agreed to the date in the first place."

Kora was right; I couldn't make decisions for Jaz. She would be ready when she felt ready. Just like how I had given her a choice today, she chose to let me please her rather than telling me to go fuck off.

"Kora, I need Terrence's number now."

I was going to make sure that man never contacted Jaz again. Not that I saw him as competition, but something about him had all the women of the East Coast falling for him, and I'm going to make sure that Jaz is as far as she can be when it comes to him.

"Why?"

"Does it matter?"

Kora pauses for a second as if she's truly contemplating giving me his number before sliding her phone out of her pocket and sending me his contact information.

"Thank you," I say before walking back to the door to see myself out.

"For what exactly?" Kora chuckles, knowing damn well what I'm thanking her for.

"Don't push it, Kora," I remark before stepping out and heading back to the apartment.

Jaz was in the shower the moment I entered the apartment. That meant I still had some time to change and get ready before leaving. I walk over to my room and get ready, but not before pulling out my phone to send Terrence a text to fuck off. I didn't know if he had texted her already, but I was going to make sure that he would be staying away if she ever sent a text back.

I grab my clothes and put myself together before stepping back out to see Jaz dressed in her shorts and one of my overused t-shirts that she loved so much. And fuck, it made me want to take her back into the bedroom and have more of her. She looked up from her phone, turning it off and bringing it to her pocket.

Was she texting Terrence?

Could I even ask her that?

Fuck.

I was going to have to bite my tongue on this one. I had already overstepped. The last thing I needed to do was act like a jealous psycho.

"Hey, um, where do you want to go for lunch?" She asks, her voice shy and mellow. Nothing like the Jaz I'm used to.

"Anything you want, my love. I'm starving." I walk over to her, leaving little space between us. My finger twists around her coil of hair.

This woman was devastatingly beautiful. From her bundle of curls, her doe brown eyes, those plump, kissable lips, her full figure, and don't even get me started on praising her beautiful glistening cunt.

This woman was going to be all mine.

"Is sushi okay?" Her voice barely reaches a whisper.

My eyes move from her lips back to her eyes, my cock pressing tightly against my jeans.

"Sushi sounds fine, my love." I nudge my head towards the door, having her follow as I walk out. Jaz leans against the hallway wall while she waits for me to lock the door. Before she can push herself off the wall, I lean my body towards hers, my arm blocking her from leaving.

"I just have to tell you that you look beautiful." Jaz's cheeks flush at the compliment. This woman needed to hear those words every day, to the point that it wasn't so much a compliment but a daily reminder.

"Thank you," she whispers.

I lean my head back to her ear, letting her know exactly what I should've said in her bedroom.

"And you looked even more beautiful laying naked on that bed with that wet pussy waiting for me."

I hear Jasmine suck in her breath as I push off the wall and head towards the elevator.

"Oren!" I hear her screech as she comes running after me.

There's my lovely Jasmine.

Chapter Fifteen

Jasmine

A couple of days had passed since the incident with Oren, and things felt like they had gone back to normal. When I wasn't writing, I was working at the bookstore, still unaware of my last day. Marvin had spent most of his time in the back looking at flights and trips he had planned on going on once he got the store out of his hands.

"I bet you it's one of these big corporate dickheads." I say, trying my best not to move my lips. I was currently sitting on the couch that Oren had in the middle of his studio, trying to stay as still as possible as he painted.

"You don't know that, maybe they're a regular person just like the rest of us. I'd go as far as betting that they are probably way better than Marvin." Oren's eyes don't leave the canvas as he speaks; his concentration is focused on the canvas in front of him.

"I just don't want to lose my job, and as much of a dick-head as Marvin is, I love that I can pretty much do anything I want in the bookstore. This new owner may start coming up with new rules and procedures."

Change wasn't my cup of tea, and not knowing exactly when it was happening or what changes would be made didn't make it any better.

"Jaz, you just need to relax; all will come in good timing. You just need to be patient and focus on that book you're writing. By the way, how's that coming along?"

Great, this was just what I needed. I wanted to let my best friend know that my novel wouldn't advance anytime soon since I couldn't give in to the one thing that inspired me.

"It's great!" Oren's eyes shifted towards me, which was more than enough to tell me that he had just called me a liar.

I clear my throat, shifting in my seat on the couch. Suddenly, the room had gotten slightly too warm for my liking.

"Can I move? I'm tired." Oren looks up with a sly grin.

"Sure, love, if I'm being honest, you didn't need to stay still. I can recall every little detail I need about you to make this painting." I run my hands through my hair, detangling some of curls before giving up and tying the thick bundle together. Oren's eyes remain on me the whole time, and I swear I can see his hunger for more ever since that day.

But regardless of what I thought or wanted, we had agreed to forget all about what had happened, which meant we would never repeat our actions of the other day again.

"Of course, you had me stuck in this *torturous position* for hours." I exaggerate, knowing it had only been a max of five minutes. I had come up to the loft after my shift hoping that just being around Oren would inspire me. But the only thing it was bringing on was sexual frustration. This man was painting me, and I found it hot to the point I was fantasizing about him bending me over this couch and fucking me.

What the hell was wrong with me?

"Torturous? I can put you in a much more satisfying position if that's what you want, love." Oren's smirk makes an appearance on his face. The sun shone through the loft's windows, making his olive-toned skin glow. This man was built to make women fall onto their knees, and I was willing to be one of them.

"What are you thinking about?"

Oren's question brings me out of my daze. "Nothing," I quickly say, opening my laptop, trying to brush off the embarrassment of Oren catching me in a daydream about me getting on my knees for him. Oren walks over and sits right next to me, obviously not having a clue about personal space.

"That wasn't nothing, Jaz; I practically caught you drooling at me." I let out a fake chuckle, hoping he would take the bait of him being delusional about what he saw. "Sorry to disappoint, but if there had been any drool, which there wasn't. It wouldn't have been because of you."

Oren's eyebrows raise in amusement, knowing damn well he's attractive enough to be fantasized about. But I wasn't about to give him any more of a reason to be flamboyant.

"You know what I've realized, love?" Oren asks, stretching over my laptop to have his face close to mine.

"What's that?"

Oren's hand touches my chin, lifting it to have me look at him.

"I think that by now, I can tell when you're lying, and the

reason you're lying is because you don't want to admit to having been caught fantasizing about me." I open my mouth to respond but choke on my words, unsure what to say.

"It's okay, you don't have to admit it. But just know you're not the only one fantasizing about your best friend." Oren's hand trails down my neck, his fingers skating towards my shoulder, playing with the strap of my top.

"In fact, I can't help but think what exactly could have happened if we had continued our little escapade that morning." Oren's face leans closer to mine, his lips dangerously near my own.

"Oren," I whisper, his green eyes staring intensely into my own.

"Yes?"

"This is a mistake."

"How come it doesn't feel like one?"

Oren's lips crash into my own, his hands fisting my hair, pulling me closer to him. Kissing me with determination as if trying to prove this was anything but a mistake.

This was perfection.

Oren shuts the laptop between us and lays it on the floor as he pushes me onto the couch. His hand trails down my body, my hands instinctfully wrap around his sturdy arms. This wasn't what we had agreed to, but I didn't care.

Oren moves his mouth down to my neck, sucking at the sweet spot in the crevice between my neck and collarbone. My back arches in response. He slides his hand underneath, holding my arch up as he grinds his hardness onto my cunt.

No sound but our heavy breathing surrounds us, and we are both too afraid to say something that would ruin the moment.

Oren's lips find their way back to my own, this time his hands moving under my shirt, grabbing onto my hips to push me closer to him. I moan at the sudden thrust between my legs. I needed more of him; I had to have more of him.

The sudden ringing of my phone breaks our kiss apart. I stretch over, picking my bag off the floor. Shuffling through the purse's interior, looking for it. Pulling it out, Terrence's name flashes on the screen. "That little fucker." Oren mutters, snatching the phone away from me and picking it up.

"Hey, give me the—" Oren's hand covers my mouth, blocking me from saying anything. I try my best to reach up for the phone. But there's only so much I can do when this six-foot man holds me down as he answers the phone.

"Hello, Terrence; what a pleasure it is to hear from you," Oren answers bitterly.

I tried to pull Oren's hand off my mouth, which was a waste of physical exertion.

"You're a dead man, Oren." Though my words sound muffled, I know Oren heard them by the smirk on his face.

"Well, Terrence, there's no need to check up on my girl anymore because she's doing fine with me."

My tongue shoots out, licking Oren's palm, hoping it would gross him out and have him release me. Oren only gives me a cheeky smile before letting out a chuckle.

"That's right, baby, lick it just like that."

My eyes practically jump out of my eye sockets as I scream in frustration. Slapping Oren for embarrassing me.

It wasn't like I had wanted to continue my relationship with Terrence. The reason for his call was probably because I had been ignoring his texts about a second date. I should've told him I wasn't interested, but I didn't know how to say it.

So, I thought ignoring him would be the best option. He obviously didn't understand that, being that he was calling me. And now he was probably thinking that I was giving Oren a blowjob while he was on the phone.

"I'm sorry, Terrence, but Jasmine and I are currently a bit busy, so we'll probably give you a call back… never." Oren releases his hand from my mouth as he hangs up and tosses the phone into my purse.

"Get off of me!" I shout, pushing Oren's body away from my own.

Oren removes himself from me allowing me to get up and grab my laptop, which I quickly shove into my purse agressivly.

"You're mad," Oren states.

"Really? I hadn't realized! How could you tell?" I adjust the purse over my shoulder, walking past him towards the loft's door.

Oren runs past me, trying to stop me from leaving, "Oren, not now. I'm very annoyed with you and want to leave."

"I don't understand. You're upset that I told him to leave you alone?" Oren looked far more annoyed than he should be.

It was more than him being a territorial dick. It was about him embarrassing me and trying to fight battles for me that didn't need to be fought. I could let Terrence know I wasn't interested over the phone myself. And if I had actually been interested, he would have ruined it for me.

We had just been kissing a moment ago, and now shit had already hit the fan. This was more than enough proof to let me know that this wouldn't work out. Just like last time, we were caught up in the moment.

"Oren, what you did was crossing the line. It was disrespectful and embarrassing. If I had wanted him to leave me alone, I would've told him that myself over the phone. I don't need you to go all alpha male on him just because we've kissed. You crossed a line." Oren reaches out to grab my hand, but I step back.

"Jaz, I'm sorry."

I CROSS MY ARMS OVER MY CHEST, "I KNOW YOU ARE, OREN. But right now, I'm a bit annoyed and would like to go home. So please move out of the way." Oren sighs but moves away from the door, allowing me to walk out. I make my way down the steps, heading back to the apartment but not to go back home. I needed to speak to someone about this.

"He embarrassed me! Can you believe him?!" I exclaim as I walk back and forth in Kora's living room. Unfazed by my outburst, Kora continues to write on her music sheets as she plays around with some notes. I had sprinted to Kora's apartment after leaving the loft, needing another opinion on the Oren fiasco.

Kora sighs, putting her pen down and playing something completely different on her piano. "I can't believe I'm basically a couple's therapist, except the couple refuses to be a couple."

"What?" I scrunch my face in confusion, unsure what she meant by her comment.

"Nothing; listen, Terrence is a great guy but he's not a saint. He won't care that you've moved onto Oren." I halt my step, looking straight at her.

"I have not moved onto Oren; we are friends. Nothing has changed."

"You're right; nothing has changed," Kora shakes her head in agreement with my statement. "Except you let him finger you, and you've kissed on two separate occasions. So something in that relationship has changed."

My jaw drops at Kora's collectiveness as she gets up to sit on the couch, patting the cushion for me to join her.

"And if I recall correctly, from the moment you entered the apartment spilling out all of the tea, you mentioned a couple of times how he's… what did you call it?" Kora brings her hand up to her head, scratching it as if in a deep thought. "Oh, that's right, your *muse.*"

I grab one of her fancy throw pillows from the couch, smacking her with it.

"Don't taunt me."

Kora giggles at my outburst with the pillow before fixing her hair. Not that there was a single hair out of place. This woman could be dragged through a muddy forest and still come out looking pristine.

"I'm just saying that you like him a little more than just a friend, Jaz. And that's perfectly okay." As I rest my head on her shoulder, Kora brings me into her arms.

"Kora, I don't know why I let him touch me. I just complicated everything. What should I do?" I prayed that Kora had some magical solution to my mistakes. To make everything disappear and go back to normal.

"That's easy, go get your muse."

"Huh?" I tear away from her embrace, looking at her in shock. I came here looking for a way out of my situation, and she was handing me more wood to add to my fire.

"Jasmine, you need to stop overthinking this. Oren is into you if he's making these moves. He's a man you can trust, and he's a man who cares about you. So go for it. Use up your muse and finish that fucking novel." I nod, not entirely sure if I'll be following anything that she says the minute I leave this apartment. But the one thing she had right is that Oren cares about me, and I trust him. So, if there was anyone I would decide to test the waters with, it would be him.

"You're right."

"I know I am. You wouldn't be coming to me if you didn't think I'd give you the right answers. Now sit on the bench with me and tell me which of these compositions you like best."

I walk over to the bench, sitting next to her while she sets up her sheets.

"What are all these compositions for?" I ask, curious about what she was working so hard on.

"It's for a competition. Whoever wins gets to join this famous classical musician Hugo Dupont's next album. Which in the classical musician industry is pretty fucking cool and intense. Hence, all of my scattered music sheets."

I look around at the scattered sheets all over the floor. "Who's your muse?" I ask, curious to see if she had anyone that inspired her creativity too.

Kora chuckles, playing around with the notes before beginning to play. "Success is my muse. And I'm going to make sure I get to it."

Me too, Kora… me too.

Chapter Sixteen

Oren

As much as I loved my sister, she could be somewhat like a leech. Except instead of sucking blood out of you, she was sucking out the life from you. When she's talking about her interests, I don't mind sitting down and listening to her. At least I don't mind pretending that I'm listening. But when she starts questioning my life and relationships, I contemplate continuing to pay for my phone plan.

"Are you listening to me?" Phoebe asks through the muffled line. This woman could not sit still for a second.

"Phoebe, I can barely listen to you when your mic is being covered. What the hell are you doing?"

Calls were not meant to be this complex. I can hear rustling from the other end of the call. Had she buried her phone in the ground? What the hell was taking her so long?

"Sorry," I hear her say. This time, it was much clearer than before. "I'm cleaning out my closet and lost you under a pile of clothes." I let out a sigh, already knowing she was preoccupied with other tasks while speaking to me.

"Why am I not surprised?"

"Hey! Just because I'm speaking with you over the phone doesn't mean I'm going to stop what I'm doing. I need to get things done." Phoebe argues, "This isn't even what I wanted to discuss. We were talking about the Fourth of July." I groaned into the phone, already knowing where this was going. Every year, my family and Jaz's family got together to celebrate the fourth, and last year, Jaz and I opted out of going because she was having a rough time after her breakup with William.

"You two better be coming. You guys canceled at the last minute last year. You could at least let a girl know ahead of time. I was stuck listening to Mom and Delilah shipping you and Jaz together all night." Phoebe groans in the remembrance of that day. Even though it wasn't the only time and definitely not the last time that Jaz and my mother got together and talked about how they'd wished that Jasmine and I would somehow realize that we were meant to be together.

If you asked me, the women were onto something, but it wasn't as easy as one could fantasize about. "You know, while you're at it. Why don't you put on your big boy pants and ask her out before some other man comes and proposes to her."

"Not funny and not that easy," I remark.

There it was somehow the conversation had gone from Fourth of July to having it be about me finally making my move. In Phoebe's defense, she had been waiting since we were teenagers. I'd always seen Jaz as more than a friend. You didn't grow up around someone as beautiful as Jasmine and not think about having her be yours. But I wanted to be the right man for her. I wanted to be successful for her and give her all that she needed in this world, regardless of whether she asked for it or not. She deserved so much more than I could have given her.

"Of course, it's not that easy because you made it hard yourself. Listen, you still have some time left before the fourth. So make it work." I roll my eyes at Phoebe's demand, not bothering to keep up with this conversation about having a relationship with Jaz.

"I'll write it down in my calendar. In the meantime, I'll have to let you go. See ya on the fourth." I mutter, ending the call before she drags me into another conversation about things I need to do.

As much as I'd love to make things work with Jaz, I first had to apologize. That was exactly my intention last night, but by the time I finished working on the painting, it had gotten late, and Jaz was asleep. On top of that, thanks to Garrett, I was behind on some last-minute work that I had to get done before the art gallery at the end of the summer. Most of the work I had set up for it was art I had worked on throughout the years. But there were still new pieces I needed to get done. But right now, Jaz was my priority.

She was all I cared about.

And I was going to make it up to her.

THERE WAS NO REASON FOR ME TO BE THIS NERVOUS TO apologize. But being that I was about to tell my best friend that I was sorry for being a territorial prick, as well as asking her to be more than friends, I think I had every reason to be. My grip tightens around the flowers in my hand, and I'm unsure if this is even the right thing to do. I enter the elevator, clicking my floor number. Just as the door closes, a hand shoots out to stop them.

"Hello, Oren," Kora chirps before the doors can even finish opening back up.

Great, this is just what I fucking needed. Kora steps in, lifting her eyebrows as she peers over at the bouquet of flowers in my hand.

"Those are cute." She says, pressing the elevator's button to have the doors close. I was not in the fucking mood to have Kora start teasing me. How did she always end up catching me in vulnerable moments? It's like this woman had a sixth sense for that crap. I nod my head at her, not wanting to reveal too much. The last thing I needed was to hear from her how badly I had fucked up.

"You fucked up pretty badly with that whole phone call." I glance over at Kora in shock.

That fucking sixth sense.

"How the hell do you know about that?" I question as the elevator door dings open for us to exit.

"Oren, you cannot expect two girls to hang out for two weeks and not immediately click and speak about everything to one another," Kora says, stopping her movement the minute she steps out of the elevator so that we can continue our conversation.

"Everything?"

I highly doubted that Jasmine was feeling up to telling Kora all the details about what happened the minute I returned from Alaska or what would've continued happening if Terrence just stuck to his own lane.

That man had some fucking audacity; he had ignored my text and still had the balls to call Jaz. But if the text hadn't been clear enough for him, our call was.

"Everything," Kora responds. "And I have to say that I am very disappointed that you didn't tell me about your little welcome home gift."

"She told you— wait, it wasn't a welcome home gift. It just happened." I correct.

"Yeah, I'm aware. But when you get in there and grovel, and she forgives you and decides to open up to you. Just remember to thank me." Kora pats me on the shoulder before sliding past me to head towards her apartment. Kora would have to keep waiting if she was expecting a thank you for being a friend. Her secluded childhood growing up had affected her when it came to being friends with people. But she was getting there.

I unlock the apartment door and call out for Jasmine's name as I enter. I hear the closing of what I assume is her bedroom door as she walks out of the hallway and towards the living room. She must've just showered because her curls were voluminous and shining. She had on a white tank top that didn't help my situation, being that her nipples were peeking through, demanding attention.

"What's up with the flowers?" Jaz asks, coming over to the kitchen and taking a seat on the counter. I push the flowers towards her like an idiot, not thinking clearly about letting her know that they're for her. What the fuck was wrong with me.

I was a fucking flirt with anyone, but every time I got around her lately, I felt like a thirteen-year-old boy asking their crush to be their Valentine.

"They're for me?" Jaz asks, taking the bouquet of Lilies away from me.

"Yeah, I wanted to apologize for yesterday." I take a step closer to Jaz, fitting myself between her legs while she continues to look at the flowers.

"I shouldn't have acted that way. I was just —"

Jealous? Pissed? Annoyed?

"Oren, it's okay, I understand," Jaz says, setting the flowers down on the counter.

"You do?"

I must've entered a new dimension because I could've sworn that just yesterday, Jaz was fucking pissed. And according to Kora, I was going to have to grovel. So, what happened in the moments between last night and right now that Jasmine no longer saw anything wrong with my actions?

Was this what Kora said I would thank her for?

"Yeah, well, I kind of have to tell you something." Jasmine grabs a piece of her hair, twirling the strand around her finger. Something she only did when she was nervous. I lift my hand to her cheek and rub my thumb across her soft skin to comfort her. My other hand reached the side of her head to massage her scalp, which always seemed to ease her mind.

"What's going on, love? You can talk to me."

My revelation of wanting more could wait a little longer. I wasn't going anywhere, and neither was Jaz.

"Oren, do you remember the other morning? When you came back from your trip?" She asks, her cheeks flushing from embarrassment even though there is nothing to be embarrassed about.

"How could I forget?"

Jaz clears her throat, her eyes searching around the room. She wasn't looking for anything in particular but just trying to stay clear of my own eyes. "Well, you see, it kind of sparked something in me."

"Sparked something in you?" I questioned, unsure what she was trying to get at.

"Yes, like inspiration… for my book."

Now, this time, my cheeks heat up from her admission. I can't help but smirk down at her, knowing that she sees me as her muse.

"I know it's weird — "

"It's not weird," I cut off. "Trust me, I completely understand."

"Really?" Her eyes jolting out in surprise, I nod my head, not wanting to overshadow the continuation of her story. That was not the only thing she had to say by the way she was still holding tight to that curl that was wrapped around her finger.

"Great, because I have something to ask you." I wrap my hand around her own, gently helping her untangle the hair that was stopping blood circulation from flowing to her finger.

"Go ahead, love, you can tell me anything."

"Oren, I want to be more." She says, tightening her hand around my own now.

"More?"

I wasn't sure what she was trying to get at. I knew this couldn't be that easy. Knowing Jasmine, she probably thought I wasn't into her, despite me gawking at her naked body like it was my first time seeing a woman's body.

"It doesn't have to be serious; it can be a friend thing, like friends with benefits." Jasmine continues to rant about her friends-with-benefits idea as I stand and stare, waiting for her to stop. There was no way that I was going to allow this woman to be my friend with benefits. I could work around that if that's what she wanted for now. But this was only going to lead to me calling her mine.

"Am I talking too much? You know I tend to blab on when I'm nervous. I just—"

"Jasmine." I cut her off, her eyes finding mine, waiting for a response.

"I don't do non-serious relationships."

Jasmine lets out a chuckle, obviously finding my statement hard to believe. "Oren, I don't think I've ever seen you in a serious relationship. You don't have to lie to say no."

"I don't do non-serious relationships when it comes to you, Jasmine. You deserve more than that." My hands find their way to her cheeks, bringing her closer to me.

"You can just say no to me, Oren; it's fine." Her voice was shaky from my rejection.

"Jasmine," I whisper. My lips leaning over her plump ones. "I will continue to be your muse. I will please you in so many different ways, love. But I won't fuck you. Not until you're fully mine. Do we have a deal?" I ask, my lips just waiting for her agreement so that I can start my part of the deal.

Jaz nods her head, her eyes focused on my lips. I wrap my hand around her throat, her eyes looking up at my own.

"Use your words, love."

"Yes, it's a deal."

With that, I crash my lips onto hers, my hand tightening

on her throat as our mouths move in sync, my teeth bringing her bottom lip into my mouth and sucking the cherry-flavored chapstick off her lips.

"Get completely naked and open those legs wide for me, love." Jasmine only gives me a teasing smile before removing her tank top and letting her tits fall into my view.

Thank you so fucking much, Kora.

Chapter Seventeen

Oren

Jasmine sat on the counter, her doe brown eyes looking up at me, waiting for my next demand like a good girl. Her curves are accentuated as she sits there naked in front of me. I could look at her like this for all eternity. Her chest rises with each shaky breath; her nipples perked up, waiting to feel my touch again. Her thighs slowly opened more every second, waiting to be pleased.

"Lay back, my love." The demand comes out in a whisper, but it's loud enough for Jasmine to hear. She lays her body on the marble counter, my breath hitching from her mesmerizing appearance.

Anyone who said that The Birth of Venus, the Mona Lisa, or any fucking old piece of artwork was the most beautiful art in the world had never laid their eyes on Jasmine. And that for any artist would be a shame because Jasmine was truly God's best creation.

Jasmine Monroe was a masterpiece. God had taken his time in sculpting every crevice, beauty mark, scar, color, and texture on her body. How could you not want to get down on your knees and praise such a beauty?

I brought my hand down to Jasmine's neck. My fingers grazed her skin lightly. Trailing down her collarbone that my lips ached to leave their mark on. But this wasn't about what I wanted or what I needed. This was going to be all for Jasmine. I wanted to see her ache for me, ache for more. I wanted to hear my name escape her lips, begging for more, begging for her release.

My fingers trace circles around her nipples. Her breath hitching as she closes her eyes.

"Eyes on me," I bring my finger and thumb around her right nipple. Squeezing it enough to have her arching her back for more. Her eyes were now on my own, just like I wanted them. I didn't want her fantasizing about anything else or someone else.

"If you want me to stop at any moment, all you have to do is say it, and I'll stop," I instruct as I release her nipple and go back to tracing a circle around them. Her skin lifts with goosebumps. Jasmine shakes her head up and down, her breath hitching as I continue to tease her senses. I grasp each nipple with my fingers, squeezing them lightly, tugging them up. Her body lifting to ease the slight ache coming from her nipples.

"Remember, you can always say stop." I let go of her nipples, rubbing them with the pads of my thumbs. Her thighs widen as a light moan escapes her mouth.

I grind my teeth, fighting off the hard-on suffocating in my jeans. Yearning to be inside of her. But even if I wanted to, even if I could, I still wouldn't do it. This moment had to be just for her. My fingers find her nipples again, this time pinching them harder and pulling on them higher.

"Up," I say; Jasmine's back arches up, the hard counter making it harder for her to find comfort in lifting for relief, but that thought alone makes me want to take her even more.

"Oren," She groans as I squeeze her nipples a bit tighter.

"Tell me what you need," I whisper, releasing Jasmine's nipples and having her fall back onto the counter. Her brown nubs begin to swell, and I drop my lips down to them, swirling my tongue around each one and sucking. I hear Jasmine's moans, encouraging me to continue to tease them with my teeth. My hand grazes past her navel, towards her already dripping wet pussy.

Fuck, this woman would be the death of me.

I bring my fingers against her folds, rubbing her pussy up and down as I continue to press kisses down her body, stopping right in between her legs.

"I want to feel you clench your thighs around me." I groan into her inner thigh.

Jasmine lifts herself up on the counter to look down at me. Her lustful eyes glistening just like her pussy.

"Oren, please. I need you." She begs. I grab ahold of her hips, tugging her towards me as I kneel on the floor, sitting her thighs onto my shoulder.

"Oren, wait, you can't." Jasmine's eyes look down, searching for my own. She looks worried as she tries to get off my shoulders. I hold onto her thighs tighter, waiting for her to relax with my touch.

"Jasmine, I promise you that I can." She relaxes at my words, but her eyes still show her worry.

"Trust me, if you feel uncomfortable, just tell me." Jaz nods in agreement, bringing her hands to the counter for support.

I grab her ass, making sure to squeeze a little more than I would to teach her a lesson. I readjust her onto my shoulders, aligning her pussy with my mouth. I knew Jasmine was putting some of her weight onto the counter, trying to hold herself up. But that wouldn't matter in a few seconds when I had her losing control and pulling at my hair for more.

"Jasmine, I want to see you looking down at me," I say before pressing a kiss to her pussy. Jasmine looks down at me as I tease my tongue around her clit. Bringing it back and forth. Not giving her enough stimulation but giving her exactly enough to start begging for the real thing. I keep my left hand around her thigh while the other teases her entrance, waiting for her to beg.

"Oren, what the fuck are you waiting for?" Jasmine snaps.

My hand slaps her round ass, making her jump slightly, not having expected that.

"I'm waiting for you to beg for me like a good girl, my love."

Jasmine bites her lip before giving me a devious smile.

"Oren, shouldn't you be the one begging me for my pussy? Shouldn't you be praising it?"

Yes, I fucking should.

I thrust my fingers into Jaz's wet cunt, my tongue continuing to circle her clit before bringing my lips around it and sucking on it. I curve my fingers up and speed up my thrusts, sending Jaz's head back, a moan escaping her lips. I release her clit from my mouth, looking up at her, my fingers still thrusting in and out of her wet pussy.

"Jasmine," I murmur.

She looks back down at me, biting down on her lips, holding back the urge to moan for me.

"Look at me when I'm on my knees for you, love. Watch me praise you like the goddess you are. Don't hold back your moans; let me hear how good I make you feel." I say as I bring her clit back into my mouth. Sucking and bringing my tongue back and forth on the bundle of nerves.

"Oren, faster," Jasmine begs, her hands gliding through my scalp, pushing me further into her. Her hips are riding my face. My other hand moves towards her ass. Gripping it tightly as I steady her on my shoulders. God, this woman was going to be the death of me. I was already becoming addicted to her.

Addicted to her touch, stare, voice, and her fucking taste.

I feel her walls clench around my fingers as I keep thrusting in her faster. I follow the rhythm of her hips, satisfying her clit as she continues to ride my face.

"Oren, I'm going to come."

I suck on her clit, this time grazing my teeth lightly on the sensitive nub as I press up onto her g-spot, rubbing it rapidly with every thrust.

Jasmine's grip tightens around my hair, pulling me closer to her, allowing me the pleasure to suffocate in her ecstasy as she screams out my name.

Jasmine releases my hair, her chest rising as she catches her breath from her orgasm.

She smiles down at me as she presses her arms against the

counter again before removing her thighs from my shoulders. My knees remain glued to the floor as I continue to look up and admire her.

The light of the kitchen enhanced the outline of her curls as she stared down at me, her eyes still full of lust, her bottom lip plump from having bitten down on it to hold back her moans. Her soft skin and dark nipples awaited my touch.

"My God, I could sculpt and paint all your beauty for all eternity." I praise.

Jasmine looks away to stop me from seeing her blushing cheeks. I get up and grab her chin, turning it back to face me.

"I mean it, you're beautiful, Jasmine. The most beautiful woman I've ever laid my eyes on, I swear it." I whisper, leaning over to kiss her lips before picking her up to bring her to my bedroom.

"I thought you said you didn't want to have sex?"

"Relax, my sweet nymph. I said I wouldn't have sex, not that I wouldn't cuddle." I respond, laying her down on the bed.

I walk over to my dresser, pulling out an oversized shirt and underwear for her to wear tonight.

"What about you?" Jaz asks, her voice soft and innocent.

My cock hardened just thinking about Jaz's lips wrapped around it. Despite my hard-on, I wasn't going to let that happen. This was supposed to be about her. Jasmine didn't have to feel like she needed to reciprocate it back. I turn back around, expecting her to be under the sheets.

But, instead, she was on the bed, sitting on her knees as if waiting for my order to open her mouth like a good girl.

Fuck.

What do I do?

Could I sleep with jeans on?

Would that be weird?

I walk over and lay my clothes on the mattress, "these are for you." I turn my body back around before sitting on the bed, my back facing her. I feel movement from behind me on the bed, assuming it's Jasmine getting dressed. But the moment I feel her breath on my ear, I know this woman hasn't even touched the clothes.

"Why are you ignoring my question, Oren?" Jasmine asks.

"It's not that I'm ignoring it, love." I turn my body to face her. "I just don't want you to feel that you need to satisfy me because I'm satisfying you. This is about giving you inspiration for your book." I explain, my finger twirling her curl instinctively.

"You're wrong," she says, bringing her face closer.

"This is all about you being my muse, so it's only fair that I get to experience what it's like to satisfy you. Unless you really don't want to, then I'll back off." Jasmine begins to back away, probably already overthinking that she crossed a line. I grab a hold of her wrist, bringing her back to me.

"I want to. I really fucking want to." I groan, the tightening in my pants becoming suffocating.

"Then let me please you," Jasmine whispers, her hands sliding onto my crotch, tightening her hold on my bulge.

"Fuck me." I groan.

Jaz giggles in my ear, "I bet you'd like that."

I turn to face her, my hands back at the base of her throat, bringing her closer. Her lips hovering mine.

"You have no fucking idea."

My lips crash into hers, my tongue teasing her bottom lip for entrance. I needed as much of her as I could get. Jasmine brings her hands to the hem of my shirt, pulling it off. The room is filled with the sound of our heavy breathing and rapid movements as I pull down my pants and briefs.

My cock springs up, in need of her touch.

"Jesus Christ." I groan as Jaz wraps her hand around my cock. I lay my head back on the headboard as Jaz gets on all fours to face me; she arches her back, letting me have a perfect view of her ass.

Jaz tightens her grip on my dick, making me look back down at her, a hiss escaping my lips.

"Now it's your turn to watch me please you."

Jasmine brings her lips to the tip of my cock, sliding her tongue around teasingly before sucking on the tip. She grips my cock and strokes the length up and down, letting her spit slide down her lips as it trails down my cock lubricating her strokes. Jasmine takes my cock in her mouth, her head moving up and down each time, taking more of me in her.

"Fuck baby, just like that." Her left hand cups my balls as she continues to stroke me with the other one. Bringing my cock deeper down her throat.

I bring my hands to her head, tightening my grip on her hair as she picks up her speed, bobbing her head up and down. Choking and gagging on my cock, bringing herself up for air just to go back down and please my needy cock.

"That's right, baby, let me fuck that mouth. Tap twice on my thigh if you need me to stop." I grab Jasmine's head forcing her down onto my cock, having her take every inch. Thrusting my hips in her mouth as she moans and gags from my harshness.

"Do you want me to stop?" I ask, pulling her off so that she can catch her breath.

"Fuck no, I want to feel you come down my throat." She says, eagerly coming back down on my dick. Jasmine takes back control, opening up and relaxing her throat, taking my cock deeper.

God, she was a fucking goddess.

"That's it, Jaz, right there. Fuck, I'm going to come down your throat, love." Jasmine lets out a moan, the vibrations sending my head back in a moan as I push Jasmine's head down and release my cum down her throat.

I look back down to see Jaz's eyes staring up at me as she swallows all of my cum, before pushing herself off.

"Fuck, that was amazing, love." I bring her closer to me, sitting her on my lap. Kissing her lips one last time before raising the bed sheets and letting her slide into them. I turn the lights off and bring her closer to me. Fuck the clothes. I wanted to feel her just like this. Naked and pressed up against me.

"Oren," Jasmine whispers.

"Yes?"

"Do you think this will only complicate things?" Jasmine asks, her voice worrisome. I pull her in closer, my hand rubbing up and down her thigh to soothe her.

"Jasmine, nothing between you and I has ever been complicated… it's always felt right." I responded.

Jaz turns around, laying her head on my chest, and in minutes, she's fast asleep. And like everything else between us, it feels perfect.

Chapter Eighteen

Jasmine

Writing has never been easier; my fingers type rapidly on the keyboard, and my eyes continue glued onto the screen. I wasn't sure if the sudden burst of motivation was due to my inspiration or because I was on my fifth latte today.

"Jesus, I think you should take a break," Kora mutters while sipping her coffee. She stares at me from across the table of the café.

"Says the girl who was glued to her piano chair for a week, composing music." I retorted, my eyes finally leaving the screen to look up at her.

"I was talking about the coffee, not the writing," Kora says, her eyebrows lifting in amusement.

Oh.

She was probably right about that one. "Sorry, I've finally

got this book rolling. I mean, I think I've actually got some-thing to work with." I remove my blue light glasses and replace the sip of coffee with a sip of my iced water, which I had completely forgotten about.

"Hey, I get it. You're finally getting some, and now you've got what you need to make this book come to life." Kora shrugs, taking a bite from her croissant, the flakes falling onto her black-knitted vest. Kora sets down the crois-sant and wipes away the flakes from her vest before peering back up at me and nodding her head, encouraging me to continue to write.

Kora had decided to meet me at the café when she had texted me to hang out. I had let her know that I was trying to catch up on my writing and couldn't give her the proper hangout she wanted. But Kora said she didn't care for the talking as long as she just had some company. The whole time that I had been downing my lattes and writing frantically, she had been enjoying her time watching people and giving out her comments and opinions here and there.

I stretch my fingers and crack them before they stiffen up on me. I had written more than enough, and though Kora said she didn't mind not talking, she still deserved my time, espe-cially when she shared her own time with me when she was busy just to listen to me go off on a tangent about Oren. Shut-ting my laptop, I look at her to give her my undivided attention.

"You don't have to—" Kora begins.

"Yes, I do," I say, cutting her off. She obviously needed a friend, and I was here to listen.

"I'm just nervous about this competition." Kora's hands reach towards mine at the table to hold onto them.

Her hands were cold and clammy, proving that Kora was very anxious about this competition. She said it was a big deal for any classical musician and that it could help her career. Even though Kora looked like she had her life put together, in reality, she needed to win this to prove something to herself and to her parents, who were very much against Kora following her dreams as a musician.

"Kora, you can't doubt yourself, not now. You've worked so hard for this. You're an amazing pianist; if you weren't, you wouldn't have families dying to have you teach their kids. They know you're good at what you do and want their child to be just as good. You've worked hard for this; you've committed yourself to this. I promise that you've got this." I encourage, holding onto her hands tightly. Kora nods her head, taking in my words of encouragement.

"You're right, I'm overthinking. I worked really hard on this. I just need a distraction. Something that will stop me from remembering that I submitted content into this contest." Kora's eyes scan the café; she looked like she was trying to find something or someone.

"Oh my god, are you looking for someone to hook up with?" I asked, swinging my body around to look at our possible contenders.

"Well, what's a better way to distract yourself than with sex? Unless you're a romance writer, then it becomes a part of your job, in a sense." Heat rushes to my cheeks at Kora's comment.

Oren and I had been enjoying our bodies as much as we could without crossing any lines. I had really wanted to fuck him, and it was getting harder every time to stop from going any further. Regardless of just sticking to nothing more than oral, Oren had found a way to make every intimate moment different and spicier.

Especially last night when I, a can of whipped cream and melted chocolate, had been his dessert before dinner.

"Have you been enjoying your sexcapade with Oren?" Kora teases, handing me a piece of her croissant without having to ask if I wanted any.

"Well, yeah, but you know we don't really have sex." I shrug.

Kora crinkles her eyebrows in confusion, "do you guys just lay together naked and hold hands? Is this some weird thing that straight people do?"

Kora scrunches up her nose in disgust, probably picturing what she had said in her head.

"No, of course not. We just do other things… anything besides… intercourse." I whisper from across the table, afraid of anyone listening to our conversation.

"Right, and why is that?"

This had been the second time that Kora and I were out in public talking about my sex life, and this time around, there was no live music to stop our conversation from entering some stranger's ears. I knew nothing was wrong with our conversation; I just wasn't used to it. Especially now that it involved Oren and I's sex life.

"We just think that it should stay that way, especially because we're just friends. Anything more than what we're already doing would make things complicated." I explain, but even as the reasoning leaves my mouth, I know it makes no sense.

"Right, because oral sex is a best friend's thing. That

makes total sense. Every pair of besties does it." Kora crosses her arms across her chest and stares down at me.

"Yes, I know how stupid it sounds. You can stop staring at me."

Despite my admission of stupidity, Kora remained in the same position. At this point, I definitely felt embarrassed at Oren and my thinking process regarding our relationship.

"Listen, I'm just respecting both of our boundaries. Oren doesn't feel comfortable having sex if he's not in a relationship." I reason, but Kora only burst into laughter, leading to people staring.

"God, I am so sorry. That was funny because whatever he said was not how you interpreted it. Because the Oren I know never gave a crap about being in a relationship with someone, especially if it was strictly sex." Kora argues. I sigh, trying to relieve the tension within my chest. This was not a conversation I wanted to have, especially because Kora was right.

Oren did whatever with whoever he wanted. Despite having different girls throw themselves at him daily, he was never in a committed relationship.

It just wasn't his thing… or maybe they weren't his.

"Jaz, I'm just saying that I think that you're only holding yourself back." Kora brings her hands to my arms to comfort me from across the table.

I understood exactly what Kora was telling me, but that was because it was something I had known the whole time. I kissed Oren, and that only escalated to more. Sex is the only thing that's holding us from changing our relationship forever, or at least that's what I was telling myself. I just can't bring myself to admit that Oren and I are becoming something more than friends.

I can't get myself to admit that I'm starting to want to be something more than friends.

AFTER THE CAFÉ, I DECIDED TO GO STRAIGHT HOME TO SPEAK with Oren. Kora had said she had plans with a friend. But by the way, she was looking around the café, searching for a distraction. I could tell that this friend was going to be much better at taking her mind off things than I would've been able to.

I open the apartment door and call out for Oren, unsure if he'd already arrived home. He had been at his loft all week working on his projects for the upcoming gallery.

I walk into the vacant living room, taking a seat on the couch, and I hear Oren walking around his bedroom, which has become more of a shared space now. The door of the bedroom opens, and Oren comes out in nothing but his gray sweats. His gaze is glued to his phone as he comes over and takes a seat beside me, his hand leading its way up to my scalp and running his fingers in a circular motion to massage it.

"Hey, love." Oren huffs, typing away on his phone with his other hand. "Are you hungry?" He asks.

I was about to respond, but my growling stomach beat me to the answer before I could say anything.

"Great, me too. Why don't you check out a place? We can order takeout." Oren continues glued to his phone, which tells me something is off. Any moment that Oren could get away from work and technology, he would take. People were constantly reaching out to him for work, and it could get a bit overwhelming, especially when you were managing it all on your own. So, he was strict when it came to setting definite work hours for himself.

I grabbed Oren's hand, which was currently giving me a nice massage to get his attention. He snaps his head over and turns off his phone. By the concerned look on his face, he probably thinks I want to talk about a personal problem.

"Sorry, love, just work stuff. How are you? How was your day?" Oren asks like he did every night when either one of us got home from work. I was starting to like this living dynamic we were making. Of course, the sexual endeavors were just a bonus.

"It was good; I was able to get a lot of work done. But I'm more concerned about what happened to you. You're practically glued to your phone." I answer by trying my hardest not to sound like a brat. I didn't want to come out as being pushy or needy. Especially when nothing had changed, we had agreed on just staying friends. So, why did it feel like I was being an overbearing girlfriend, wondering why he was on his phone so much?

Oren shrugs before bringing me closer, picking up my legs to bring them over his own. "It's nothing, really; something just came up for my shoot tomorrow, so I'm just trying to find a way to figure it all out."

"What happened?"

I was trying my hardest not to get into his business, but I wanted to help in any way I could.

"It's nothing; the model just decided to cancel at the last minute, so now I need to find a replacement who would be willing and free to shoot tomorrow." Oren begins scrolling through his phone again, skimming through what looks like his list of contacts.

I had no clue Oren had a photoshoot planned for tomorrow; he had kept anything going into his gallery a secret, so I didn't pester him to tell me what exactly he was working on or to show me any of his work. It would only lead to him asking for my manuscript. But something about having him read a book based on my sex life wasn't something I was comfortable with showing him just yet.

But having Oren looking at potential models for his shoot irked me a bit. For some reason, I wanted to be the one in front of the camera.

"I'll do it." I blurt out, not even thinking of what exactly he would have me do tomorrow. Oren stops scrolling on his phone and looks over at me.

"What was that?"

"I said I'll do it. I'll be your model. I know you don't want me to look at your work before it's all put in the gallery, but if you really think about it, I won't actually be seeing the outcome. I'll just have been part of the process." I rationalized in hopes of having him agree to the idea, just so I didn't have to think about him eyeing another woman in one of his projects.

Not that I thought that Oren would be unprofessional. He wouldn't. But I knew that Oren wasn't blind, and if some pretty model with a phenomenal personality was in front of him, he wouldn't even have to think twice before making his move.

That blonde woman from his Instagram feed… *Renee James.*

She was the perfect example. Granted, I didn't know if she

and Oren had slept together, but by the way he looked at her in that picture, I could tell he was thinking of it.

My mind was overcrowded with jealousy, and I didn't like it. I had never felt this way, not when I was with William and certainly not ever with Oren, until now.

"Are you sure you're okay with that?" Oren asks, breaking me away from my thoughts.

"Huh?"

Oren grabs my hand, clasping his fingers around mine. "I asked if you were sure about being my model for tomorrow."

No, I wasn't, but I wouldn't tell him that.

"Yes, of course! I can't wait; quick, let's find something to eat. I'm starving." I unclasp my hands from his and remove my legs off his lap before heading to the kitchen to grab a folder full of takeout menus that we hoard within our kitchen drawer.

"You're amazing, Jaz. Thank you." Oren says, coming over to me by the counter and kissing my head before looking at the menu options in front of us.

And as Oren continues to look through the menus and talk about his favorite place. I can't help but continue to stare at him rather than at the menus. My heart beating faster with every breath that I took.

What had I just agreed to?

Chapter Nineteen

Jasmine

To say I hadn't thought this through would be correct. I really hadn't. And now I was nervous out of my mind, wondering what exactly Oren had planned out for this shoot. I had begged him all last night and this morning to give me a hint as to what exactly we would be shooting. Oren just said I would have to remain patient and wait for tomorrow.

Oren held onto my hand tightly as he pulled me through the crowd of people on the street. He had stopped at a café to get us coffee and breakfast, but I hadn't really touched the muffin he had gotten me; instead, I chugged down the iced latte that was now making me even more nervous about the photoshoot.

Oren opens the door to the loft, moving to the side to let me in first. I make my way up the stairs rather than taking the elevator. Oren seemed to have set up the set the night before because he had his camera set up on a tripod in the middle of the room facing a white backdrop. Fake flowers were placed in a pile on a table next to his camera supplies and some rope.

Looking back at the white backdrop, I see a thick metal rod attached to the ceiling. I couldn't say that I had seen it there before because I hadn't stopped to look up at the ceiling before, but it must've been there the whole time because it seemed pretty sturdy and attached.

Oren makes his way to the camera, and it seems he is already beginning to set it up for the shoot. He adjusted the lights, first asking me to stand in the center of the room to gauge the lighting for the shoot. Setting up the final light stan,d he makes his way towards the closet and pulls out a latter, bringing it over to where I am standing.

"Could you bring me that rope over there?" Oren nudges his head over to the table full of supplies. I walk over to the table and grab the rope, bringing it over to him. Oren begins tying the rope in an intricate knot onto the metal rod and tugging it several times, ensuring it's secure. I watch him take another rope and repeat the same knot onto the rod.

The veins on Oren's arms protrude as he tightens the rope. Oren was wearing his white slacks and light blue linen shirt, his dark curls falling delicately over his face. He had let his hair grow out a bit more than usual this summer, and it only made him look sexier. If he continued to look this good while doing his job, I don't know if I could control myself from getting on my knees for him.

"Are you ready?" Oren asks, climbing down the ladder.

I look over at him, taking a deep breath to calm the nerves

stirring up in my stomach. Oren leans onto the latter as he looks down at me, waiting for my response.

"Yep, as ready as I'll ever be."

Oren's cheeky smile rises as he moves closer to me.

"Great, get naked." Oren snaps the latter close, grabbing it and bringing it over to the side as if he hadn't just asked me to remove my clothes.

"What?" The question barely leaves my mouth as a whisper, but somehow, Oren registers it. He walks back over to me, his finger gliding down my collarbone.

"I said, get naked. You know… undressed, naked, your birthday suit—" I grab ahold of his hand to make him stop his teasing.

"I know what naked means, Oren. I just hadn't realized that this was that type of shoot." I explain. I wasn't aware that Oren did these types of shoots at all. I had no idea he was looking at naked women on the regular, even at work.

How often was that?

Did he just have a line of models open to getting completely naked in front of his camera?

"You don't have to do it if you don't want to. I'll just substitute this work with something else for my gallery." Oren reasons.

But I didn't want him to do that. I wanted to be up on that wall in his gallery. If other models could do it, there was no reason why I couldn't.

I wanted to do this.

I grab ahold of the bottom and pull it off. I wasn't wearing a bra, so my breasts plopped down thanks to gravity. But the way Oren sucked in his breath and looked straight at them told me he didn't see a single thing wrong with it.

I unclasp my jeans, lowering them down along with my underwear. I step out of them and kick them off to the side, looking up at Oren. His gaze still locked onto my bare body. I clear my throat, unsure what to say exactly, to let him know I'm ready to start the shoot whenever he is.

Oren's eyes look into my own, his cheeks brightening into a soft pink from getting caught staring at my tits.

"I don't think I truly thought this through when you agreed to participate in this shoot." Oren clears his throat before walking over to the supplies on the table and bringing over a step stool and the flowers. He places the step stool between the ropes before nudging his head so I can get on top of it.

I follow his silent instructions as he begins taking the rope and wrapping it around my body in an intricate manner, making it into some sort of harness as he brings it around my curves.

Where had he learned this from?

"This is Shibari," Oren explains as he concentrates on tying me.

"Bondage?" I ask, unsure what about tying someone up was a form of art.

"Yes, but it's more than that. The way I see it, humans are a form of art. Whether we were made from cells or a higher being. We were created just like anything else. We all look so different, from our hair, skin, and eye color to their texture and personalities. We are all so different. And an art form like shibari accentuates that even more." Oren's face lights up as he speaks; he is truly a modern-day Renaissance man. Passionate and in love with his career. And undoubtedly sensational at it all.

"What I'm trying to tell you is that shibari is a form of juxtaposition. You see this rugged rope against someone's smooth skin." Oren tightens the rope, accentuating my curves like he had said. The rope stings my skin a bit. But it's not something I mind when the only thing I can concentrate on is how wet I'm getting just by Oren's touch on mine as he concentrates on the rope's knots. "You can't stop but see how the two shouldn't be near one another but how undeniably good they look together." Oren continues, bringing the fake flowers and placing them between my skin and the rope to cover me up a bit.

Once Oren seems pleased with everything, he places his foot on the stool I'm standing on and looks at me.

"If you feel uncomfortable or it's all too much. Just let me know. We can take breaks or stop the shoot completely. Do you understand?" Oren asks, his hands brushing the curls away from my face.

"Yes, I understand," I reply. Oren nods before letting me know that he's going to remove the stepping stool. He shoves the stool away, and my body falls slightly. The rope tightens around my skin as it swings me from side to side. The sting subsides as the rope begins to still.

Oren holds his hand under my chin, lifting my head to look at him.

"Jasmine, you look so fucking sexy. It's going to be so unbelievably hard to get through this shoot without wanting to fuck you tied up like this." My nipples harden at his words, my pussy throbbing. Wanting him to do exactly what he had said.

"Let's get this photoshoot started. The faster we get this started, the quicker we finish, and I can get a taste of that sweet pussy on my tongue." Oren backs away and walks over to the camera, unhinging it from the tripod before snapping the first couple of pictures.

AN HOUR HAD PASSED SINCE WE BEGAN THE SHOOT. EVERY couple of minutes, Oren would have me take a break to ease any discomfort. But the biggest discomfort I was having didn't really have much to do with rope. Oren had changed my position with the rope a couple of times, and as his skin grazed my own, I couldn't help but crave more.

I needed him closer.

I wanted him closer.

"I think we've got a good amount of photos to work with," Oren says, placing the camera on the table before striding over to me. Oren grasps the rope and swings me close to him.

"How did you enjoy it?" Oren's gaze travels down my bare body. Although Oren had seen me naked many times now, this time, it felt different and much more vulnerable.

"It was nice." I manage to say, but the crack in my voice doesn't go unnoticed by Oren, whose lips curve into a smirk. Oren grabs ahold of the harness on my chest, pulling me closer to him. His lips hovering over mine dangerously.

"I want to kiss you so fucking badly; seeing you hanging here naked in all those positions was so fucking hard. You have no fucking idea, love." Oren's minty breath touches my lips, and I can't help but stretch up as much as I can to reach his lips, but Oren pulls back, leaving me swinging back and forth.

"Hey, what was that for?" I ask, not understanding why he rejected my kiss. From what I gathered, he was fantasizing about fucking me the whole time he was doing the photoshoot.

"Jaz, I meant what I said. I won't fuck you until you're mine."

The swinging of my body comes to a slow halt. My eyes peer into Oren's. I know that so far, Kora has been nothing but right regarding Oren and me. And maybe she's also right about this. Maybe this is something I should bring up. It's obvious Oren wants more. But since when? And what if it didn't work out?

Oren's hand reaches out, his fingers wrapping around my neck, tightening his grip on it.

"God, I fucking want you. Are you going to make me beg, love?" Oren's lips tease my own. He knew I needed him, and though he was asking me if he had to beg, he was making sure that it would be me begging for more.

"Oren…" I trail off; he lifts his eyes to look back up at me rather than continuing to stay focused on my naked body.

"Yes?" He asks smugly, already knowing how much I craved him.

"Fuck me." I plead.

Oren grunts as he grabs the rope around my legs and untangles them. My legs widen, and Oren stands right in between them. I wanted to reach out to him so badly and hold him closer. But my arms were still tied behind my back.

"Is this what you want, Jasmine?" Oren asks, his hand finding itself back on my neck, his other hand trailing down towards my wet pussy that was craving more than just his fingers. "You want me in between your legs like this? Worshiping that wet pussy? You know I'd worship that pussy anyway. Fuck I already worship the ground you walk on, my love. I'm just waiting for you to notice."

Oren's lips begin trailing down my neck, stopping right on my shoulder. His hot breath hitting my cool skin every so often.

How do I tell him I noticed? How do I tell him I want him?

"Fuck." Oren groans, stepping aside to remove his clothes feverishly. Oren's toned skin glistens as the natural light from the window caresses his skin, accentuating his muscles. Oren removes his belt and pants, sliding them down. The bulge in his briefs doesn't go unnoticed as he tugs them down, his erection hard and ready for me. A bead of pre-cum glistens at the tip of his crown.

Oren steps back in between my legs, his length teasing my entrance this time. My pussy clenching, yearning for him to be inside of me.

Oren's hand trails down my body, teasing my hardened nipples. My hips roll into him in response. Oren's eyes darken as he lowers his mouth to them, tugging at each nipple. "Next time, I'll make sure to get you some nipple clamps to make sure they're getting more attention, my love."

Before I can respond, Oren's lips collide with my own, his teeth finding my bottom lip to suck on. A moan escapes my mouth. Oren slides his member up and down my entrance.

"Fuck, Oren, enough teasing. Fuck me." I beg; I need him near me. I need him closer.

"Fuck." Oren steps away, my feet touching the ground this

time. Oren steps over to his desk opens the bottom drawer and takes out a gold foil. He rips it open, removing the condom and sliding it onto his length.

Oren walks over to me, lifting me back into his arms. I wrap my legs around his waist, bringing him closer.

"Jasmine." Oren's voice is strict and serious, the tip of his cock pushing into my entrance. But not enough to extinguish the yearning I have for him.

"Yes?" I ask.

"Say you're mine."

Oren's voice is demanding, but his eyes are almost pleading. He needs to know that this is more. This is different, and as much as it scares me, I need it just as much as he does.

"I'm all yours, Oren," I whisper.

Oren slams his length into my pussy, my back arching in response as the pleasure spreads throughout my body.

"Fuck, being with you should be forbidden." Oren groans, his hips thrusting deeper inside me. I moan out his name and lift my hips to collide in unison with his thrusts. My clit rubs up against him with each thrust. My pussy clenches around his length, sending Oren's head back in bliss. The grip of the ropes tightens around me, but the pain only satisfies me even more.

"Fuck, you're so fucking tight, love."

Oren brings me closer to him, one arm around my waist as he pounds into me; his other hand reaches up to grip my throat. His grip tightens with every thrust; our moans fill the loft.

My thighs begin to shake as all three sensations make me combust; my eyes roll back as I shout Oren's name in praise.

My body goes still, greedy for more of this euphoric

feeling passing through me. Oren releases his grip around my throat and moves his hand to my hair, tightening his grip as he moans out his release.

Oren's head rests against my shoulder, his lips kissing me gently before stepping back to remove the condom and throw it in the trash. Reaching up, he untangles the rope, removes the harness he wrapped around me completely, and drops it to the floor.

Picking me up, he brings me over to the couch, sitting me on top of him. I lay my head on his chest as he caresses my skin. The silence in the room is comforting; there's nothing much to say but the truth.

Oren was mine now, just as much as I was his, and there was no turning back.

Chapter Twenty

Oren

Jasmine was my girlfriend. My mind was still trying to wrap its head around the mind-blowing sex that unfolded in the studio. This hadn't been the plan. But who was I to stand in fate's way?

Seeing her naked in all her glory and tied up made the photoshoot torture. With every image I captured, I had to contemplate ending the shoot just to have her.

I run my fingers through her hair as she lays her head on my chest. I reach over to the bag I left on the couch last night, which is full of any other supplies I'd need for today. I remove the lotion, squeezing some onto my hand and bringing it over to Jaz's wrists.

"I'd usually set up a bath and add the lotion after, but being that we aren't at home, this will have to do until then," I explain.

Jasmine's body stiffens as I rub the lotion up her arms towards her shoulders.

"What's wrong? Does it hurt?"

Shibari was something I learned right after college with Garrett. He was writing an editorial on the art and thought the best way to understand and speak about it was to learn it. It was creative and fun and came in handy many times before.

"Well, I wasn't aware you usually fucked all your models after a shoot," Jasmine says, her response cold and annoyed.

Fuck.

I hadn't even realized how I had phrased my words. I wasn't an angel, but I made sure to be professional in my career. I had never fucked anyone that I was working with. I made sure to keep my personal and work life separate.

That's a rule I'd only break with Jasmine.

"Trust me, love, you're the only model I've done this with. I make sure not to mix business with pleasure. You're just worth breaking the rules for." I tease as I apply the lotion on her legs.

"Really?" Jasmine asks.

By the tone in her voice, I could tell she was concerned that I was lying to make her feel better. But Jasmine was my best friend; she was more than that now.

"Yes, really, Jasmine. You're the only one." I promise.

Jasmine's arms wrap around me as she pulls herself closer to set her head against the crook of my neck. I tried to wrap my mind around how to bring up what had just happened. I wanted to make sure she knew that I was serious. We were the real thing, and I wanted to make it known. But, I didn't want to scare her off, not when I'd just got her.

"Jasmine," her name barely comes out in a whisper, but I know she's heard me because she tilts her head to look at me.

"I think we need to talk," I murmur. Jasmine lifts her head in response, waiting for me to say something else.

"I meant what I said, Jasmine, you're mine, and I'm yours. This thing between us isn't fake. I meant it that night at the party. There's no more pretending between us." I say, caressing her cheek. I couldn't stop myself from finding a way to touch her. I needed to feel at peace, to feel her near me.

I hadn't realized how much I needed Jasmine near me until I had gone to college out of state and realized that not having my best friend near me fucking sucked. It had also been the reawakening of my feelings for her. Of course, I wasn't a fucking idiot. I was very much aware of her beauty. Despite her being my best friend, it fucking hurt like hell having to hear her talk about other men or how her dates with such men went.

And just thinking of William being engaged to her infuriated the fuck out of me.

"What about Renee?" Jasmine's question breaks me away from my thoughts that were leading me to a list of ideas of how to murder William.

"Renee?" I furrow my eyebrows, confused about why she would be asking about Renee.

What did she have to do with any of this?

How did she even know about Renee?

"Yes, the blonde girl in your Instagram story." Jasmine peers her eyes around the room, ignoring my stare.

But that doesn't stop her cheeks from reddening from embarrassment. My lips grew into a knowing smirk. She had stalked my social media because she had been curious about who I was hanging out with.

No.

She had been curious about who I was fucking.

"Renee is nothing but a work companion, my love. In fact, she seems to be Garrett's new enamor." I reassure.

"So, nothing ever happened between the two of you?" Jasmine asks.

A chuckle escapes my lips as I press my forehead against hers.

"I promise you nothing has ever happened between us." I would be sure to repeat it as many times as she needed in order to make her feel secure.

"Hm, I would've never guessed that Garrett was into blondes, especially ones that work for him."

"I think Garrett is into anything that's a woman. Regardless of their hair color and if they work for him."

Garrett never cared for relationships or love. In his eyes, it was all just a waste of time and a distraction. His relationship, or whatever it is, with Renee is probably the best thing for him. They're both extreme workaholics who don't care much for anything but their work, which is why they're the best at what they do.

I was heartbroken when I returned from school to find Jasmine engaged to William. I knew they were dating but didn't think it was serious. And when she showed me her ring, I had to pretend like I was fucking happy for them. Regardless, I had taken a train back to Boston that same night and went over to Garrett's place and drank for days straight, and each night ended up with me passing out on his couch.

The only reason I had gotten my shit together was because

Garrett was fed up with having me naked and drunk on his couch with random girls. But had roles been reversed, I would've been just as annoyed. At the time, it was the only thing filling the void of losing Jaz.

But now, I didn't have to fill any void because Jasmine was mine. And I was more than willing to be all hers.

Chapter Twenty-One

Jasmine

Writing had become a breeze. I was halfway through my novel now. My sex scenes were becoming raunchier. Sex with Oren had been amazing the day of the shoot. After our discussion, Oren brought me home and ran a bath for me. As much as I tried to argue with him and tell him I preferred to just shower, he said he wouldn't allow it. He ran a bath and made sure to add bubbles and lavender essential oils.

After lying in the tub for a bit, he returned to help me dry and moisturize my skin again, as he'd promised. The rope caused some markings on my skin, but they weren't bother-some; they were more of a reminder of what we had done.

The marks on my skin were all gone now, but Oren had stated he would be more than willing to tie me up again just as long as we cut straight to what had been the finale of the photo shoot when he was buried deep inside me.

Oren went back to staying at the loft all day, working on the opening of his gallery. Despite my neediness, I was grateful for his self-restraint because I needed to focus on finishing my book.

I had stuck my phone in the bottom drawer of my desk to stop myself from any distractions. But, it wasn't doing the trick because the constant vibrations from the drawer were only becoming more of a distraction every few minutes. I save my latest draft before opening the drawer and pulling it out.

William's name flashed on my screen.

I was sure after I had ignored his calls last time he was done trying to reach me. I contemplate ignoring his call again, but maybe it'd be best to just answer and let him know that it's time he let this all go.

I picked up the call bringing it to my ear. "Hello?" I answer, waiting for his response. The line is silent for a few seconds before William's voice echoes through the phone. "You answered," he says, his voice sounding hopeful. I know he was hoping that I would be aching to hear his voice just as much as he was aching to hear mine.

I definitely would have been before this whole spectacle with Oren, but now I had to give him the closure he needed.

"Yes, but probably not for the reason you think," I say, holding back from saying anything else while he takes in my words. He needed to prepare himself for what I was going to say.

If whatever he said that night about his engagement with Eloise was true, he needed closure to move on and focus on his relationship with her.

"William, I loved you. I saw my future with you and thought you were the one. And I'll admit that it had never crossed my mind that Oren would be more than my friend. And that's because I had never seen him that way."

William doesn't make any response to what I've said, but I know he's listening. I can hear his breathing at the other end of the line, letting me know that he's there listening.

"But you left, William. You said that it wasn't working out. You didn't tell me why it wasn't working out, just that it wasn't. And just like that, you left. A couple of months later, I find out that you're engaged to Eloise. I didn't know what to make out of that. I had just assumed you cheated and chose the better woman." I swallow the lump building up in my throat. I couldn't cry; I had to rip the band-aid and let this all go.

"Jaz—"

"No, I'm not finished." I croak, "William, what I'm trying to say is that regardless of why you left, all that matters is that you left in the first place. And Oren stayed; he helped me. He was there for me like always. And at some point, I'm not entirely sure when it turned into more. All I can say to you, William, is that I forgive you, and I think it's best that this ends here. No more calls. No more texts. You'll have your life, and I'll have mine." A tear escapes my eye, and I don't try to stop it this time. I didn't need his explanation; I just needed him to listen.

"Jasmine, please. I know you still care. We—"

"Goodbye William." I say before ending the call and blocking his number completely. For the first time since talking to him, I didn't want to bawl my eyes out or lay in bed questioning everything I could've done differently. I wanted to continue to write and wait for Oren to come home for dinner.

OREN HAD YET TO COME HOME, BUT I HAD GOTTEN STARTED on dinner. I wasn't sure if telling him about William's call today was a good idea. I didn't want him to feel like William was still someone of importance in my life.

"Hello, beautiful." Oren says, walking over and kissing my lips. He grabs my ass and brings me closer to him, furthering the kiss to a make-out. I push away, trying to get back to my cooking.

"Hold on, the food's going to burn," I say, walking over to the stove.

Oren's arms wrap around my waist as I focus on the food; his teeth nibble on my ear, sending me into a fit of giggles as I try to move away.

"I want to spend eternity like this, with my arms wrapped around your waist and your laughter filling my ears." Oren peppers my cheek with kisses. Something he did every night once he got home from work, which led to more than just sweet, innocent kisses on the face.

"Aren't you a poet today." I turn around and wrap my arms around his neck, stretching to kiss him. I'd thought that being in a relationship with Oren would change things or at least just make things awkward. But being with him like this as more than friends felt perfect.

Separating from our kiss, Oren moves over to the sink to wash his hands before taking over in the kitchen, a habit we had started to develop since I'd moved in. I would usually start the cooking, and by the time Oren came back, he would take over and finish everything up.

"You know the Fourth of July is this upcoming Friday, right?" Oren asks.

I lifted myself onto the counter to sit as I watched Oren cook. He didn't have to go into detail about the fourth because I already knew what he was saying. Every year, our families get together in the summer to celebrate the fourth, and this year, we'd both be showing up as more than friends.

"Yeah, I remember." Oren turns off the stove before walking right in between my legs.

"Are you ready for that?" Oren asks.

Translation: Are you ready to tell everyone our business so soon?

"I don't know, are you?" I ask. I wasn't opposed to waiting before telling everyone, especially at a function where our families would be. It's not that I didn't have faith in Oren and me; it was just that it was all fairly new. I didn't want to disappoint anyone if the relationship didn't end up working out.

"You know I'd publicize our relationship in an instant." Oren's green eyes stare at me with a pleading expression. I knew he would want to tell everyone. He wasn't one for caring about other people's opinions.

I'd be the first girl Oren introduces as a girlfriend, so our relationship must mean a lot more to him than any other one he's had, especially if he wants his family to know.

"Okay, then I'm ready if you are," I say. Oren's mouth spreads into a wide grin. He grabs my hips and brings me closer to him, giving me a long kiss on the lips.

"This all feels like a dream, Jasmine; you have no idea," Oren mutters into the crook of my neck. I run my fingers through his head of curls before kissing the top of his head.

"I promise you, all of this is real."

Oren's contagious smile appears as he grabs me off the counter. " Come, let's eat, and then you can show me how real all of this really is." Oren gives me a wink before grabbing plates to serve us food.

This all felt like some sort of dream, but if it was, I never wanted to wake up.

Chapter Twenty-Two

Jasmine

I was more nervous than I thought I would be about heading to our parent's house for the Fourth of July. Our families always had big parties full of family and friends in one of our backyards. This year, it was taking place at Oren's parents' house. The drive this time around hadn't been too long.

In previous years, we had always gotten stuck in traffic for what felt like days. This time around, no one seemed to be on the road. During the drive there, I hoped I'd have time to think through how I would tell my parents about Oren and me.

Not that they would have a problem with it. Ever since we were children, my mother was the first to jump on the Oren bandwagon. And my dad adored Oren like a son already. He probably liked him more than he had liked William. That's not to say he didn't like William; I mean, he had gotten my father's blessing.

But then again, Dad was never the type of man to make a big deal about things. If William was what made me happy, then he wouldn't try to stop me from continuing to be happy.

"Are you nervous?" Oren squeezes my thigh with his right hand, which he had placed there the whole drive to his parent's house.

"That's an understatement; I just don't want it to be awkward." I pick at my cuticles, trying to distract my mind from the car nearing the street where we grew up.

"Jaz, it's just like it's always been." Oren flicks the turn signal and turns onto our street. My heart pumps faster and what seems to be louder. "Nothing has changed, love. You're still my best friend, but we added a few more advantages to our relationship this time. I like to think of it like a bonus." Oren pulls into the large driveway, which is already full of cars. Unbuckling his belt, he turns to look over at me, still picking at my cuticles.

Oren grasps my hands, pulling them away from one another. "Stop that; you're going to hurt yourself. Don't worry about anything; I will handle our mothers." Oren brings his hand up to my cheek and stretches over the middle console to kiss me.

This kiss, unlike our previous ones, was delicate and comforting. His tongue pushes into my mouth, our kiss becoming more demanding and full of lust.

A loud screech has us break away and face the front of the car. There in all her glory is Oren's sister, Phoebe. She and Oren looked exactly alike. Her green eyes were a bit darker than his, and her hair was more wavy rather than an actual curl. But other than that, she was the female version of Oren.

"Finally! It took you long enough!" Phoebe screeches, stomping over to the passenger side door to open it up for me. I unbuckle my belt and slide out of the car to greet her. Even though Oren was my best friend, Phoebe was a close second. She was two years younger than Oren and I and is currently finishing up school in upstate New York.

"You look amazing, Jaz!" Phoebe shrieks, bringing me into a tight hug. I giggle, hugging her right back.

"Okay, Phoebe, don't kill the girl." Oren steps in front of us, holding the drinks we bought to contribute to the party. Phoebe lets out an annoyed groan before releasing me and stepping back to shoot a murderous glare at Oren.

"If there's anyone I would kill, it would be you." Phoebe walks over to Oren, shoving his shoulder before pulling him into a hug. Unlike me, Phoebe was just a few inches shorter than Oren.

"Why are we killing me exactly?" Oren asks.

Phoebe pulls away from their hug, her sweet smile becoming a scowl. "Um, because you didn't tell me that Jaz and you were finally a thing. I was getting impatient." Phoebe grabs my hand, steering me to the front door while Oren follows us with a cheeky smile. He was enjoying this way more than I was. I didn't want to make a big deal about this. I hadn't even told my parents about Oren and I. But now that I have seen Phoebe's reactions, I definitely should've sent them a text ahead of time to let them know that Oren and I will be showing up as a couple.

Phoebe walks me into their parents' house. I can hear

voices coming in from the kitchen, which makes me aware that my parents are already there.

"Is that who I think it is?" My dad's voice trails down the hallway as he walks over to me.

"Hey, Dad." I walk into his arms, and him a hug. Oren follows right after me, patting my dad on the back. Dad, just like Mom, barely showed any signs of aging. The only difference was that Dad's hair was already graying. It was the only feature of his that hinted at his age.

"Just so you two are aware, Phoebe has let us all know that you two are now living together. So, it's

definitely the talk of the moms." Dad wraps his arm around my shoulder, bringing me closer to him.

"If it was about money, you could always ask Jaz. Your mom and I would help." Dad whispers for only me to hear, but despite whispering, Oren hears him. Before I can respond, Oren clears his throat and grabs my dad's attention.

"It's not about the money, Steven. It's more about us." Oren says, bringing me closer to him.

"Damn it, looks like I'm losing money." My dad mutters, heading into the kitchen.

"Losing? You mean they're together?" My mother's voice asks as she enters the kitchen and closes the door leading onto the deck.

"Ask her yourself, " my dad says, nudging his head towards Oren and me. My mom looks over at us with a shocked expression.

"Is it true?" Mom asks.

The look on her face already told me the answer she was hoping to receive. Since there had been some sort of bet that my dad had lost, my only guess was that it meant that my mother had been the winner.

"Yes, Mom, it's true." Oren squeezes my shoulder, letting me know he's right there with me. Mom lets out a screech like Phoebe's and walks over, bringing Oren and me into a hug.

"I knew it was going to happen! Wait until I tell your mom, Oren." My mom lets us go from her grip and walks over to the door; as soon as she opens the door, she hollers for Oren's mother.

"Mariam! The men owe us money!" My mother cheers.

I look over at Oren in shock. "They all bet on us," I say.

"I would've, too, if I had known they were betting." Phoebe cuts in. Mariam walks in, cheering. Oren and Phoebe had gotten their hair from her and their height from their father, Matthias. Mariam was shorter like me, and her skin was lighter than her children's, another attribute they'd gotten from their father. But with those green eyes, there was no doubting those were her children.

"My baby, finally! I thought Oren would never ask you. He was drooling like a dog for years and never did anything about it." Mariam brings me into her arms, obviously excited to see us together. I hadn't realized that the reason they wanted Oren and me together wasn't because we were friends but because he had been noticeably pining after me, and I had been blind to it.

"I'm hungry, so while you guys bombard them with questions, I'm going to go eat." Phoebe walks past us and walks outside to sit down and eat. Oren grabs my arm before anyone can say anything and drags me back outside to the heat. Oren's dad is by the grill, plating the last burgers onto the aluminum tray. "Hey, Dad," Oren says, grabbing a hold of the trays to help Matthias bring them to the table.

Matthias pats Oren on the back, murmuring something to him that I couldn't quite catch, but whatever it was made Oren smile and look right back at me. I take a seat next to Phoebe while Oren takes a seat on my other side. Matthias walks over to me, greeting me with a kiss on the head and a hello.

As soon as he walks away, I quickly look over at Oren. " What did he say to you back there?" I ask.

Oren lifts his sunglasses onto his eyes before looking up at me. "He said they were the best five hundred dollars he's ever lost." Oren snickers.

"Five hundred?!" Phoebe and I shout in unison.

"That's what he said," Oren replies, stretching over and grabbing two plates to serve some food to himself and me.

"Damn, I wish I was part of this bet," Phoebe whines, stuffing her face with fries. I thank Oren for my plate and take a bite out of my burger. Oren stares at me intently, his gaze not leaving my face once as I continue to eat. I look over at him, lifting an eyebrow to question his stare.

"Did you put on sunscreen? Your nose is getting a bit red." He asks.

Phoebe bursts into a fit of laughter behind me, mimicking Oren's question. "She's got you wrapped around her finger." Phoebe teases.

"She does, and I like it there." Oren retorts. "Besides, where's that *lovely* man, Jacob? I thought he would be coming to the family function." I nudge at Oren and tell him to stop.

Phoebe and Jacob were high school sweethearts, but there was nothing sweet about them together. They were constantly on and off, and Jacob was known for being a dickhead.

Phoebe deserved better, but she was hung up on her first love, and it was hard for her to let that go.

"That's none of your business," Phoebe remarks, returning to her phone.

"Let's not do this today," I say.

The last thing I needed was to break up a fight.

AS SOON AS WE FINISHED EATING, MORE PEOPLE STARTED showing up, and soon, the yard was full. It had taken awhile for me to be able to escape back inside when everyone kept stopping to ask about Oren and me. But as soon as I got the chance to escape the crowd, I slipped back inside to lay down in the comfort of the air conditioning.

Oren had remained outside, continuing to be bombarded by questions. Phoebe, on the other hand, had stepped out after saying that she was going to go visit Jacob at his parent's house. Neither Oren nor I thought that was such a good idea, but it wasn't any of our business to stop her. Especially not after Oren pissed her off.

I hear the patio door open, and the sound of a pair of footsteps walks closer to me in the living room. "Fireworks are going to start at nine," Mariam says, coming closer to me and taking a seat on the sofa. If Mariam was here, so was my mother. I open my eyes and lift myself up, giving Mariam and my mother room.

"So…" my mother says, stretching out the vowel to indicate that she wants answers.

"I don't know, Mom, it just happened." I lay my head onto

her shoulder, parting her curls away from my face. I was not going to sit here and tell Mariam and my mother that Oren and I got together because we couldn't keep it in our pants.

"Well, what was your first date like? How did he ask you?" Mariam asks, her accent peaking through.

"Well, we haven't really gone on one yet," I answer truthfully. Oren and I kind of jumped a lot of steps to get to where we were, and we just made things official this week.

Mariam gets up from her chair and walks back to the sliding door. "Oren!" I hear her shout.

I get up to go after her, but my mom grabs my wrist and holds me back. "Let her be a mother to him; I think she misses reprimanding him." I roll my eyes and lay my head back down on her shoulder. "Besides, it's almost time for the fireworks; let's grab some things before heading to the park. If we don't get there early, we won't have anywhere to sit." Mom stands up, and I follow, even though I'm already dreading returning to the heat.

"I just don't feel like it's right that he gets reprimanded for something that's really not a big deal; we just haven't gotten around to it," I say, looking over my shoulder to see Oren cornered in the room listening to his mother's lecture.

"Jasmine, he's a grown man. I think he can handle it. Besides, I think Mariam just wants him to prove himself, even if you were already friends before being more. Now, let's go." I walk right behind my mother as she leads us to the hall, and I can't help but look back at Oren. His desperate eyes meet mine, begging me to get him out of his mother's grasp. She must've been quite upset about him not taking me on a date because she threw away the English and started speaking in Greek.

I give him a shrug and turn back around, feeling his stare as I make my way out of the house.

Chapter Twenty-Three

Oren

I look around the park, searching for Jaz's head of curls. The woman left me in the kitchen to deal with my mother's rant. Though having her lecture me like a child was annoying, she was right. I should've taken Jaz on a date as soon as she agreed to be mine, or at least the next day. But I had been so caught up working on touching up the photos I had taken of Jaz. I wanted to ensure they were ready for the gallery by the end of August.

By the time my mother's lecture concluded, everyone at the party had passed right by us and left for the park. I ran over as fast as I could, hoping to find Jasmine in the crowd, but I hadn't realized how many people showed up on the Fourth of July around here.

My eyes locked onto a head full of dark coils and the voluptuous body that was being hugged by a pale green dress.

My mouth had fallen to the floor the minute she stepped out of our room wearing it. But then again, that was my reaction to anything she seemed to wear or not wear.

Jasmine leans against the tree and looks over the town's river where the fireworks will take place. I walk over, grabbing her from behind. A tiny yelp escapes her, but she settles into my arms when she realizes it's me.

"You were able to make it, huh?" She giggles.

"Yeah, thanks for abandoning me out there. If it weren't for her wanting to see the fireworks, I don't think she would've let me go that quickly." I twirl her around to face me. She had to be the most beautiful woman in the universe; no one would ever compare.

Everything about her was mesmerizing.

"She was right, though." I say, "I haven't taken you out on a date yet, and that's all going to change."

"Oren, it's not that big of a deal. We've been out together on dates many times before—" I slam my lips onto Jasmine's, stopping her from uttering any more nonsense. Her lips were always plump and sweet, making kissing her even more addicting. I bring her bottom lip in between my teeth, sucking on the strawberry-flavored chapstick she must've put on before leaving the house.

Fireworks burst in the background as my tongue enters her mouth; I reach around, gripping her ass to bring her closer to me. This woman could ruin me, and I wouldn't give a fuck.

Jasmine deserved everything in life, and I was going to make it my life's purpose to grant her anything she fucking needs— no, anything she fucking wants.

I push Jasmine onto the tree to give us more privacy for any onlookers looking at us rather than the fireworks show.

A soft moan escapes her lips as I grind myself against her. I wanted to take her under the tree. I just wanted to feel her tighten around my dick as the fireworks lights danced across her skin.

Phoebe had been right; Jasmine had me wrapped around her finger. But I couldn't care less; I wanted to be there. I wanted to praise this woman for all eternity. I spent years waiting for her, and now that I had her, I wouldn't be letting her go.

I break away from our kiss. Jasmine's eyes open, and a smile spreads across her face as she slides her hands up my chest.

"Jasmine, I need—" I'm cut off from what I'm about to say when two hands slam up against my side.

Suddenly, my body hits the floor, and all I hear are Jasmine's screams. I look up to see Williams' body hovering over me. He raises his fist before slamming it into my face.

This fucking dick.

Before he can lay another one on me, I grab his wrist and pull him down onto the dirt. Getting up, I slam my fist into his jaw; despite his groans and Jasmine's begging, I continue to slam my fist into his face.

"Oren, please stop." Jasmine's hand wraps around my wrist, holding me back from colliding my fist a dozen more times into this arrogant prick's face.

"Oren, please." She begs.

I lift William up by his collar, bringing his face closer to my own. The smell of iron from both of our wounds was prominent in the air between us.

"Leave her the fuck alone. Correction— leave us alone." I let go of his shirt, letting him fall onto the ground. I look around and see the crowd surrounding us in concern. The fire-works continued to burst out in loud cracks in the sky. But it seemed William and I were much more entertaining to watch at this point. I grab Jasmine by her hand, pulling her out of the crowd.

"Jasmine, wait." William's voice shouts as he follows us through the crowd.

You have got to be fucking kidding me.

I keep pulling Jasmine along with me until I feel her stop; I turn around and see her facing William. Blood was dripping from his nose, and his face was bruising already. I probably didn't look any better.

"No, William, that's enough. I told you it was done that day on the phone. It's over. Do you understand that?" Jasmine asks him. My heart pounds in my chest from hearing those words. I hadn't even known that they had talked on the phone. But that shouldn't have even mattered.

She chose me.

She was choosing me.

Jasmine looks back at me, her eyes glistening. I wanted to be selfish and ask if those tears were for him or me. But the green-eyed monster had to be put away. This wasn't about my feelings. Of course, she still fucking cared for him. They were going to get married. Jasmine wouldn't have even thought to agree to the proposal if she didn't love him.

"Can we go home?" Jasmine's plea comes out in a whisper as she tugs at the hem of my shirt. I nod, bringing my arm around her shoulder and pulling her close to me, leading her back to my parent's house to get the car.

The walk wasn't too far, but it felt longer than usual as we walked in silence. There was so much to be said from both sides, but I didn't want to bring it up. I didn't want my jealousy to make her feel worse. I didn't understand why she hadn't told me about her call with William. The day he had shown up to her job at the bookstore, she had let me know. And at that point, we were only just friends, despite my flirtatious innuendos.

Did the change in our relationship mean that we didn't tell each other anything anymore?

I remove the car keys to unlock the car and open the passenger door for her. I wait for her to take her seat before shutting it and making my way back around to the other side and getting into the driver's seat. I turn the car on and turn on the air conditioning to let the car cool down a bit. It had been hot today, but it seemed like things had gotten even hotter after the fight.

I looked in the rearview mirror, taking in the bruise that would become more prominent in the morning. My split lip didn't help my look either.

"Does it hurt?" Jasmine's voice pulls me back to her. Her eyes remained glossy, but no tears were streaming down, which was way better because if she began crying, I was going to go back over to the park in hopes of finding Will and slamming his head onto the ground.

"Not as bad as it looks, trust me," I say.

I reach over and bring her hand in mine. I just needed to feel her. I wanted to know that she was still here with me.

"I'm sorry about him; he shouldn't have done that," Jasmine says, biting her lip. There was no way this woman was apologizing for that prick. It was just like Jasmine to apologize for someone else's wrongs.

I fucking hated that.

"Jasmine, my love, you never have to apologize for someone else's wrongs. If anything I'm sorry for embarrassing you. That prick just pissed me off. All I saw was red."

Jasmine nods her head in understanding. But it was also her way of letting me know I was forgiven without verbally stating it. I knew that much after many years of pissing her off.

I tighten my grip on her hand to get her attention again. "Can I ask you something?" My voice comes out a bit shaky at the question. I felt like an idiot for even having to ask her about it. It's not like it was some big deal; it was just a call.

Jasmine furrows her eyebrows in concern, nodding her head for me to continue. Fuck, why were my hands clamming up? It was just a stupid question.

"Why didn't you tell me about the call?" I shoot out. Jasmine sighs; this time, she tightens her grip on my hands.

"I know I should've told you. And I was planning on telling you, but that same day you came home from work, you were so excited about the Fourth of July. I didn't want to bring up something that didn't matter anymore. You were the only thing that mattered." Jasmine groans in annoyance, propping herself up in the seat.

"Oren, what I'm trying to say is that you're my boyfriend. I only care about you. That call with William was one that I answered to let him know that I was done. He needed to leave me alone, and then I blocked him."

My heart stops at those words. She had called me her boyfriend. That had been the first time she'd referred to me as that.

"Say it again," I whisper, leaning over the middle console to get closer to her.

Jasmine lifts her brow in confusion. " Do you want me to repeat my whole speech to you?"

"No, my love. I want you to call me your boyfriend." My hand finds its way back to her neck, pulling her close to me. " Say it," I demand.

"Oren, you are my boyfriend. You are mine, and I'm yours." My lips slam into hers. I knew she was turned on, and fuck, I needed her near me.

Jasmine pulls away from our kiss, her chest rising quickly with every breath."Not here," Jasmine says, "let's go home. I'll text Mom and let her know we left early because I wasn't feeling good."

Without another word, I swing myself around, grab the belt, and buckle in before swerving the car onto the road and speeding home. The whole time picturing how fucking mesmerizing Jasmine was going to look when she was riding my face.

Chapter Twenty-Four

Jasmine

The rustling of the sheets stirs me awake from my sleep. I turn over as Oren slides back into bed. I wasn't sure of the time, but it was definitely the morning, by the way the sun shone into our bedroom through the windows. Oren slides his hands around my naked frame, bringing me closer to him. I moan in delight, pushing myself even more towards his groin.

"Did I not tire you enough last night?" Oren whispers in my ear, his hands sliding further up my torso towards my breast. Giving them a squeeze.

He had tired me out last night. Oren had flipped me at every angle he could, but not before eating me out like I was the last thing he'd ever consume again.

"Are you ready for today?" Oren asks, snuggling his head into the crook of my neck.

"You mean, am I ready to spend my day tied to my desk, writing chapter after chapter?" I correct.

Oren lifts his head back up to look over at me. "Usually, I would be the first to support you in staying in and working on your novel, but since I have plans for us today, the writing will just have to wait."

I move over, letting my back fall onto the mattress so that I can look up at Oren.

"Absolutely not," I argue. "Oren, I need to continue working. I have this amazing scene involving suffocating my male character with my female character's pussy." I tease, even though it wasn't much of a lie.

"Hm, I wonder what could've ever inspired that scene." Oren laughs, "But you're still coming with me on a date, so the suffocation can wait a day."

I sigh in defeat and lift my hand to his neck to bring him closer to me and give him a kiss. Oren pecks my lips before lifting himself and giving his head a nudge for me to get up and ready to go.

"Where exactly will you be taking me today?" I ask, shoving the sheets off of my naked body. I pick up Oren's shirt from last night off the floor and put it on. The blood stains on the front were all dried up, but it was still a reminder of last night's unexpected event.

"I'm taking you on our first date as a couple." Oren stands up from the bed, heading over to his closet to pull out his outfit for the day.

"A date? Is this what this is about?" I ask.

I knew Oren wouldn't let this go. His mother made it clear to him that she was disappointed that he hadn't officially taken me out as his boyfriend. And if there was ever anything of importance to know about Oren, it was that he hated disappointing his parents. So, he would make sure that I experienced the best date ever.

"This is about me wanting to go on an official date with you. Is it so wrong of me to want to take my girlfriend out?" Oren throws his clothes onto the bed. Jeans and a nice shirt, at least I know I don't have to go all out with my outfit.

"Come on, go get dressed. By the time we leave the house and get to the first place, we will be there just in time for lunch." Oren says, stepping into his jeans and buckling them. I shrug and turn around, heading to the other room that still has all my stuff. Oren's hand lands on my ass in a loud smack. I let out a yelp in response and turn around to glare at him. But Oren only winks and gives me a sly smirk.

I shake my head and walk out of the room. Something told me that even though Oren had less than twenty-four hours to prepare for this date, it was going to be quite fascinating and beautiful.

OREN PUSHES MY CHAIR AND SITS ACROSS FROM ME, PICKING up the menu and staring intently at it as if we had never been here before. In fact, we were seated in the same spot that night when William and Eloise approached us.

"They have a variety of options." Oren comments, continuing his act.

What on earth was he doing?

"Yeah, I know… because we've been here before," I say, hoping it didn't sound snarky. I wasn't complaining about revisiting the same place we had eaten at before. I was confused about why he was pretending as if we had never been here before.

"I'm aware." Oren says, "I'm in the mood for spring rolls. Do you think they'll taste any good?" Oren asks with a clueless expression on his face.

"I'm sure the recipe hasn't changed since we've last had them, Oren." I flick through my menu, looking for something different to try.

"Why exactly are you pretending as if this is our first time here?" I ask.

Oren sets his menu down, so I do the same to give him my attention. "This is where it all started," he begins. "As much of a little shit William is, if it weren't for him coming up to our table that night, we wouldn't be here right now. But, it was also the beginning of a lie." Oren looks around, taking in the restaurant around us.

"I wanted to be here together as a couple this time. No pretending. I wanted to recreate one of the best moments of my life, but this time, I want to make it real between us." Oren's eyes glistened as he spoke.

He had meant every word he uttered. He wanted to replace the shitty memory of our time here with William and replace it with something meaningful like our first date.

"How do you think the dumplings taste?" I ask, knowing damn well we had scarfed them down quickly last time before we could even get the taste of them.

Oren's smile broadens as he takes my hand in his from across the table. "Something tells me they're very delicious," Oren says.

"Well, we can't ignore our intuition now, can we?" I pick

the menu back up and cover my face as I look at the option again. Even though the menu covers my view of Oren, I don't need to look at him to know he's grinning from ear to ear.

AFTER LUNCH, OREN TOOK ME BACK TO THE PARK WE HAD walked through that very same night to get ice cream. Now, we were just walking around the city, but at some point, Oren stopped going around random blocks and started walking as if he had somewhere to take us. My guess would have to be his loft because we were only getting closer to it.

"Are you taking me back to the loft to make part two of our bondage photoshoot? Because personally, I think the first time around was perfect, but if you feel that it's something we have to redo, I won't go against you on it. I think we should skip the photos and go straight to the fucking." Oren bursts out in laughter, and I can't help but join him.

"Though that was not my intention, we can definitely do it after," Oren says, halting in front of the bookstore.

"After what?" I ask.

Oren grabs a set of keys from his pocket and looks through them, separating one from all the others. He inserts it into the bookstore's door and opens it.

Why was the bookstore closed anyway?

My hours were getting cut even more every week, but from what I was told, Marvin was in everyday.

Wait. Why did Oren have the keys to the bookstore in the first place?

Oren holds the door open for me to step inside. I look

around the bookstore, trying to distinguish any difference that there could be for Oren to have brought me in here. Everything was still intact. Nothing had been packed, so Marvin was still working around here. I guess he just closed the store whenever he felt like it.

Oren shuts the door and locks it before turning around to face me.

"What are we doing here, Oren?" I ask.

"I thought you'd like to see the bookstore, so I thought I would give you the key as well." He says, pulling out one of the other keys from his keychain before handing it over to me.

Why would I need the key? I work here. I already had a key, if not a dozen copies, because I always lost them. "I already have the keys to the bookstore, Oren. I work here."

Oren grins as he grabs my hand and places the key in my palm. " Not anymore. I changed the locks. Jasmine, the bookstore is yours."

I freeze in my spot, trying to figure out exactly what to say to him. There was no way that this was all real. How the hell did he go about purchasing this whole bookstore? That had been the reason why my hours had been cut. There was no other owner. Well, technically, I was the future owner, but this wasn't something I could accept. It just didn't feel right. I couldn't continue to mooch off of Oren like this. He was my boyfriend, not my bank account.

"You bought the bookstore?" I ask, in hopes that I had heard him incorrectly.

"I bought *you* the bookstore." Oren clarifies.

I drag my hands across my face and pace around the bookstore. There was no way he had done this. Oren had already done so much with having me live in his apartment rent-free, and now he's gone and bought the bookstore.

"Oren, you can't keep doing this. You can't keep wasting your money on me." I say, trying to get him to rationalize this whole situation. Oren takes a step closer to me, bringing me into his arms.

"Jaz, why won't you let me be a part of this with you?"

"Because it's a lot," I say. "Oren, how did you even afford this?" I was aware Oren had money, but not this type of money.

"I saved. Besides, when you first started working here after high school, you used to say how much you would've loved to have your book café at this exact location. You said it was perfect—so that's what I did. I worked and saved to give you perfection." Oren holds my face in his hands, lifting it to look right at him.

"Jasmine, I will make sure that you have anything you want. If you even look at something for more than a second, it'll be bought and in your hands. You, my love, deserve the world."

Tears brim in my eyes at Oren's declaration. Oren had worked and saved all these years because of a stupid comment I had made about liking this bookstore. He wanted to give me the world, but Oren didn't understand that he was my world. I didn't need anything else, not if I had him.

My lips crash into Oren's; without a second thought, Oren kisses me back, pushing our bodies against the bookshelves. I hear the falling of the books, but I could care less when Oren's hands are squeezing my ass and pushing me closer to him. "Get naked," Oren demands, moving away and removing his clothes. I do as he says, getting completely naked.

"On the floor, show me how grateful you are for my gift, my love." I lower myself onto my knees right in front of him. Oren slips the belt off from around his waist and brings it around my neck. He had done this before, but each time, my pussy soaked as if it was our first time trying it.

"My love, you look so fucking beautiful. Show me how ready that mouth is for me." My focus continues on him as I stick out my tongue; Oren drags his jeans and underwear down, his cock hard and ready for me. Oren smacks the tip onto my tongue a couple of times before bringing his length as deep as I could take it into my mouth. I bob my head up and down, sucking his cock.

"That's right, love, let me fuck that throat. You look so sexy with my cock in your mouth. You like it there, don't you, baby?" Oren's words have me moaning as I push his cock deeper down my throat. Oren tugs on the belt, pulling me away from his cock as I gag in response to deepthroating it.

"That's it baby, you want me to fuck your mouth?" Oren asks, the pad of his thumb rubbing my plump lips.

"Oren, fuck my throat, and then make sure you fuck my pussy even rougher." Oren's eyes roll to the back of his head as he lets out a moan and thrusts his dick into my mouth. Thrusting in and out. The more I gagged, the rougher he fucked. He loved seeing me this way, in distress for him. Craving for more. Oren pulls his cock away from my mouth. Despite having tears and spit all over my face, Oren looked at me like I was the most mesmerizing creature on this planet.

"Get up." He growls.

Oren's arms wrap around my legs to lift me. I oblige, tightening my grip around his waist. Oren teases my entrance with his length, sliding it up and down my wetness.

"Your pussy is so wet and ready for me, baby." Oren groans, pushing his tip inside my entrance. Oren suddenly halts, looking back up at me.

"I don't have a condom," Oren explains. "But I'm fine with it if you are. I'm clean, I promise."

I didn't doubt that Oren was clean, and I had been on the pill for a while. He wasn't a one-time thing. Oren was it; he always had been.

"Oren, please just fuck me," I beg.

Oren presses my back against the shelves and slams into me. My pussy tightens around his cock, craving for more. Oren's rough thrusts shake the shelf behind me, sending books falling to the ground. But nothing fucking mattered besides us.

"I can't get enough of you. You're tits, your ass, your curves. You're going to be the fucking death of me." Oren brings his fingers to my mouth while the other arm holds me in position, my legs still wrapped tightly around his back as he slides in and out of me.

"Suck them."

I take his fingers into my mouth, bobbing my head back and forth like I would his cock.

"Fuck me, you're a greedy little slut, aren't you?" He teases, pulling his fingers away and bringing them towards my clit.

Oren picks up his speed as he slams into me, this time rubbing my clit. I grab onto the shelves, pulling myself up and down to follow his rhythm. Fuck, I was going to come, and by the tightening on my hip, I could tell he was too.

"Oren, I'm going to come." I moan, clenching around him.

"That's it, baby. Clench that pussy around my cock and come for me." Oren's demand sends me into a burst of pleasure. Oren's groan follows my own as he spills his cum deep inside of me.

"Fuck, that was the first time. I've ever done that." He kisses my shoulder before dropping one leg down at a time.

"Come inside, someone?" I ask.

"Fuck anyone bare." He corrects, pulling me to him and trailing kisses down my neck.

I was sure that Oren was always safe when he slept around, but knowing I was the only person he'd been with that way felt nice. He fucked me bare and came inside me. That had been two firsts for us.

Oren lays me down on the bookstore's couch with him. Playing with the strands of my hair once again. "I can't believe you bought the bookstore; thank you," I say.

"Well… technically, I bought the whole building, which is why I also have my loft upstairs," Oren says casually. I lift my head from his chest to look at him.

"You bought the whole loft?"

Oren shrugs, "it was for sale."

"When was this?" I asked him, and I was surprised he had kept this from me for so long.

"The purchase was finalized in May." Oren's persona remained nonchalant.

I couldn't be upset at him for keeping it a secret, not when he was waiting for the right time to tell me about it. "Well, are there any other secrets you want to tell me about?" I mutter jokingly.

"Well, I guess you should know that all the cameras around here are all set up by the security company I hired,"

Oren admits, but that's not exactly what he was trying to say. In other words, he told me he'd seen William here that day.

"You mean—"

"Yes, I saw William acting like a fool around here. Since I'm being so honest, I should also tell you that I called Marvin to come and disrupt the reunion." Oren's eyes darkened at the telling of the story; just picturing William with me together pissed him off.

"So, he didn't look at the cameras in the back?" I ask for reassurance.

"No, I would never allow that perv to have access to any footage of you." Oren scrunches his head at the thought of Marvin looking at me through the cameras.

"So you were just stalking me?" I ask, sitting back up.

Oren lifts himself to sit up and look at me. "Jasmine, I just had the cameras installed because I also had them installed in the loft upstairs. I just wanted to take precautions with the bookstore as well. This has nothing to do with stalking you, I promise." Oren says, dragging me back into his arms.

"Fine, you're forgiven."

Oren hums in agreement, wrapping me up in his embrace, "although I would be lying if I said I didn't enjoy looking at your ass bounce every time you had to stand on your toes to put something on the top shelf."

"Oh, shut up." I slap his arm playfully.

"Open those legs and make me," he murmurs near my ear. I open my legs in response, looking over at him.

"Go right ahead." Oren gets down on his knees, bringing his head right between my legs. Pleasuring me until all is forgiven.

Chapter Twenty-Five

Jasmine

Fucking until my legs felt numb was not the best idea when you still had to walk back home right after. In Oren's defense, he had offered to order an Uber, but I had rejected his offer. "There's still one more surprise I have in store for you," Oren says, pulling out the keys for the front of the apartment.

"Another surprise?"

Oren was ensuring this would be the best date I've ever been on. He was ruining another guy's chance of ever trying to woo me. Not that there would ever be another guy.

Oren was it for me.

Oren pulls open the door and walks over to the mailbox, opening it with his key and taking out the hoarded letters. We rarely checked it, so I could only assume our mailman *loved* us.

"Yes, but before you see anything, you have to understand that denying the gift is not an option, and you'll have to accept it no matter what." Oren holds his hand for me to take as he walks us to the elevator.

"Oh, now I'm curious about what you've done." I stand still, tapping my foot on the elevator floor as it rises. My mind races through different ideas of what Oren could've gotten me.

"Don't think too much about it. You're about to see it, and it's not that big of a deal. I'm just warning you because you're a bit dramatic." Oren steps out of the elevator, leading us over to our apartment. Opening the door, I step inside expecting an extravagant change, but nothing seems out of place. Everything is just as it was when we left. Oren moves towards the kitchen, dropping the mail onto the counter.

"Stay right here," Oren says, walking into our bedroom to get what I assume is the last gift of the night. I take a seat on the counter and pick up the scattered mail. A gold-bordered envelope with Oren and I's name written on top of it captures my attention. I slide the envelope out of the stack and drop the rest onto the counter.

What the hell was this?

Could I open it?

I hadn't really gotten much mail here, but then again, I'd never checked the mail often enough to know. But this was a handwritten letter with both Oren and my name on it.

I let curiosity get the best of me and open up the letter. I pull out the card to see William and Eloise's engagement photos. They seem to be the same ones on her Instagram. Turning the card, I read the invitation for the wedding this August.

Was she inviting me to the wedding?

When had she even sent this out?

"What's that?" Oren asks, approaching with a blue envelope. I lift the invitation with William and Eloise's photos.

"I just can't escape this man, can I?" In annoyance, Oren lets out a huff of air, taking the card away and turning it around to read the invitation on the back.

"This is most likely William's doing," Oren says.

"Possibly, I mean, it doesn't matter. It's not like we're going."

Oren looks up and tosses the card back onto the counter. "You're right," he says, handing me the envelope.

"Besides, I think we'll be too tired once we come back."

"Where would we be coming back from if we'd be too tired to attend a wedding?" I ask him.

Oren hands me the blue envelope, nodding for me to open it. I tear the seal open and take out two sheets of paper. They have next week's date printed on them, along with the flight information to Greece.

There was no way.

I look up at Oren, my mouth opening to deny this absurd gift from him. But Oren grabs my chin, pulling me closer.

"Not a word, Jasmine." He reprimands, "I want to do this. We've both been working hard. I'm so proud of you, love. And also disappointed that you refuse to let me read that manuscript."

My cheeks turn red at Oren's accusation. I hadn't sent Oren my manuscript because, on one half, I was embarrassed that it wasn't good enough to read. And on the other hand, I was embarrassed for him to see how he had inspired me. My male character was Oren, from the way he looked to the way he acted and the *things* he did.

Having him read my erotica would feel like having him read my fanfiction from when we were twelve. My novel hadn't been close to being finished, and it was still just the first draft. I was better off waiting until the book was completed to show him.

"You'll read it someday.".

Oren's face spreads with a grin as he lets out a chuckle. "Trust me, love, even if I have to wait for it to be published, I will definitely be reading it."

Oren brings himself closer and kisses my forehead, "So, being that you haven't argued with me. I'm guessing you'll be coming to Greece."

I chuckle as I look at him. "It's not like you've given me much of a choice," I say.

Oren's smile widens, grabbing my chin and kissing me. "Jasmine." His lips touch my own subtly as he whispers my name in praise.

"It's just you and me, no one else in Greece. I want no distractions, no interruptions. I want to enjoy my time with you without thinking about work or people." I knew exactly what Oren was trying to tell me without having to bring up Willliam's name. He wanted time for us to grow and to be together as a couple without having Willliam try and slither his way between us.

He just wanted time with me, and though I felt that leaving for Greece to spend some time alone together was a bit of an exaggeration, it's what he wanted, so I was going to be more than willing to give him that.

"It's just you and me, Oren. I promise."

Oren's lips press back onto my own, his hands already leading down my body to unfasten my jeans. This man was going to be the death of me, but I was more than willing to allow him to do it as long as I had the chance of being his.

Chapter Twenty-Six

Oren

Kora's face held nothing back as she stared at me dumbfounded after I told her about this past weekend.

"So let me get this straight." Kora props herself up straight on her couch before continuing. "You're finally official; you take her to meet the parents she's already known for years, her ex-boyfriend shows up and beats the fuck out of you, then you proceed to take her out on a date after your mother knocks some sense into you, and there— at said date— you reveal that you're a lovesick puppy that bought her a bookstore and a trip to Greece, while also admitting that you're a psychotic stalker?" Kora scrunches her nose as if questioning her last sentence, obviously trying to wrap her head around why I was looking at the bookstore's cameras.

Honestly, did people not understand that this was precautionary? I needed to make sure that everyone was safe. Yeah, I checked the cameras more often when Jasmine was working, but it was only because I cared about her and wanted to make sure she was safe.

I nod my head towards Kora, agreeing to her words as she continues to process it. "Yeah, pretty much, minus William beating my ass. I don't know where you got that from."

I was not going to have anyone think that I had let that man beat the shit out of me. I let him have one shove and a hit, and that was me being gracious. The prick had no respect; he was about to be married to Eloise and was running around trying to get Jasmine back. If he really loved Jasmine, he wouldn't be waiting to break things off with Eloise. He wouldn't be waiting on Jasmine's response to decide for himself.

"Your bruised cheek," Kora answers, lifting herself off the couch and walking to her kitchen. This place was huge compared to my apartment. From what Kora had told me, it was all thanks to the trust fund that her grandfather had left her. Her parents refused to help her after she chose to pursue a musical career rather than a business one.

I raise my hand to touch the tender area that was already yellow and fading. "Trust me, he doesn't look too pretty either." With the way I had left him, I didn't think he'd heal completely for his wedding.

"It's moments like these that I am very grateful to like women." Kora walks back into the room, holding two bottles of water and snacks. I had left Jasmine alone in our apartment to work on her book. I didn't want to be any more of a distraction than I already was.

There wasn't a moment when I didn't feel the need to

keep her close to me, and at this point, that was only going to slow both of us down in our work.

"Have you read it?" Kora asks me, I turn my head and grab the water she passes over to me. I shake my head, not needing her to clarify what she was talking to me about. The only thing she'd be referring to when it came to reading was Jasmine's book.

Jasmine had refused to let me read her work so far for whatever reason, but I wasn't going to make a big deal out of it. I would read it when she was ready for me to. I don't understand what made her so shy about it. I mean, it's not like I'd be reading something that I hadn't already seen or done before.

Besides, what was there to be shy about when I had her practically riding my face most nights?

"No, she hasn't shown me yet." Kora nods her head, holding back a smile as she looks away to open her snacks.

"What is it?" There had to be a reason behind that reaction, and I hadn't said anything funny.

"Nothing, I just think I know why she hasn't. But, let me tell you that the minute you read it, you'll enjoy it." Kora sits back, setting her feet on my lap.

"Don't you have some music to write?" I ask, annoyed at her teasing.

"This is my apartment. Don't you have some sculptures to go sculpt or whatever it is you modern Renaissance men do?" I roll my eyes and move her feet off my lap as I stand up.

"You're not wrong, but listen, I need to ask you a favor, and I can't do it 'cause I refuse to talk to that dipshit Terrence." I look down at Kora, waiting for her to refuse my favor.

"Ah, I knew you didn't just come here to braid each other's hair and share secrets. What is it that you need, exactly?"

I run my hands through my hair, thinking of having to ask Terrence for anything at all.

"I need you to ask him to find a literary agent interested in helping Jaz. But do not say a word of this to Jasmine. She's doing great with her writing, and I don't want her to feel rushed. Just see what he can do." Kora sits up in contemplation. I roll my eyes at her little act, knowing damn well she likes Jaz too much not to do me this favor.

"Fine, I guess I can contact him." Kora sighs dramatically as if I had just asked her to find a solution to world hunger.

"Amazing, but not a word to Terrence about me being the one asking for this favor," I say.

"Why exactly don't you ask him yourself?" Koras asks.

"I don't think he'd make it easy for me, especially after the last time he and I spoke."

He would not do me this favor if I asked, but if Kora did, he would be more inclined to look into it for her.

"Ah yes, you men and your possessive tendencies." I roll my eyes and make my way towards her door to leave. I look over my shoulder and call out her name to have her turn back to me.

"Yes?" She asks.

"I'm going to have so much fun when it's you pining over a woman," I say.

Kora only chuckles and looks away. "Keep waiting; it's never going to happen." I shake my head at Kora's ignorance before stepping out.

I had no doubt that if Terrence didn't have a literary agent to help out, Kora was going to bring out her Rolodex full of people that she knew, thanks to her father's name. She wanted Jasmine to succeed just as much as I did.

Regardless of how things turned out between us, I wanted to make sure that Jasmine came out on top. Her dreams were going to come true, and I was going to do anything to ensure that they did.

Chapter Twenty-Seven

Jasmine

Oren and I had landed in Athens, and the minute we left the airport, it felt as if Oren was where he belonged. As soon as he got his hands on the rental car, he drove us straight to the hotel. My mouth completely dropped the moment Oren brought me up to our room.

Correction— our suite.

This was basically the size of our apartment back home. It must've been a fortune. I walked around the suite, looking at the view of the city from the windows. It was all unbelievably beautiful.

"Oren, this must've been expensive." I turn away from the window to face him. Rather than admiring the beautiful city, he stared at me as if I were just as mesmerizing as Greece.

Oren shrugs, not bothering to look away.

"It wasn't expensive at all. This is the room I get every time I visit family in Greece." Oren answers nonchalantly, as if that had been the answer I was looking for.

"Oh, so every time the Greek American comes and visits his country, they offer the best room in the hotel?" I wrap my hands around Oren's biceps and pull him closer to me as I tease him.

"More like every time his nephew comes, my uncle tends to offer me the best stay in the city rather than having to drive out to the rural area of Greece, where they all live an hour away." I furrow my eyebrows together, looking up at Oren. I wasn't aware that his family had this type of money to own a hotel, especially because his parents immigrated to the States for a better living than what they felt they had here. But I guess that didn't exactly mean that all of his family struggled when it came to having an opportunity to work.

"He owns all of this?" I ask him.

Oren shakes his head and chuckles at my question,"He's a manager here, so he has a few perks up his sleeve. I also did the owners a favor when it came to decorating the room with art, so they don't really mind my stays here either. My uncle lives an hour away with the rest of my family."

The mention of his family made me a bit nervous. Oren had mentioned that he wanted to take this trip to focus on us but that if I was ready, he would be more than happy to introduce me to his whole family. I hadn't given him a definite answer yet; I didn't want to rush anything. A side of me was also worried that they wouldn't accept me.

I had zero Greek in me, and I definitely didn't look it, either. Not that Oren or his parents ever made me feel like that mattered. But I just didn't want to be a disappointment.

"Come on, there's more I want to show you." Oren tugs at my wrist and pulls me out of the suite with him, leading me to the elevator that brings us up to the rooftop.

Oren steps out, and I follow, looking around. Everything is beautifully decorated with peonies and candles. The area looked like a restaurant, but it was completely vacant. Oren steps up to the man behind the podium who takes out two menus. Oren and the man begin to speak in Greek amongst themselves as we're brought to a table with a beautiful view of Athens. My jaw drops as the acropolis's perfect view sits right before me.

"Do you like it?" Oren asks, pulling out my chair for me to sit. I sit and push in my chair as Oren walks around to sit across from me.

"Oren, I love it; this is so beautiful." I can't say anything else because everything feels like a dream. I wasn't expecting a trip to Greece to begin with, and here I was sitting across from Oren.

A little lie that Oren had started led to all of this.

"Jasmine, I'm really glad you like it. I can't wait to bring you around my favorite places here." Oren reaches his hand across the table, and I bring my hand to his. His rough hands rub against my soft ones, my heart fluttering in my chest.

"Jasmine, there's something I've been meaning to tell you." Oren murmurs; I nod my head for him to continue, tightening my hold on his hand to reassure him that anything he says is safe between us like it always has been.

"I wan— " Oren's speech is cut off by a deeper one coming our way. I turn over, and walking toward us is what looks like an older version of Oren. The only difference was that the gray hair was beginning to grow out on both his head and beard. Oren greets him back in Greek before getting up and bringing him into a hug. I stand up, unsure of what to do. If I were meeting his uncle, I wouldn't have looked uninterested.

The two continue to speak for a minute before Oren looks over at me and brings me into his arms.

"This is Jasmine, my girlfriend." Oren introduces, "Jasmine, this is my uncle Kostas."

"Hello, Jasmine. It's lovely to finally meet you. Oren and his parents have told me so much about you already." Kostas reaches over and brings me into a hug. I wrap my hands around his body instinctively to hug him back. His English is perfect; the only thing that stands out is his accent.

I assumed Kostas learned English to maintain a job in this hotel. However, Oren begins speaking with Kostas in Greek once again, which I assume is because despite knowing English, Kostas probably prefers his native language.

Kostas leans in to kiss Oren goodbye before turning over to me to do the same. "It was nice meeting you, Jasmine; I hope to see you around again very soon. I know that the family is dying to see you," Kostas says, bringing me back into his arms for another hug.

Kosta makes his way to the elevator, leaving Oren and I on the rooftop again.

"I didn't know your family over here knew English," I say, sitting back down. Oren brings his chair in before giving me a shrug, "I guess I didn't think it was a big deal. Besides, only Kosta speaks English because he spent time in England in his twenties. Then he came back and used the English to his advantage." Oren says, gesturing his hand around the restaurant.

"But, he still loves being out in the rural town because family is there." Oren takes a sip of the water that the waiter had come by to pour in our glasses while Oren was speaking.

"Well, that, and he says he likes it more than the city; he says there's way too many tourists," Oren says, picking up the menu. I pick up my own and look through the menu, not focusing entirely on the menu but rather on how Oren's family wanted to meet me. From what I could gather, Kosta seemed to like me, but then again, he could've just said that to be nice.

"What are you thinking so intensely about?" Oren asks, flipping through the menu. I am well aware that he is still looking at me through his peripheral vision.

"Your family wants to see me," I answered honestly. After meeting Kosta, it would only be rude of me not to show up and meet the rest of his family. Oren sighs and closes the menu to look up at me.

"Jasmine, you do not have to meet my family yet. I had told Kosta's to keep it a secret, but he went and opened his fucking mouth. But don't worry, I'll just let them know that we couldn't come around to see them because we were busy being tourists." Oren looked sincere; he really didn't care if I met his family or not. He wanted to bring me so that I could spend some time with him and get to know the country that he was from. But, looking at it now, it wouldn't be fair to see his country and not the people who surrounded him with love.

I clear my throat and take a sip of water before looking back at Oren. "You know, I guess it wouldn't be too bad to meet your family since I'm already here." I compromise, considering that maybe Oren would love to have me meet his family.

Oren's wide smile spreads. " Really? " he asks astonishingly. His reaction furthers my point and only validates how much I truly know Oren.

"Yes, I would love to meet the rest of your family."

Oren reaches across the table and puts his hand under my chin, bringing me closer to him so that he can peck my lips.

"You are the most magnificent woman I have ever met. And hopefully, someday, you'll be all mine." Oren says, taking a seat back down on his chair.

"I already am all yours."

"Hm, I would like that in a recording so I can listen to it on a loop." Oren teases.

I roll my eyes and set the menu down on the table. " Choose something you'll think I like," I tell him.

Oren's eyebrow shoots up in question, "Anything?" He asks.

"That's on the menu," I emphasize.

Oren lets out a chuckle before closing the menu and calling the waiter to come take our order. Oren speaks to him in Greek, and the waiter jots everything down. I wasn't sure exactly what Oren had ordered, but I knew it had to be good.

"What was that thing you wanted to tell me before?" I ask Oren, recalling our conversation before Kosta stopped by.

Oren lays back in his chair and shrugs his shoulders. "I don't remember, " he replies, looking out towards the view of the landscape.

I shift awkwardly in my chair at his lie. There was no reason he had to lie. Not when he admitted to it being about something he wanted to say. Something important doesn't get forgotten in the few minutes we get interrupted or distracted by something else.

I want to question him and ask him why he won't just tell me, especially when he was planning on doing so before. Instead, I opt out of it, not wanting to start an argument, especially not when we came here to enjoy our time together as a couple.

I wouldn't bring it up, but if the same words slipped his lips again next time, I would ensure he finished his sentence.

"Get out of your head, Jasmine. I promise it's nothing bad. The time just isn't right. It will be soon, and then you'll know. But for now, please enjoy our first day here in Athens with me." Oren reaches over and caresses my hand on the table.

"Plus, I want to go through our itinerary list for this week. I want to show you some of my favorite places, and of course, the historical ones, too." Oren continues, and though I know he's trying to distract me from what he wants to tell me, I let him do so just because I really wanted to know what he had planned for this week.

"Fine, I guess I'll allow you to distract me," I say, giving into him. Oren lets out a breath of air before continuing to list all the things he has planned. But despite his change in subject, my mind couldn't help but wonder what it was that Oren wanted to say and why he was waiting for the perfect moment to say it.

Chapter Twenty-Eight

Jasmine

I continue to nibble on my cuticles as Oren makes his way around the winding roads of the rural land. We enjoyed our first couple of days together with no distractions. But today was the day that I would be meeting his family. And even though I had talked myself into a calm mindset about the upcoming interaction, it didn't seem to stop my anxiety from making its presence as we drove over to their house.

"Stop that," Oren grabs my hand away from my mouth and pulls it back down to my lap, interlocking our hands together and tightening his grip. Oren hated it when I was anxious, especially when it caused me to get back into the habit of biting my nails.

"You'll be fine; they all know about you from years of

stories. You don't have to be so caught up in your mind about what they will think and how they will act." Oren reassures.

I knew Oren was right; he was annoyingly never really wrong. But I couldn't help the way my mind worked when anxiety started to make itself known. I just don't want to disappoint his family, not like I was with William's parents. Neither of them ever bothered to look at me, so getting to know me was out of the picture.

Maybe our relationship was never meant to last, to begin with; I wouldn't have wanted to live my life being ignored and looked down upon by my in-laws. At least with Oren, I knew Matthias and Mariam liked me and treated me like one of their own.

The only people's opinions that mattered were already given, and they supported and encouraged our relationship.

Oren pulls his car into a gravel road leading to a white stone house. "This is it, " he says, putting the car in park and unbuckling his belt. I quickly follow and do the same. Opening my car door, I step out while Oren makes his way around the car to meet me.

"Just remember that they're very big on hugging, so if they start suffocating you, just let me know," Oren whispers, and before I can answer him or even question why he's whispering, the door of the house swings open, and a wave of people come out of the house, greeting us with smiles and open arms.

An older woman I remember as Oren's grandmother from the photos brings me into her arms and kisses me on both of my cheeks and murmurs something in Greek I didn't understand but by the smile on Oren's face told me that it hadn't been anything bad.

"She called you beautiful," Oren translates, bringing his arm around my waist to bring me closer to him. His cousins take turns introducing themselves one by one. I had known that Mariam came from a big family from the stories she told, but never this big. It was a lot different than what I was used to. I only had my mom and dad, and I barely got to see my mom's extended family because they all lived in different areas.

On the other hand, Dad was a single child just like me and barely had any family to go around. It had always just been the three of us, and I think that's what brought us so close to Orens' family. They were used to coming from a larger home and being so far away from their loved ones, and reducing themselves to a family of four had them open their arms to new people to call a family.

"They all think you're beautiful, Jaz. They're already asking for the wedding date, and I haven't even proposed." Oren teases as he leads me up the stairs to the house, and everyone continues to banter around me.

"Where are we going?" I ask, unsure of where we are heading.

Oren only chuckles and points to his grandmother, "Don't expect to come to see my Greek family and not expect them to bombard you with food, especially my grandmother."

"Got it, of course. Your mother must've gotten it from somewhere." I tease.

Oren brings me over to the kitchen table before pulling out the chair so I can sit in. "My love, it's in our blood." Oren sits beside me as his family gathers around, bombarding us with questions.

Oren had been right. This was overwhelming, but seeing

him laugh and smile widely while he talked made it all worth it. Oren always had me in his mind, focusing on what would make me happy and doing everything he could to accomplish that. So, meeting his family was nothing compared to all he had done. But it was a start to many things I would work for to make him as happy as he makes me.

 OREN'S FAMILY WANTED US TO STAY LONGER, BUT OREN TOLD them he wanted me to experience the most I could while in Greece. I told him I wouldn't mind staying longer to spend more time with them, but Oren said he had already made important plans and couldn't cancel them.

I had asked him about where he was taking us, but like everything with Oren, it had to be a surprise. By now, I was already used to the response, so I didn't even know why I bothered asking when he wouldn't ever tell me.

Oren continues his drive to the secretive location before moving to the side of the road, reaching into the car's middle console, and pulling out a silk blindfold.

Oren slides the blindfold onto my lap. I look up in confusion as he nods his head, insinuating that I should put it on. "Absolutely not. I refuse to look like an idiot like I did back home when you were showing me the loft." I argue, lifting the blindfold and placing it in his lap.

Oren groans and picks it back up, extending it back over to me. "I promise that you won't look like an idiot. We are close to the place, and I want it to be a surprise when we get there. Trust me, it won't disappoint." Oren pleads.

I look at his pleading eyes, sighing in defeat. I grab the blindfold from his hand and wrap it around my eyes. Oren pulls back into the road before slowing down and lowering his window to speak with someone. I wasn't nervous, especially because I trusted Oren, but I was curious to know exactly what he didn't want me to see.

"We're here," Oren says.

I remove my seat belt and wait for Oren to walk over to my door and lead me out the car because I certainly wasn't leading myself out in the dark. I probably looked stupid just walking around with a blindfold. At least with Oren, it looks like he's actually leading me somewhere.

Oren grabs my hand, leading me to his surprise. I can tell we're at the beach by the sound of the waves crashing and the sand brushing against my feet. This wouldn't be the first time he'd brought me to the beach since we arrived, but there had to be some sort of reason why this one was more special. At least special enough to have my eyes covered.

My heart thumps in my chest as Oren leads me down the path. "Don't worry, I've got you, love." He whispers in my ear, "The whole reason I wanted to blindfold you is because if you were looking, you'd already see the signs telling our destination. And I wanted to see the look on your face as you're surprised by not only the place and the actual date but also the words I have to say." Oren grabs the blindfold, loosening it completely to uncover my eyes.

I gasp at the scene in front of me, already aware of where Oren had brought me immediately.

It was Astir beach.

Oren had mentioned how beautiful it was to be there at sunset, so I was hoping we'd be coming to see it, but I gave up on the idea when it wasn't mentioned in the itinerary list.

I look at all the vacant lounge chairs and then at what I assume is ours, which is filled with scattered rose petals and trays of food between the two chairs.

"Is this all for us?" I ask Oren.

"Well, I didn't buy off this whole area for others to come and enjoy it themselves." I turn around wide-eyed at Oren.

What did he mean by buying off the area?

"Stop overthinking; I wanted this to be special. I needed this to be special." Oren declares, bringing me into his arms.

"Jasmine, I've been trying to say this for a while." Oren begins.

My heart drops at those same words he mentioned just a few days ago. I bite my lip and lay out a tiny prayer in my mind that there'd be no interruptions.

"What is it?"

"Jasmine, I know it's only been a couple of weeks since we became official. But... fuck you're making me nervous." Oren slides his hands down the fabric of his shirt, trying to dry off his sweaty palms, which only made an appearance when he was nervous, which, for Oren, was never.

Except now.

Somehow, I, a woman he'd known for years, was making him anxious.

"Jaz, what I am trying to say is that I love you." Oren raises his hands to my cheek, holding me still, and his eyes look into mine, waiting for an answer.

This hadn't been the first time we had verbalized our love, but I knew that this time, it was different. This wasn't the love you say to someone you care about and will always be there for. This was the type of love that owns you, the type of love that merges your soul with another's in hopes of having an eternity together even after we are nothing but stardust.

"I love you, too." The words escape my lips in a whisper.

Oren's lips rise into a grin as the pad of his thumb plays with the bottom of my lip.

"You, Jasmine, have always been my definition of love." Oren's whisper meets my lips as he presses his own against mine. Our lips moved in a graceful dance, unlike our previous ones.

This was raw and vulnerable; this was *real.*

I push Oren onto the lounge chair, our lips never once separating, his hands gripping my hips as I straddle him.

I pushed myself back up to look down at him; the sunset's hues danced across his skin. My heart skipped a beat with every second our eyes focused on one another.

The sound of the waves pushing against the shore blocked out the sound of our heavy breaths. This moment was nerve-wracking; it felt like many of our firsts again. But none of the other firsts really mattered anymore because the only thing that mattered now was us.

Chapter Twenty-Nine

Oren

Jasmine looked mesmerizing. I couldn't stop staring. The way the sunset colors arranged themselves behind her accentuated her form.

My God, I was looking at a goddess.

This had to be some unbelievable trick being played on me because there was no way this woman was all mine. Years that I silently yearned for her, and here she was looking down at me, all mine.

I move my hands down from her hips to her bare thighs, my fingers playing with the hem of her dress.

No words needed to be said.

This moment was for us, and we were taking it. Jasmine glides her hands up her thighs, pulling the skirt of her red dress up to reveal the black laced panties that were now enticing me for more.

Jasmine grinds herself against my hardening bulge, my grip on her thighs tightening. I wanted nothing more but to be inside of her at this very moment.

I move my hand past her laced panties, circling my finger around her clit before inserting two inside of her. Jasmine's light moans delicately fill my ears as she rides my fingers. I curve them in, hitting the spot that has her soaking for me in minutes and craving much more than just my fingers.

"I need more," Jasmine moans as she continues to ride my fingers, burying them deep within her.

I wanted to give her more; this time, I wouldn't make her beg. This wasn't about adventuring into our sexual fantasies in hopes of creating the spark that had her complete the next chapter in her novel.

This moment was only for us.

I remove my fingers from her wetness and quickly unbuckle my belt. Jasmine removes herself from above me, giving me room to take off my pants as she removes her panties before bringing herself right back on top of me.

My cock, now teasing her entrance, sliding up and down her slick pussy. I move my tip gently against her clit, her head moving back at the sensitiveness. Her nipples hardened against the material of her dress.

Fuck, I needed her.

I bring my cock to her entrance before thrusting upward, feeling her walls clench around my dick. My hands remain on her thighs as Jasmine takes the lead, finding the right rhythm as she glides herself up and down my cock. Her tits bouncing in that dress. The darkening of the sky fills her figure out even more as the moon begins to take its place, its light reflecting onto her.

Fuck she looked incredible, taking all of me within her. Jasmine moves herself up and down, rubbing her clit on me as my cock pulses inside of her.

Jasmine's moans move in sync with the clashes of the waves. I lift myself up, her movement continuing up and down my cock. I lower her dress looking at her plump tits. My tongue licks around her nipple, teasing her skin before bringing the nipple into my mouth. Sucking and pulling on them gently. Her back arches as she takes even more of me deeper inside of her.

My hands grab onto her ass, pulling her closer to me. I needed to feel all of her. I needed to have even more than I already was. I was greedy for her. The sweet taste of her skin, combined with the salty air of our surroundings, engraved itself into my mind, creating an archive of nostalgia.

I wouldn't be able to see a beach the same ever. The sound of the waves and the scent of the salty waters would always bring me back to this moment with her.

I release her nipple from my mouth, my hand clenching around her curls, bringing her closer to me.

"I love you," I whisper in between every deep thrust.

Jasmine opens her eyes, looking back down at me as she picks up her pace on my cock. Her lips widened into that beautiful grin I wanted to see for the rest of my life.

"I love you more." She declares, my thrusts becoming rougher and quicker. Jasmine throws her head back into a moan, clenching herself around me.

"Óti i agápi mou eínai adýnati. Eísai mia theá kai eímai móno énas ánthropos pou tha synechísei na se epaineí méchri tin teleftaía tou pnoí. Esý, Giasemí, eísai i aioniótitá mou. I zoí den échei nóima gia ména an den eísai mésa se aftín."* I whisper in her ear.

"What does that mean?" Jasmine asks between thrusts.

"It means that I am forever yours," I say, shooting my load deep inside of her as we climax together. Her body continues to ride me, enjoying every second of ecstasy that her orgasm gives her.

Jasmine's chest rises as she begins catching her breath as she comes down from her climax. Her skin glistened, and her hair wisps blew away in the night's wind.

Neither of us dared move just yet. We wanted this moment to last forever. This had been the beginning of everything and the declaration of forever.

My Jasmine, forever mine.

And I, Oren, forever hers.

---

* "That my love is impossible. You are a goddess, and I am only a man who will continue to praise you until his last breath. You, Jasmine, are my eternity. Life has no meaning to me if you're not in it."

Chapter Thirty

Jasmine

The trip had gone by too quickly, and even though I wanted to stay longer, both Oren and I had much to do. I hadn't worked on a single thing for my novel while on vacation, so I would be playing catch-up to make sure I had the first draft of this novel finished. I had sent my last few chapters to Kora, who, each time she read them, encouraged me to keep going and to start coming up with ideas for a sapphic novel.

The minute we arrived back home, Oren filled his schedule with all the work he had to get done before his gallery. He had said he wasn't really behind but wanted everything to come out perfect. It all had to tell a story, and he wanted to make sure that his new work was finished in time for the gallery.

He'd still refused to let me see the photos of our shoot, but

I wasn't as worried as I thought I'd be. If Oren found them beautiful and perfect enough to add to his gallery, then I had no worry that they wouldn't come out looking beautiful.

The knocking at the door startles me as I stir my coffee. It was part of my morning routine before gluing myself to my desk and writing all day until Oren arrived back from his art studio. I hadn't been expecting anyone. Kora had an important meeting with a fellow musician that she wasn't so happy to be working with. She had finally heard back after sending out her compositions, and though they were interested in working with her, it wasn't how she had thought it would turn out.

I opened the front door without even thinking to look at who was there first. It would at least have stopped me from looking dumbfounded to see Eloise standing there.

She was put together like the last few times I had seen her. Her blonde hair fell perfectly against her pink silk blouse. Her large Louis Vuitton bag was in hand, and her heels were always glued to her feet. She seemed like a life-size Barbie doll right in front of me.

Not a strand of hair was out of place.

"Hi," her voice soft and unsure. "I know this is weird; I promise I'm not here to harass you. Can I come in?" She asks.

It was probably best to close the door and tell her to leave me alone. William had done enough trying to slither his way between Oren and me, and the last thing I needed was Eloise here doing the same.

But the glossy look in her eyes told me otherwise. I sigh and open the door further so she can step in. At this rate, Oren and I would have to look for another place to move to where people wouldn't knock on our door every other day.

"Um, I know I had sent the invitation out at such short notice… but I never received an answer from you guys." Eloise steps into the kitchen as I close the door and look back at her.

There was no way this woman had come over here to ask us for our answer to her invitation. I was sure no response was already an answer to her question.

"Well, not everyone wants to see their ex get married, Eloise." I head back to the counter to finish making my coffee.

"Yeah, I can understand that." Eloise sighs, placing her bag on my counter as if her visit was going to last longer than it should. This had to be the most uncomfortable situation of my life, and neither Oren nor Kora would be barging in through the door to take me away from it.

"Listen, I know this is weird. I just need to have you there." Eloise pleads, stepping a bit closer to me.

I bring the mug to my lips, take a sip of the coffee, and stare at her with a concerned look.

Was she okay?

She was asking me to be there. She wanted her soon-to-be husband's ex at the wedding.

"This engagement is a complete sham," Eloise explains.

"So you aren't getting married?" I ask her.

"No, we are, but that's the thing. I don't want to." Eloise finally lets go of the tears that have been waiting to fall since she arrived. I can't help but hug her, letting her cry out on my shoulder.

How the hell did I get into this situation?

I was comforting my ex's fiancée because she was upset about having to marry him. "Eloise, I don't understand any of this or what it has to do with me going to the wedding," I say delicately, not trying to bring the girl into a sobbing hysteric.

Eloise pulls away, wiping away her tears. The girl who had looked so perfect every time I saw her was now so vulnerable in front of me. Her hair is disheveled, and her mascara smeared.

"Our parents are making us get married to merge their companies. They feel that if they bargain away our love life, then there is no way their partnership will turn against each other. William is only doing this because he wants his father's business after he resigns, and I'm doing this because I have no choice." Eloise continues to break down into a sob.

I rip off a piece of paper towel from its roll and hand it over to her, rubbing her back to calm her down.

"The only way my father will let me out of this stupid arrangement is if William calls it off, and he won't do that unless he knows you still want him."

I stand frozen in my spot, unsure of what to say. I didn't want to get in between them. This was none of my business. This whole time I was trying to do my best to push William away; I fucking blocked him so that he'd leave me alone.

Oren and I finally felt like something real; we were something real. I wasn't willing to ruin what I had been working so hard to obtain and strengthen with Oren to make William see that he was making a mistake by marrying Eloise, especially not when it would only raise his hopes.

"Jasmine, why do you think I've been so insufferable?" Eloise pleads.

I shrug nonchalantly. "I just thought you were like that." I didn't think that past her hard, posh exterior, a woman was breaking down because of the hell that is her family.

"I mean, I don't think I'm the best person on the planet. But if I was interested in William, why would I encourage him to talk to his ex? And then invite myself to your house party? I just needed him to see that if he didn't make a move now, he would eventually lose you." Eloise sobs.

She wasn't much of the psychotic, overbearing person that I thought she was.

She just wanted a way out.

"My whole life, I have had to follow everything my family has demanded of me. Schools, diets, clubs, friends, and now even my husband. There's never an end. I don't even want to be a lawyer; I just picked it because it was one of the only options my father had given me in order for him to pay for my education." Eloise blows her nose onto the piece of paper, trying to catch her breath between sobs.

Eloise was exactly what Kora had said. She was a puppet to her parents. They didn't care about her wants; it was all about how they could use her to benefit themselves.

"I know you don't owe me anything," Eloise reaches over to hold my hands against hers in a plea. "But Jasmine, at this point, I'm desperate. I don't want someone to marry me because of a business contract. I want someone to marry me because they actually love me." Eloise's red, puffy eyes made me feel even worse about this situation.

"Okay, don't worry, Eloise. I'll do it, I'll be at the wedding, but I can't promise you anything." I say, giving in to her pleas. Eloise brings me into her arms, hugging me and thanking me for everything.

I would do this one thing for her, just to help her. But Oren couldn't find out about this. He wouldn't understand and definitely wouldn't care if it was just to help Eloise.

Having me be anywhere near William would send him into a frenzy.

This was just between Eloise and I.

Eloise pulls away, rubbing away the mascara from under her eyes. "How do I look?" She asks, her hair still disheveled and her eyes puffy and red, surrounded by the remnants of her smeared mascara.

I fixed her up a bit before giving her the okay. Eloise grabs her bag from the counter and walks back over to the door. She opens the door and stands still for a bit before turning back to me.

"I wish a man looked at me the way he looks at you," Eloise says.

I scrunch my eyebrows in confusion, "William?" I ask.

Eloise scoffs and shakes her head, "No, Jasmine… Oren."

With that last response, Eloise makes her way out of the apartment, shutting the door behind her.

I feel guilty, and my chest pounds as I think about how I'll get around this without Oren finding out.

What did I get myself into?

Thirty-One

Jasmine

Talk about money. This wedding venue looked like it could pay all the debts in the world. It was only an hour away, which wasn't too bad. But having to lie to Oren this morning and tell him I had plans with Kora rather than tell him the truth made my heart ache.

Maybe I could've told him the truth. He would have understood if I had really tried to get him to see what I saw. But it was already too late. I was already at the venue, waiting in line to give my name to security so I could get this over with.

I wasn't even going to bother with the actual wedding ceremony. I just needed to find William and speak to him. I had unblocked his number and tried to reach out, but now it seemed that he was the one doing the ignoring. Then again, I hadn't reached out to him when Oren busted his face in, so I'd ignore him, too.

"Your name?" The security guard, who looked too buff for my liking, asks me, not bothering to look up at me.

"Jasmine Monroe," I responded.

He takes his sight off the clipboard and looks over at me, his piercing brown eyes looking at me as if trying to decipher if there's any lie to my identity.

Was I getting into a fucking wedding venue or the White House?

"You can go ahead, " he murmurs before looking back at his clipboard and asking the person behind me for their name. I move past their barrier and towards the entrance of the mansion, which is the opposite way from where all the guests are currently gathered.

But I wasn't here to mingle with the guests. I was here to break off the wedding. And that meant I had to find William. I make my way past the caterers, the shouting wedding planner, and what I assume to be bridesmaids in their robes.

This place was huge. There was no way I would find William on the first try. I look over to my right at the angry wedding planner who seems to be arguing about the center-pieces with someone on the phone. I walk over to her and tap on her shoulder to get her attention.

"Give me a second— Do not hang up! Can I help you?" She asks brusquely.

"Oh, um, I need to know what room the groom is in."

The wedding planner looked me up and down; I wasn't necessarily dressed for a wedding. I just grabbed the first nice floral dress I saw in my closet and threw it on.

"Who are you exactly?" She retorts.

I open my mouth to let out any excuse that comes to mind but am immediately cut off by her phone's ringtone. "God damn it, what is it now?" She mutters, answering the phone. "Give me a second," she mutters into her earpiece before looking back at me. "He's on the second floor, west wing, sixth door to the right side of the hall." She says it before storming off and bickering with whoever was on the other end of the call.

I make my way up the stairs towards William's room. I stand at the door, taking a deep breath. I try gathering all my thoughts, thinking of what exactly I'm going to say to him that can persuade him to call off this wedding. My fists meet the door three times before I hear it unlock. The door opens, revealing William in his tux, his wavy hair more prominent than usual.

"Can I come in?" I ask, looking around to make sure no one is looking. For some reason, I felt guilty just being alone in the room with him, despite being here at Eloise's request.

William pushes the door back, allowing me to step in. He closes the door the minute I step in, locking it for what I assume is a precaution. The last thing he needs or wants is rumors flying around that he was seen with a woman in his room before the wedding.

Though that wouldn't be much of a rumor, just the assumptions of what we could be up to.

"What are you doing here, Jasmine?" He asks, his voice stoic.

"You can't do this to Eloise, William." I blurt out; there was no walking around it. I didn't need him thinking I came all this way because I wanted to give us another chance.

William gives me a sly grin before moving past me to sit on the velvet vintage sofa.

"So that's why she was there," William murmurs more to himself than to me.

"You knew she was at my apartment?".

Had he been following the poor girl, too?

"She's my soon-to-be wife, Jasmine. I have eyes on her to ensure she doesn't run into any issues." William admits.

Something was wrong; this wasn't the William I knew. This wasn't the same man I had known for years. It for sure wasn't the man I was planning on marrying.

"William, you have to call off the wedding. Don't do this to Eloise." I beg, trying to get him to see where I'm coming from.

"Jasmine, you made your choice very clear. You chose him," he mutters. "The only thing I wanted besides you is my rightful position at my father's company when he leaves. You made your answer very clear, leaving me with the only thing I know I'll never lose, and that's my company."

William's eyes darken with every word. There's no remorse for how this will affect Eloise. He only cares for himself, and nothing I say will change that.

"You're taking her chance at love away," I say.

William rolls his eyes before standing back up to stand right in front of me. My phone buzzes in my pocket, and I pull it out to take a quick look at who it is. Kora's name flashes on the screen, but I hit the ignore call button and make a mental note to call her back later.

"Is Oren calling? He's probably wondering where you are. You should probably get going. The last thing you want is him finding out that you're in my room trying to get me to call off the wedding," William says with his new snarky attitude.

"Go to hell, William," I mutter.

I remove the ring I had brought with me from the pocket of my dress and place it on the coffee table. This was it for us. William doesn't even shift in his seat. He remains stoic and impressionable as he stares up at me.

That ring would be our final goodbye. After this, I never wanted to see him again. I turned back around and walked towards the door.

"She'll be fine, you know," William begins. As much of an arrangement as it is, that doesn't mean I won't respect and protect her," William says as if respecting and protecting her were enough.

I turn to look back at him, my hand at the door. "If you think respecting and protecting her is enough, then you never really loved me, William. Because if you did, you'd realize what you're taking away from her." William's eyes drop at my words, his jaw clenching as he takes them in. I unlock the door and step out into the hallway, shutting the door behind me. I make my way towards the steps but stop when I see a hint of white in my peripheral. My eyes meet Eloise from across the hall. She looked like a fairytale in her dress. Despite her glowing beauty, her eyes held so much hope. She hoped my answer would have her jumping out of her gown instantly.

I shake my head, and that's the only thing needed for Eloise's hope to diminish right in front of me before giving me a brief nod and turning away.

All of this had been for nothing.

I make my way down the steps, pulling out my phone to

call an Uber to bring me back home. My eyes remain on the phone as I make my way towards the entrance of the mansion, but my body instantly smacks into a hard chest.

"Oh, I'm sor—" I look up, and before I can finish, my breath leaves my lungs in an instant as I stare up at Oren.

What the hell was he doing here?

"Funny little thing," Oren rasps. "I bumped into Kora a few minutes after you left; she was on her way to a meeting."

I close my eyes, hoping that this will all be just a dream if I open them. There's no way Oren is here in front of me. He's obviously assuming the worst after finding out that I lied about where I was and just having seen me come out of William's room.

"Oren, it's not what you think." I try to explain.

Oren lets out a scoff before turning away to walk out of the mansion. I quickly follow him, calling out his name in hopes of him stopping to talk to me. I don't care how pathetic I look running after him. I needed him to know that this wasn't because of any remaining feelings between William and me.

Oren turns around, his anger raging within him. I don't think I had ever seen Oren like this before.

"Then why didn't you just tell me you were coming?" He remarks.

The eyes are definitely on us now, but I couldn't care less. I needed Oren to listen to me and understand.

"Because you wouldn't have understood. I was doing this for Eloise—." I freeze, taking a look at the crowd around us. The last thing I wanted was to publicize Eloise's issues.

"Can we talk somewhere else?" I plead.

Oren only shakes his head as he brings his hands across his hair, pulling at the roots.

"You're never going to see me the way you see him," Oren says.

I look up at Oren, unsure of what he's trying to get at.

"Oren, what are you talking about?" I ask, trying to reach out to touch him, but he only steps back. I freeze in my spot, unsure of what to say or do. Oren didn't even want me touching him. The man who constantly finds a way to have his hands on me didn't want me anywhere near him.

Oren's eyes begin to water, his jaw clenched to hold back tears. This wasn't about the lie; this was all about what Oren thought I had been lying about. I just needed to go somewhere private to explain everything.

"Oren, please—"

"No." Oren cuts me off, clearing his throat. He looks around at everything but me. I need you to hear what I have to say, Jasmine."

I nod, my heart thumping loudly as I wait to hear his words.

"I never really understood how much you meant to me until after I left for college." Oren's voice croaks, his eyes on the people walking toward the venue rather than at me.

"I realized then how much you really meant to me and how much you truly deserved. I wanted to give you the world, Jasmine, and I made sure I could give you that when I finished school." Oren continues, his eyes shifting to mine, my breath hitching in response. Afraid that any sudden move-ment would have him walk away.

"When I came back, it fucking hurt to see you with him. But fuck, Jaz, he made you happy. And I wanted so badly to be him. I wanted so badly to be yours. But you had said yes to his proposal. And I couldn't wreck the world that you were so happy with just because of my selfish need to want you to be mine."

Oren's glossy eyes shed a singular tear that he's quick to wipe away, but it's already too late. My heart shatters at just the thought of being the one to have caused him all this pain.

"And even when I can finally call you mine, you're somehow still his, and I don't know how I'll ever compete with that. Not when you won't let him go." Oren's murmur is low, but I swear his words traveled through the light breeze toward me, sending shivers throughout my body.

"That's not fair; you're not letting me explain." I try to reason.

This wasn't fair, I always heard him out, and here he was, playing sweet and innocent as if he had never lied to me. This wasn't right.

"I think we need some time apart." Oren's words collide with my heart, breaking it completely.

"What?" I manage to croak out.

"I'll stay at the loft for now, and you can stay at the apartment. I think we just need some space." Oren says.

I only manage to nod as he turns around and walks away. I'm frozen to my spot, watching him walk away until he's no longer visible, hoping he'll turn back around and speak to me.

Instead, I stood there while everyone walked past because, just like that, it was over. Just as quickly as it had started. I thought what I felt with William was heartbreaking, but I was wrong. This with Oren had been heart-shattering. My soul had been ripped out of its home. I wanted to cry; I wanted to fucking scream.

I just wanted him to hear my heart shatter so he could understand how real my feelings for him were.

But Oren kept his head forward, not once turning back to look at me; I continued to stare until he disappeared from my field of view.

And as he did, just like that, I lost not only the love of my life but my best friend.

Chapter Thirty-Two

Jasmine

Heartbreak didn't seem to get easier the second time around. But maybe that's just because my love with Oren was genuine. It had sprouted from our friendship, giving it even more importance.

This was destined to be a failed relationship, no matter how much we wanted it to be real and forever. You couldn't go from being platonic to romantic partners overnight. Oren and I just wanted to prove the impossible.

I wanted to blame myself for allowing this to go as far as it did. But I also wanted to hunt Oren down and scream at him for not letting me explain myself and for not allowing our love to continue.

I remove the covers from my face, to peer around the room. Not that anything had changed in the past four days. I had little to no motivation to continue to write.

The last thing I wanted to do was write about someone falling in love with the man of their dreams, especially not when mine had just broken up with me.

My phone flooded with texts and calls from Kora and Phoebe. The only reason I knew it was them is because I had checked every time my phone made a noise, hoping it was Oren.

The sudden, consecutive banging on my door began to twist my stomach. Just thinking of having to talk to someone had my chest pounding and my stomach churning. I just wanted to be alone, but Kora obviously didn't get that.

As much as I'd like to pretend that I'd see Oren the minute I opened that door, I knew it would be too good to be true. Regardless, I still hold my breath as I open the door, mustering any hope I have left that it's him.

But instead, my first guess is the win. Kora's standing there with a bag full of snacks, similar to the first time we had hung out together.

"I brought the best sweets that are said to mend a broken heart," Kora says, making her way in and taking a seat on that nasty orange couch that Oren would not get rid of.

But in all honesty, now, it was one of the few things in this apartment that reminded me of him. A sob breaks out of me as I close the door and make my way over to Kora.

"Oh, Jaz." Kora coos, opening her arms for me to hug her. I fall right into her, laying my head on her shoulder as I continue to cry. Kora rubs her hand up and down my back, trying to comfort me, but it only leads to louder sobs.

"It's alright, Jaz, this too shall pass," Kora reassures.

I pull away from her embrace, taking deep breaths in and out to calm myself. "No," I managed to croak. "Not without

Oren. I need him to stay." I say through sniffs and gasps of air.

"He will stay. He just needs time. Remember that men are idiots. And Oren, in this case, is very much an idiot, but he's hurt." Kora's hands caressed my arms to bring me some sort of physical comfort, but it was nothing like Oren's touch. Kora was a great friend, but at this very moment, I needed my best friend.

"I should've just told the truth of where I was going; I just thought he wouldn't understand.".

"Well, why did you go?" Kora asks.

I told Kora the truth, letting her know how Eloise came to me for help and how their families were forcing this marriage between them.

"Well, it doesn't surprise me. That's how all these big-money families work. Their children are just another asset." Kora says.

I didn't expect much of a surprise from her; Kora had been involved in this type of lifestyle before she left.

"I'd like to say that Oren is an idiot and should've heard you out. But you were also an idiot for not being honest in the beginning. The least you could've done is let me in on the secret. It caught me off guard when he started hounding me for answers." Kora rationalizes as she begins pulling out the many snacks she brought.

"You're right; I'm sorry I put you in an uncomfortable position," I say.

I never intended to get Kora caught up in the mess. It hadn't occurred to me that Oren and her would run into each other. Kora was usually out of her apartment before either of us. That day, fate had just decided to go against me, like usual.

Kora shrugs, opening up a bag of salt and vinegar chips. "It doesn't really matter. Things happen, and I think that when big events like this happen,, it's for you to grow and make the most of it." Kora says between munches.

She offers me some, but my stomach revolts at the thought of eating. I shake my head, lay back down onto the couch, and plop my feet on top of her thighs.

"This is a perfect time for Oren and you to heal. You guys need to focus on yourselves as individuals for a while," Kora says, her voice light to make the statement as comforting as possible.

I knew what Kora was trying to say. In other words, I couldn't stop my life from continuing to complete my goals because Oren wasn't here. I'd bet money he was at the studio using all this time and all these emotions to get things together for his gallery.

His gallery.

He had been so excited for me to be there the day of the opening. Was I even still invited? Had he taken me off the list by now?

I brush past the thoughts of Oren not wanting me to be there during a big moment in his career. I was only hurting my own feelings at this point. We still had time to fix things; we just needed time. And I couldn't stand around and continue to mope. I had much more important things to do.

"You're right." I declare, pushing myself back up on the couch to face Kora.

She looked me up and down before giving me a knowing

nod. "I know I'm right, babe, and you might want to start with taking a shower, " she comments.

I take a whiff of my shirt, not smelling anything but knowing that she's probably right.

"Go ahead and take a shower; I'll be here when you get out. We got to get you back and running. You also left me on a bit of a cliffhanger in your last chapter, and I'd like to figure out what the fuck is happening." Kora teases, making me let out a genuine laugh that was well-needed.

Getting up I head back into the room to pick out a new set of clothes. I was going to do as Kora said. I had to use this time to grow and allow Oren the space that he needed. At some point, he had to talk to me again, and when he did, I was going to make sure that he listened this time around.

I wasn't going to give up on us.

Chapter Thirty-Three

Oren

I had given up on us.

I had spent years waiting for her to look at me the way I had looked at her. I wanted her to want me like I wanted her. The flirting, the touching, the protecting, all of that had been done out of deep desire for her. And somehow, I was still just the best friend at the end of every day.

And even when she finally begins to see me as more, I still get put on the back burner the minute that slimy douche of a man comes back into her life.

There was nothing she could've said to defend her lie about going to see William at the wedding.

She had said she would be out with Kora, but Kora had no clue what the fuck I was talking about when I ran into her. It hadn't taken me long to figure out why Jasmine would've lied about her whereabouts, especially when the date of William and Eloise's wedding suddenly appeared in my mind in a glowing red neon sign.

I had held on to what little hope there was that Jasmine would be anywhere but there. And when I saw her come out of that door and towards the stairs, I didn't even know what to think.

Why hadn't I just let her talk?

I deserved a fucking answer, but I was too fucking pissed to speak to anyone. The only people I had bothered answering had been Kora and Phoebe. And that's because both women had no fucking concept of personal space.

I just needed to be on my own. These past four days, I have been distracting my mind with work, whether booking dates for some freelance work or creating new works to add to the gallery.

Most of my art was ready to go. The gallery space would be available to me in three days, and then all I had left to do was set up all the art I had worked on throughout the years. All this led to this big moment where I could tell my story at my first-ever art exhibit.

I wanted to be excited, but nothing felt right if Jasmine wasn't there, and right now, I couldn't even think about speaking to her. I wasn't ready to see her just yet, and hearing her would just break me.

It had taken so much out of me not to want to turn back to her the moment I had left her at the wedding venue. But I couldn't do it anymore. I had been chasing after Jasmine for years; this time, I just needed her to come after me. I needed her to show me that I was just as important to her as William had once been… or still is.

"What the fuck is wrong with you?" Garrett's voice

echoes through the loft; my shoulders drop at its sound, bringing out a groan from within my chest.

"What do you want?" I was being straightforward.

The last thing I needed was Garrett coming to breathe down my neck to have me participate in another one of his works or to just screw around and get in my head.

He was a close friend throughout college, which is why I have chosen to work with him from time to time. But he could be such a fucking prick. And that only made me want to punch him in the face even more.

"Relax, just so you know, I tried calling you, but you've been ignoring my calls. And also, your door is unlocked downstairs, so I made sure to lock it before some psycho decides to come fucking murder you." Garrett reprimands me by walking over to my table, where all my supplies are currently scattered.

Everything around my studio was disorganized and chaotic; I'd be lying if I didn't admit to coming here right after my argument with Jaz and wrecking the loft.

On the third day of my moping, I finally picked up all of my broken items and left them in a corner to throw out later. That was a step for another day. I was lucky enough to have gathered everything to a corner in the first place.

"No one is going to come and murder me," I say, grabbing a wet rag that I kept on the counter to wipe off my hands that were covered in paint.

"Well, not anymore, 'cause I locked your fucking door." Garrett chastises.

"Fuck off."

Garrett was right. I must've accidentally left the door

unlocked when I came in the other day, but I had other shit eating up my mind that wasn't my door.

I also wasn't a fucking child.

"Woah, relax. What's got you pissed and trying to disappear off the face of the Earth?" Garrett's eyebrows furrowed in confusion, unaware of why I had a hellish attitude and a look that could kill on my face.

"Jasmine and I broke up, well technically, we're on a break, but I don't even know what the fuck that entails." I sounded stupid as if I hadn't been the one to decide on the break.

"She broke up with you?" Garrett asks, giving me an understanding nod as he gives me a once-over.

Fucking prick.

"No, you dick, I— "

Damn it, I sounded so fucking stupid. There was nothing good about me breaking up with Jaz, and here I was, trying to get the story straight. But the last thing I wanted to do was talk about this. I needed to devote my time and mind to something else. I needed a distraction from the problems encircling around in my mind.

"Forget it, it doesn't matter. What are you doing here?" I question, trying to get out of the topic of my breakup.

"You mean you don't remember asking me for help last week to fly over and help you set up your gallery?" Garrett's sarcasm sinks in my stomach.

God, I was such a fucking dickhead.

Garrett had agreed to take some time off of work to come and help me out with setting up, and here I was, being a total douche. I drag my hands down my face, letting out a groan before looking back over at him.

"Let me hear it." Garrett sighs over-dramatically.

"I'm sorry," I mutter.

"All is forgiven; besides, I can understand a broken heart, too."

I scoff at Garrett's response; that man had never experienced love to know what true heartbreak was.

"Did Renee leave you already?" I ask, my curiosity getting the best of me.

"Actually, no, we are working out quite well," Garrett reassures with a surprised look on his face as much as it is on mine.

I don't think I've ever seen Garrett with anyone for more than a weekend, so this relationship between Renee and him must've been serious.

"Hey, but just because I haven't ever experienced that type of love or heartbreak doesn't mean I haven't seen it. And I'm here for you." Garrett brings his hand to my shoulder, giving me an assuring pat and letting me know that he isn't leaving any time soon.

And as much of a dickhead as I wanted to be, I couldn't because I needed him here. When I was hung up over Jaz in college, Garrett had been the only one I could talk to and overall the only person who was ever really there, granted he was my roommate. But he hadn't signed up for that shit, but somehow he was still there when I needed him.

"Thanks; I think I need the company," I admit, taking a seat on the stool near my table and pulling one out for him as well. Garrett lets out a chuckle and takes a seat on the stool.

"Not for nothing, but I practically have people begging for my company."

Cocky bastard.

"Now show me some of this work that you're keeping hidden away from the world." Garrett extends his arms in a gesture toward all the work I have covered in sheets. Everything that would be shown at the gallery was work I had set on the side throughout the years, never allowing anyone to see it.

There had been a time when I thought I'd never reveal it to anyone, but I had already committed to the gallery, and there was no turning back.

I motioned my head towards one of the covered art pieces. It was one of the biggest pieces I had, a bronze sculpture that had taken me months to perfect until I was finally happy with the way it had turned out.

"Can I?" Garrett asks. The aching look of wanting to get off the stool and take a look was plastered on his face. I let out a chuckle before nodding.

Garrett shoots out of his chair, practically running to the covered gem. His finger grazes the ends of the sheets before looking up at me to ensure I'm okay with showing him my work.

But it was irrelevant now; if he didn't see it now, he'd see it in three days when he moved it to the gallery.

It only takes half a nod before Garrett pulls the sheet, revealing the bronze glory from underneath it. Garrett's mouth drops, his eyes widening in shock.

"Holy. Fucking. Shit." Is all that escapes his lips as he stares at the detailed figure.

My lips can't help but widen into a grin at his reaction. Maybe Garrett was exactly the person I needed right now, not my best friend but a friend nonetheless.

"Come on, get your sorry ass off the fucking stool and

show me more; I think I already know what to expect." I lift myself off, walking over to tear off all the sheets, allowing them to be seen for the first time by anyone other than me and my curator.

But finally, being able to show someone close to me all my work made me feel accomplished.

Even if it wasn't the one person that I really wanted to show it to.

Chapter Thirty-Four

Jasmine

My fingers cramped by the end of every night after writing consecutively. My book felt like a pile of vomit on several pages, but I was hoping that once I had begun the editing process, it would make me feel a bit better.

Though Oren had been my muse and inspiration, this book was now my distraction from him. I had tried calling him once every night these past few days, but the calls would go straight to voicemail.

In some ways, the calls each night encouraged my consistency. I had to show him how much he meant to me, and this book would say it all. It wasn't until I got to the epilogue that I felt accomplished but lonely.

I had written my first romance novel. I had constructed a

world and its characters; I built a loving relationship that I lacked creating in my own life.

Regardless, it wasn't the lack of a love life that made me feel numb; it was the lack of Oren in it. I had finished my novel and didn't have my best friend to turn to anymore.

The buzzing on my phone brings me away from my self-pity. I reach out for it quickly, my hope skyrocketing, only for it to plummet down at a message from Terrence rather than Oren.

> **TERRENCE**
>
> Hey, Kora sent me a copy of your manuscript. Though I do not work with romance novels, I do know someone who does. I decided to forward it to her, and she loved it.
>
> I hope you don't mind. I gave her your info, and she said she's willing to see where this can go. So she'll be reaching out real soon.

KORA DID WHAT?!

My heart stopped at the words on the screen. I had sent her those rough drafts with the agreement that she wouldn't show anyone.

I was going to kill her.

And then…

I was going to hug her endlessly.

I would've never asked Terrence for a favor like that, not after ditching him for Oren. Even if I hadn't continued things with Oren, we weren't as close for me to ask him for any favors at all. But even though Kora asked for me, he had decided to help me anyway.

JASMINE

> Oh My God, I'm going to kill Kora for this.

> I had no idea she had sent you that; I'm so sorry.

TERRENCE

A thank you will do. I read it before I even thought about sending it to Mel…. I don't send things unless I like them.

She's good at what she does. If you give it time, I think she might just be able to get you published.

Thank you.

THERE WAS NOTHING MORE I HAD TO SAY. TERRENCE HAD done me a favor, but not because he liked me or valued his friendship with Kora. It was because he enjoyed it.

He had enjoyed my book or the little piece that was sent to him.

My fingers quickly slide into the messages on my phone, pressing on Oren's name to tell him about the surprising news before they halt in motion. This wasn't how I wanted to tell him. This wasn't how I wanted things to go at all. This was going to be something I would tell him in person. So, instead, my fingers glide towards Kora's name, sending her a friendly threat for going against my wishes and a quick thank you for doing something I wouldn't have even thought about.

Too scared of the thought of being rejected.

Until I got my message from Terrence's friend Mel, there wasn't much I could do. Now that I had accomplished writing my first draft, I would focus on the one important thing I needed to get back.

I needed to prove my love was real to Oren.

I open my email, type in Oren's email address, and upload my manuscript onto the email.

The subject name: I finally did it!

Chapter Thirty-Five

Jasmine

He hadn't responded, granted it had barely been a whole twenty-four hours. But he was bound to check his email throughout the day. I was getting impatient, waiting around for some sort of response. Even a *great* or a *I don't care* would've suffice. Just as long as the ignoring came to some sort of end.

I received a couple of emails throughout my morning, most of them promotional, except the one from Terrence's friend Melanie Lombardi, with whom I set up a meeting for this upcoming Monday.

"How do I get you out of that head of yours?" My dad's voice rings as he walks over to me by the history area of the bookstore. I returned home this morning to spend some time with my parents in hopes of having them make everything feel better.

I hadn't told them about what had happened, but I don't think that was necessary. They were my parents. They always knew when something was up, even when I tried to hide it.

"How do you know I'm in my head and not interested in learning about U.S. History?" I tease, picking up an overly heavy book with what I assume is an image of one of the founding fathers.

"Yes, because my daughter is highly interested in learning about the establishment of the white patriarchy of this country that seems to continue to put her on the back burner when it comes to the importance of being a woman, let alone a black woman." My dad iterates, looking down at the book in my hand. I pucker my lips, placing the book back down on the shelf.

What else could you expect from a white history teacher married to a black woman? On top of that, he had a daughter who, from as far as my memories could go, was constantly lectured on the importance and value that came with being a woman.

"Got it, you caught me," I say. Making my way down the aisle, my dad's arm reaching over my shoulder to pull me in.

"Now, are you going to tell me what's wrong?" Dad questions, and even though I'm looking forward, I can feel his stare.

"Why would you think something's wrong?" I ask, pushing open the store's door to head back outside.

My dad and I had been to this bookstore many times; it was our favorite thing to do. We would do the same thing each and every time we hung out. We'd make our way to the bookstore, and usually, we'd end up buying more books than we could read before stepping out and heading to our favorite ice cream shop at the corner of the street that served the best soft serve. It was our little dessert before going back home for dinner. It was also our little secret, or at least Dad would say that, even though I'm pretty sure he would tell Mom all about it afterward.

Just like I was sure she would tell him all about her and I's little secret of going out for brunch every Sunday even though she told him we would be running errands.

"Come on, Jaz. The minute you called and told your mother you were coming over to spend some time with us, she was worried that something happened to you." I rolled my eyes at my father. In other words, I wouldn't be home unless something had happened, which was not true at all.

I was just always busy before, and now… God, I'm a terrible daughter.

"I'm sorry; I'll come visit more often," I promise, hoping it makes me feel less guilty for being here.

"Jasmine, that's not what I'm saying. I know you have your own life now, and I know that you're busy. But I also know that you decided to stop by out of nowhere, which is always nice. But, this whole day, you've been unlike yourself. Starting with the fact that you just walked out of the bookstore without a book in hand." My dad's words hit me right in the chest.

He knows me well enough to know something's wrong, but I felt like such a loser to admit to him that Oren and I were no longer together after introducing ourselves as a couple just a few weeks ago.

"Oren and I aren't really together— anymore." I clarify, swallowing the lump that's formed at the center of my throat. Dad stops behind the line of customers that's leading into the ice cream shop. The line has always been long, at least I think it has; it's been a while since we were last here. But waiting next to my dad, who's silent at my reveal, makes it feel much longer than usual.

The line moved up a couple of times in the past five minutes that we stood here, and not a word left his lips. The man started humming to the songs that played out of this place's speakers, completely ignoring my revelation.

Was he getting to the point in age where his hearing was starting to fade away?

"Aren't you going to say something?" I finally ask, more annoyed that he hadn't tried to say something sooner or at least comfort me.

Dad looks down with a grin before giving me a shrug, "What's there to say? It won't last."

I roll my eyes at his stoic response. Had that not been what I just said? That we hadn't lasted?

"Dad, that's what I'm saying; we didn't last." I reiterate, moving further up the line and into the shop.

"That's not what *I'm* saying," He says, pausing before looking up at the man behind the counter to order our usual. The man returns with a cherry-dipped soft serve in a cone and rocky road filled into a cup. "What I am saying is that there are going to be fights and arguments, and after a while, you realize they're not worth having." Dad pulls out his card, hovering it over the payment terminal to pay. I step outside, away from the crowd, waiting for him to join me.

Dad takes a bite out of his ice cream, humming with delight. I take a bite of mine, scrunching my nose up at the odd taste. Something just wasn't right about it. The taste was off.

"You don't like it?" Dad asks, scrunching his eyebrows as he tries to piece together how I stopped loving my favorite ice cream.

"I don't know, it tastes funny," I say, continuing back onto our path to get home.

"The world must be ending for you not to like your favorite ice cream." Dad teases, but that's exactly how everything has been feeling lately.

Nothing was how it should be, and everything seemed to be falling apart. I throw my ice cream in the nearby garbage bin as the tears start streaming down my eyes again.

"Oh crap, no, don't cry. We can get you another one." Dad murmurs, bringing me into his arms as I sob into his shirt. Were men so oblivious? Better question: was my father so oblivious to the reasoning behind my tears?

"It's not the ice cream, Dad," I mutter, pulling away to wipe my tears. "Oren was meant to be my best friend, and I ruined it. Now I've not only lost my boyfriend but the one person that's always been there for me."

Dad sighs and brings us over to a bench on the sidewalk. "You didn't ruin a thing," he says, gently caressing my hair.

"This is all just an argument that will blow over soon enough." He assures, but both of us knew how untrue that really was.

"No, you just don't get it. This is different. He was my best friend—he is my best friend. This isn't like you and Mom or any other couple, for that matter." I rub my hands down my face, unsure of how to explain the situation to my father to make him understand that Oren and I were just never meant to be more and that because of our foolishness, we had corrupted something beautiful that was already there.

"What's so different? That you guys are friends? You think your mom and I aren't friends?" I lift my head up from my palms to peer over at Dad, who's enjoying his rocky road as he speaks.

"What?" I croak.

"Your mother and I may not have started out as friends, but that doesn't mean she never became my best one. That's why we have lasted as long as we have because she's my best friend." Dad leans down towards me to whisper something in secret. "If you ask me, that's the key to a happy marriage."

I chuckle before wiping away the remainder of my tears. Maybe Dad was right. Regardless of my situation with Oren, it didn't take away that our love was only made more special because of our friendship.

I was moping around, waiting for a call back from Oren, my boyfriend, hoping he'd hear me out. But I was Jasmine, his best friend, and if this were any other situation, I would've gone right over to his loft and forced him to listen.

"I'm going to kill him," I mutter, upset that Oren hadn't stuck around to listen to my side of the story.

"There it is; that's what I want to see. The female rage taking charge." Dad gets up from the bench, giving his head a nudge for me to follow. "Let's go; I don't want to be late for dinner. If you're here, that means your mom is making something really good tonight, and I'm not missing out."

I laugh and catch up to him, not letting go of my thoughts about Oren. I was going to go to him and I was going to make sure that he listened.

Chapter Thirty-Six

Jasmine

I think of all the excuses I could give the security guard at the door for him to let me in. If nothing seems to work out, I'll have no other choice but to cry my eyes out in hopes of them taking pity on me.

"Name?" The security guard questions as I get closer.

"Jasmine Monroe," I respond my breath a little shaky at just the thought of seeing Oren.

The minute I had gone home from visiting my parents, I showed up at his loft unannounced in hopes of finding him and making sure that he listened to me. But to my surprise, he wasn't there, and though it could've been just some type of fluke, in my heart, I held onto the idea of it being fate.

The security guard opens the door, allowing me to pass through. I was wearing a floral dress because adding more clothing sounded atrocious in the summer heat. But I wished the gallery had taken place in the fall so I could wear my jacket and hide my shaky hands in its pockets.

A woman at the front of the gallery handed me a pamphlet with Oren's face on it. His bright smile and green eyes looked photoshopped onto the glossy cover.

But I could vouch from experience that he was just as perfect in person as he was in the pictures; he was just insanely photogenic.

I enter the first room, my feet completely freezing as my eyes take in the art before me. A bronze sculpture stood there right in the center of the room.

It was the outline of a woman's body

No.

It was the outline of my body.

I move closer to the sculpture, taking in the physical attributes added to the face.

This was me.

I look down at the plaque that read;

My Love
— Oren Samaras

I look around, taking in the other pieces surrounding me, a multitude of paintings hanging on the walls.

All of me.

If they weren't portraits, they were paintings of objects and places that were only ever related to Oren and me.

I look over to one of the paintings leading into the next gallery room. It was a painting of the bookstore, and I was by the window. I look at the side, viewing the plaque beside it, glued onto the wall.

Our Dream
— Oren Samaras

Right next to it was a painting he had begun doing when I visited his loft after my shift at the bookstore. Oren captured every strand of hair, the sun's glow on my skin, and the glint of lust in my eyes that had been stirring up deep within me that day as I began thinking of him as more than just a friend.

Torturous Position
— Oren Samaras

I hadn't even known that he had gotten around to finishing the painting at all. And now here it was in the gallery amongst all the other ones. I feel stares at my every move as I continued to move through the gallery. Heat rises to my cheeks at the thought of everyone knowing that I'm the woman in the paintings.

That I was his muse.

But, surely, just because I looked similar to a painting didn't mean that I was the woman painted onto the canvas.

Entering the room, I look over at the wall being hovered by groups of people. I stand on my toes looking amongst the crowd, and there I am.

A multitude of portraits and candid photographs scattered the gallery's walls.

My Mind Away From Her
— Oren Samaras

There are several photographs; they must've all been

pictures he had gathered throughout the years. Some of these extended to high school and middle school. For years, Oren had used me as his muse, and I had no idea.

And now that I did, everyone else did as well. I looked away from their stares, not caring enough about their opinions, as I continued to look at the photographs that recalled distant memories from within my mind.

"You know my favorite has to be that one over there." A fair muscular arm points over to the wall on the right, which was beginning to gain attraction like this one. I look over to see Garrett. His coppered beard was trimmed, and his hair was pulled back. The round shape of his glasses formed his face even more.

I had met Garrett a few times when visiting Oren in Boston or whenever he came down to visit Oren, but I wouldn't say we were close or knew each other very well.

"Well, hello to you too," I respond before walking over to the wall where he had declared his favorite. My mouth completely drops at the sight of my nakedness as I'm bound by rope, the flowers hiding away the areas I would've been too uncomfortable to show. But the thought of what had happened right after the shoot had me heating up.

Was the air conditioning even on in this place?

"It's not because you're naked," Garrett says, clearing his throat and dragging my attention back over to him.

"It's because I know this work holds more value than all the others because even when he was giving them over to the curator, it took him a while to let go. So I know there's a lot of importance there."

Garrett looks away, staring back at the pictures of me on the wall. Which I had to say was quite odd, being that I was naked in them. Looking over at the plaque, my heart squeezes at the words.

Bound to me
— Oren Samaras

Somehow, those words still felt true despite the break between us.

"He misses you," Garrett murmurs. "He's just a stubborn prick." Garrett's words fill me with hope that there will possibly be a chance for Oren and me. All I needed to do was find him.

"If I can gather everyone's attention, please." A woman's voice breaks through the gallery's murmuring. Our bodies face a petite woman dressed in all black, and right next to her stands Oren.

He looks mesmerizing in his olive green suit, which brings out his eyes even more. He looks around the crowd as the woman, who I assume is the curator of the gallery, continues to speak. Oren's eyes lock on mine. The shocked look is there for an instant before he wipes it away after being introduced by the curator.

"Hello, everyone," Oren clears his throat, his eyes remaining on mine as he continues to speak.

"I first want to say how appreciative I am of you all being here. All the works in this gallery have been stacked up throughout the years, pushed into a corner of my studio covered for no one to see." Oren's stare remains consistent, though I'd normally look away, afraid of anyone noticing our interaction. For some reason, this time, I didn't really care. I wanted to hear his words, and I wanted to continue to look into his eyes.

"The gallery is based on one singular muse throughout the years, whose love I had for her kept on growing fonder. She became the center of my Universe; there was no value to life without her in it. And whether she was mine or someone else's, I just needed her a part of my life as a neighbor, friend, or roommate." Oren's chuckle at the last word sent my heart fluttering into a fit.

Its thumping increases with every breath. "Maybe this gallery isn't exactly what you'd all expect. But it tells the story of a boy who begins to fall in love with a girl, and now that he's a man, he continues to fall in love with the girl who is now a woman. And even though the years have passed, his mind still thinks of her, and his heart still beats for her."

At some point, Oren's speech stopped being for the crowd but rather for me. The tears in my eyes threatened to fall, but I held them back, aware of everyone staring at Oren and me.

"I hope you enjoy and value the vulnerability of an artist in love. Thank you." Claps erupt throughout the gallery, Garrett's and mine included. I took a couple of steps to walk over to Oren, but he was quickly bombarded by multiple people who looked to be important.

I wasn't entirely sure who they were, but I did know that they saw Oren's talent, and I couldn't have been prouder of him. Oren's eyes looked over at me to make sure I was still here waiting for him.

I gave him a short nod, letting him know I wasn't going anywhere.

We were bound together.

Chapter Thirty-Seven

Oren

These rich nuisances needed to get the fuck out of my way already. I was tired of shaking hands and learning names I would forget as soon as they left. The whole point of giving everyone a pamphlet at the door was so that they had my contact information right at hand. It was also a great way to ignore all these meet and greets.

I probably wouldn't have cared so much if Jasmine hadn't been standing in the middle of the gallery looking like part of the collection.

I needed to speak to her, but instead, I had to deal with this man whose name was Victor, or Vincent, or maybe Vinnie.

Fuck, if I knew.

I was thinking of how to make everything up to Jaz and hoping she'd forgive me. Garrett had pulled some sense into me these past few days, and though I wanted to be upset at her for meeting up with William, I couldn't. She had done nothing wrong, and when she had tried to explain, I had denied her any chance to do so.

I had let my jealousy define her actions rather than listening. I was the one who caused all the pain in the end, and now I so desperately wanted her back.

I had received her email earlier this week with her draft. I had been so fucking proud of her. Kora had told me that Terrence was able to find a literary agent who was very interested in working with Jaz.

Granted, she had said all that after berating me like the scum that I was. I had been so pissed when William hurt her, and now here I was doing the same thing. I was no better than him, but that didn't mean that I wouldn't beg her to forgive me and continue to show her every day of my life how much she deserves to be loved.

"Oren, you remember Robert." My curator Sofie asks, introducing me to an older man who looked, if not retired, on his way to it.

I didn't know who the fuck this Robert was, but regardless, I was going to have to sit through each conversation that everyone wanted to have with me while I watched Jasmine wait patiently for me.

Garrett was keeping her company, but if he got any closer to her, I would walk over there and knock some sense into the idiot.

I had caught him staring a little too long at the photographs of Jaz and I's shibari photoshoot. Even though I knew everyone would look at the pictures, they didn't need to stare at them for hours, especially not Garrett.

And as soon as the thought went through my mind,

Garrett's eyes looked up to meet mine, and that fucking bastard sent me a wink along with his devious smirk.

I was going to kill him.

I HAD BEEN HELD UP ALL NIGHT BY PEOPLE, AND SOFIE hadn't done a great job of making it easy for me to leave. At some point, I had lost sight of Jasmine, but I knew she was still around because she hadn't just come here to see my work; she was here to talk.

As the last of the people begin to leave, Garrett walks over to me, coming out of the room with the copper statue that everyone has been head over heels for. But there were only a few items that I didn't allow to be sold, and that was undoubtedly one of them.

That replica of beauty was all mine.

"She's in there, try not to screw it up. I'll handle the rest around here for tonight." Garrett says, giving me an encouraging pat on the back.

I rolled my eyes but muttered a "thank you" before walking over to Jasmine, who was facing the bronze figure.

"You came," I say, unsure of what to say.

"I wouldn't miss it for the world." She says, looking over at me, her doe eyes soaking into mine. God, I could see her hurt, all the hurt that I had caused.

"Jasmine, I'm sor—"

"Don't." She says, cutting me off, pressing her hand directly on my chest.

"But I need to tell you how sorry I am and that I should've

listened and that—” Jasmine groans, dropping her hand away from my chest, my body aching for her touch to be close once again.

“God, Oren, let me speak!” She shouts, taking me aback. I don't think I'd ever heard Jasmine shout like that before. I screwed up this time. I rub my hands against the fabric of my suit to stop my palms from sweating from the nerves.

“I know I'm a pessimist,” Jasmine begins. “I constantly stop myself from succeeding and pursuing what I love and want. And that's mostly because I think I'm a failure.” My throat tightens as I try to hold back my tears.

I fucking hated that she felt that way. Jasmine was perfect in many ways, and I wanted her to see that.

“Jasmine—” I say, but she cuts me off again before I can say another thing.

“No, just listen.” Jasmine's croaks.

“Oren, with you, I don't feel that way. With you, I feel like anything is possible and easier. So for the first time in my life, I'm going to go after what I want, or better yet— who I want.” Jasmine steps an inch closer with every word, and I want to tell her how sorry I am and how much I love her. I want to bring her into my arms and make love to her right here in this gallery, surrounded by my crazed obsession with her.

“Oren?” She whispers.

“Yes?” I ask, bringing my hands up to cup her cheeks.

“I love you. I want to be with you. Not as friends, not as a lie, but the real thing.” Jasmine reaches up, her arms wrapping around my neck to bring me down closer to her.

“Just you and me.”

Her lips graze my own as she whispers those last words

before I bring my lips onto hers. Kissing her as if it were our last time together on Earth. I had gone days without speaking to her because of my hurt ego, and somehow, she was here, making me feel better after I had hurt her.

I pull apart from our kiss, my fingers entangling themselves in her curls as I look down at her.

"What is it?" Jasmine's voice falters as she asks the question, obviously trying to understand why I was pulling away from her when she had just forgiven me so quickly.

But I didn't want to be let go that easily, not after what I did.

"Jasmine, I need you to hear me out now," I say.

Her lips curve into a smile as she nods, already aware of the apology coming her way.

"I should've listened to you that day. I just hadn't understood why you had lied, not when you could've told me the truth, and I would've been there to support you. And when I got there, the wedding planner directed me to where you had been, and my heart sank when she said you were in William's room. I began to believe the worst."

I fucking hated myself for not letting her explain herself that day.

Why had I been such a dick?

"Hey, I understand." Jasmine's hand grabs mine, bringing it to her lips.

"Oren, I know you were hurt, and you're sorry. All I want and need right now is you." Jasmine brings her other hand onto her shoulder, lowering the sleeve of her dress.

Fuck me. I didn't deserve this.

But I was going to take it.

My lips crash back onto Jasmine's, pulling her closer to

me as if the more she was pushed up against me, the more I could take back those days of loneliness and hurt.

My hands reach the bottom of the dress, pulling it up over her head. I needed her bare underneath me while I fucked her. I pull off my clothes, hating the layers that came with wearing a fucking suit.

"Wait, what if someone's around?" Jasmine asks, her sense taking over as she begins peering over at the entrance of the room. I pull off my underwear that's currently restricting my hard-on.

"Don't get shy on me now, love. People were gathering around to look at this sculpture and those sexy photos I had of you." I tease, bringing her lips back to mine, sucking on that plump bottom lip that begged to have my teeth marks on it.

Jasmine lets out a groan as my hands palm her ass, bringing her even closer to me. "Lean down and get your hands on the bench in front of the sculpture. I want your ass facing me." I growl, my hand smacking her ass, making her jolt in my arms before doing as I say.

Jasmine's back arches so fucking beautifully for me, waiting for me to please that beautiful pussy. I make my way over to her, my hardness yearning to be inside of her. But she wasn't ready yet. I was going to stretch that pussy out before making her tremble around my cock.

My left hand glides upwards, meeting the nape of her neck. I clench my fist around her hair before pulling her up towards me. My right-hand rubs gentle circles around the bundle of nerves that have her arching her back for more.

"You want my fingers deep inside you, don't you love?" I ask, giving her hair a tug for a response.

"Yes, please, Oren, I need you." She moans, shoving her ass closer to me.

My fingers glide up and down her wetness before inserting them in her pussy. Thrusting in and out of her slowly.

"Oren, please." Jasmine's moans make my cock stir. She needed me deep inside of her. I thrust my fingers in and out of her slick, curving it at just the right angle.

I couldn't wait any longer to be inside of her. I remove my fingers and grab ahold of my cock, inserting my tip at her entrance before grasping her hips and slamming her right into me.

"Fuck, Oren, I need more." She gasps as I pump in and out, feeling her pussy clenching tightly around me. I grab Jasmine's hair and have her face up at all the art within the gallery. I needed her to see how crazy she drove me. I hadn't even tasted her or fucked her, and she had somehow already engraved herself in my fucking mind.

"Look at how crazy you make me; you are the goddess I want to worship for all eternity, my love." Jasmine's pussy clenches around my cock at my words. Her hips moved forward and backward, following my rhythm.

My cock furthers itself deeper into her.

"Do you like how fucking crazy you make me love?" I ask, knowing damn well that I won't be getting any response from her. Not with her eyes rolling to the back of her head as she begins to come around my cock.

"Fuck me!" The words leave her mouth as her thighs begin to shake with her orgasm. I grab onto her hip as her hands grip the bench, my thrusts becoming harder and faster.

"Oren, I can't—" I smack my hand against her mouth, blocking out her words.

"You can and you will, my love," I demand, releasing my grip and switching positions. I sit on the bench and situate her right on top of me. I grab my cock and bring it back into her warmth, letting her sensitive cunt adjust itself around me again.

"That's right, love. Up and down, just like that." I encourage her as she picks up her pace. Her darkened nipples taunt me as her luscious breasts jump up and down. I bring them into my mouth, biting and sucking. Jasmine throws her head back, a moan escaping her lips and getting even louder as I start to thrust up into her. By the clenching and screams, I can tell she's close again, and this time, so am I.

A groan escapes my lips as I spill myself within her.

"Fuck, I could stay like this forever with you," I mumble into her chest as she runs her fingers through my hair.

"You sure you wouldn't get tired?" She teases, her chest rising as she catches her breath from our intense fuck.

"Have you not learned anything from this gallery? I'm obsessed with you. You're the only woman I ever want to laugh with, fight with, cry with, and you're definitely the only woman I ever want to sleep with." I grab her face, bringing her closer to hear my words and really take them in.

"You, my love, are it for me."

Chapter Thirty-Eight

Jasmine

In these passing days, I missed the warmth in the bed. But it had shown me how much I loved waking up to Oren in the mornings. It felt right to have him here again.

After the makeup sex in the gallery, we came back to the apartment to continue it on our bed. Multiple rounds had us knocked out for the majority of the morning.

Well, it currently had Oren knocked out this morning.

I wanted to wake him up to have breakfast together, but I enjoyed seeing him rest. I was proud of his work last night but hadn't told him so until we got home.

Oren responded by sitting me right on top of his face and showing me how much he missed me. Nothing else mattered to him at that moment—not the gallery, not the people he spoke with tonight, not the art itself. The only thing that mattered at that moment was us.

"What are you thinking about that has you blushing like that?" His hoarse voice sends shivers down my bare arms and legs, and I can't help but feel how my cheeks heat up at being caught fantasizing about last night.

"Well, if you must know, I was just thinking about how I need to get started decorating this room to my liking and actually make that the whole apartment.

Oren closes his eyes, humming in contentment at my excuse while sliding his hand up my thigh and squeezing it.

"I'm sure thinking of paint, drapes, and whatever the fuck you need to revamp the apartment is what had you clenching your thighs together a few moments ago." Oren murmurs.

I slap away his hand and let out a giggle as he grabs my waist and tugs me closer to him. His body is now pressed against me, and his lips create a trail of kisses from my shoulder to my neck.

"Terrence texted me a few days ago." I blurt out, unsure of how to bring it up. Oren pauses his movement but doesn't say a word, but his lips hover over my skin, awaiting my words before continuing.

"He found an agent interested in helping me get published," I explain, not wanting him to think it was anything other than a work message.

What Terrence and I had was short and nothing.

"Hm, did he now." Oren's lips go back to laying kisses on my neck. Though Oren is calm, he isn't shocked at my revelation, as if he had already known.

"It was you." I voice aloud as the thought comes into my head.

"What was me exactly?" Oren moves his kisses lower now, back to my shoulder and moving down to my breasts.

I grab his chin, pulling him up to look right at me. "You asked Terrence for help." I accuse, my lips forming into a giddy smile at Oren, pushing down his dislike for Terrence just for me.

"God, no." Oren's face scrunches up in disgust at even thinking about speaking to Terrence.

My smile stammers as I mentally scold myself for even thinking that. "I told Kora to do it for me." He admits, his eyes falling back down to my bare chest.

He was devouring every second of my nakedness before leaning down to continue his trail of kisses.

"That's the same thing!" I exclaim, but Oren only shrugs and continues moving downward.

"Oren— "

"No."

"But— "

"Jasmine, let me enjoy my breakfast." Oren's kisses grace my thighs as he opens them wider.

"Technically, it's lunch," I correct.

"I don't fucking care what it is, just that I want to have it every day that I wake up." Oren's breath tickles my inner thigh before he brings his mouth onto me, eroding away any questions I have for him.

None of it mattered, just him.

Oren led us back to the gallery, which was closed for the day. But Sofie, the curator who had introduced him to the audience last night, was there changing things around.

When he agreed to the gallery, Oren made it clear that he wanted only a few things back, and those would be available for viewing only. Everything else would stay in hopes of getting sold, even though I highly doubted anyone would want to have a painting of me in their home.

According to Oren, I was wrong. He had already made a couple of sales the first night. I was just relieved it hadn't been the sculpture or the risky Shibari photos. Though I didn't mind having them in his collection for viewing, I wouldn't have been too thrilled to have them in the hands of a random stranger.

"Hello!" Sofie's cheery voice rings as she opens the gallery door and lets us in.

"Hey, Sofie," Oren greets as he tugs me inside.

"Hey," I say, giving her a wave.

"It's so nice to finally see the muse in person; technically, I saw you last night, but with all the people bombarding Oren and me with questions and opinions, I didn't have the time to introduce myself. I'm Sofie, by the way." Her smile lit up her rosy cheeks, enhancing her skin's fairness. Her round, wide, rimmed glasses fell to the tip of her nose, which she kept pushing back up.

She seemed like a sweet woman who enjoyed what she did.

"I'm Jasmine," I say, keeping up with her and Oren's steady pace as she leads us into the back room.

"I had some of the workers last night bring the work that you wanted back here so there wouldn't be any confusion. But they didn't bring over the sculpture for some reason, which is odd because I was sure I told them too." Sofie explains, organizing the canvases and photographs that were on the table into a neat pile for us to carry.

My eyes shoot out at the thought of one of the workers having spotted Oren and me having sex, which had obviously derailed them from continuing their tasks. Oren's smug smirk plays on his lips as he chuckles.

"Hm, maybe they just forgot, or maybe it was just too heavy," Oren suggests, peering over at me.

I hate him.

I roll my eyes and look towards Sofie to ensure she isn't looking before flipping him off. Oren's smile widens as he turns his attention away from me and back to Sofie.

"Don't worry about the sculpture. Keep it around for a while, and then when you feel like it should go, just give me a call," Oren says, gathering all the items in his arms.

Sofie's eyes light up at the gesture, not failing to show her excitement of keeping the copper figure around longer.

"That'd be amazing. I think it was a favorite last night; it was definitely mine. If you want, you can take a look around. If there's anything else you still want to keep, just let me know. I'll be over in my office." Sofie nods over to a door at the end of the room.

"Thanks, Sofie; I think I'm good with what I picked, but if *the muse* wants to keep something, I'll let you know."

Sofie gives her head a slight nod before walking away. Oren turns around to face me as he gathers all his work into his arms. The Shibari photographs are placed right on top of it all.

"Did you want something for yourself, or are you ready to go?" Oren asks.

I reach my hand out, grabbing the first photograph of the collection. "I'm curious about something," I state.

"What's that?" Oren asks.

"If your whole gallery was based on me, how come you had another model planned for the photoshoot?" Oren's lips turn into a sly grin, already giving me the answer I needed.

"You lied," I murmur.

"I did." Oren admits, "I wanted this photoshoot for my exhibit, but I also knew you wouldn't do it if I had just asked you."

My jaw remains on the floor as Oren reveals the truth. "Plus, I just wanted another excuse to see you naked." My hand reaches out and slaps Oren's arm before putting the photograph right back on top.

"You're a pig." I jab as I turn around to walk away with Oren beside me.

"According to that first draft you sent me, baby, I'm your muse." I stop walking to peer back up at him. He hadn't replied to my email, so I assumed he hadn't read it.

"You read it," I whisper in disbelief.

"Three times... and I liked it." Oren leads us out of the gallery and towards the car, the building door locking automatically.

"Three times?" I ask, making sure I heard him right. Oren places everything in the back seat before opening the passenger door for me.

"Three times, my love, and I can't wait to read it a million times more."

I enter the car and buckle myself in. Oren walks over to

his side of the vehicle and buckles himself in before bringing himself over to the middle console. He gives me a peck on the lips before starting up the car.

"Just so you know, the next time around, I better get the first draft before Kora. She may be your friend, but I'm still your best friend." Oren says, pulling out of the parking spot and laying his hand on my thigh.

"I promise you I will."

And I meant it.

Chapter Thirty-Nine

Jasmine

I open the front door, immediately welcomed by the smell of tomato and herbs. Oren said he would get started on dinner for us tonight and let me know he was making eggplant parmesan. Which usually meant he was making the tomato sauce from scratch.

"It smells delicious." I rave as I walk into the kitchen, setting my purse down on the stool. Oren faces the stove but looks incredible just to stare at from the back. The sculpted muscles on his back take shape through his white shirt, which had been a risk to wear since he was handling tomato sauce.

"I hope you like the taste just as much as you like the smell," Oren turns around to face me. I take a couple of strides towards him, his hands already meeting the back of my neck to inch me closer, his lips locking with my own.

I moan as I gently press my hand against his chest to

move him away. "How much longer? I'm starving." I ask, trying to ignore the grumbling of my stomach. I hadn't eaten anything all day because I had been a bit worried about meeting Melanie for the first time.

I hadn't thought that she'd be a monster, ready to terrorize me as soon as I entered her office, but since Terrence hadn't said much about what to expect, especially when I asked, it only made me get even more anxious about the whole meeting.

But in reality, everything had gone super well. We talked about my ideas for the novel and what was coming next. She was also quite excited about having my first draft completed. She had let me know that I'd be hearing back from her in a few days, but in the meantime, I could continue with my revisions.

Oren also gave me some numbers of contractors that he wanted me to look at before starting renovations on the bookstore. I would start looking at those tomorrow, as well as compiling my Pinterest photos into a file to choose the exact look for my bookstore café.

Everything seemed to be manifesting itself before me. Everything that had once been just an aspiration had become my reality. And all because the man of my dreams, who had been in front of me the whole time, decided to start a little lie.

"Here, help me set the table. Kora said she was on her way about a few minutes ago, so she should be here any second." Oren says, passing over the plates to me and turning back around to grab the utensils.

We set up the table for three as we wait for Kora to walk in at any minute. We had invited her over to share the news about Melanie and the beginning of the renovations in the bookstore.

I'm sure she'll try to persuade me that the café needs a piano for live music, but I'll just have to make it known that it won't fit our budget.

"Honey, I'm home!" Kora sings as she walks into the apartment, holding a pastry box that I was sure contained her favorite cookies.

"Finally, I'm starving." Oren groans, bringing his cooked meal to the center of the table. I sit right next to him as Kora sits across from me, already devouring the food with her eyes, as anyone would.

"This looks delicious; thank you, Jaz." Kora smiles and grabs the utensils to serve herself.

"Why are you thanking her?" Oren grumbles, "I'm the one that cooked."

Kora rolls her eyes, passing me the serving spoon. " Yes, but she's the one who invited me."

Oren and Kora continue to bicker, so I end up serving Oren food, too, before digging in. Oren looks at me as I'm halfway through my plate before ending their unnecessary banter.

"Sorry, love. It's a neighbor thing," Oren defends as he takes a bite of his own meal.

"No, it's not," Kora argues, mouth full of food.

"We shouldn't have invited her; she has an attitude." Oren jokes, or I assume he is by his playful tone.

"Um, I am just as much in this relationship as you two are, so if this is major news, I need to be here," Jasmine argues before tearing her eyes away from Oren to give me her full attention.

"No, you aren't," Oren says.

God, this was never-ending.

"Hey, if it weren't for me, you two would still be moping around, upset at fate for making you friends instead of lovers. God, you guys were so insufferable." Kora grumbles through her chewing.

Oren's eyes and my own meet as Kora continues to imitate us, asking her questions about the other, our faces heating up simultaneously. Once Kora's teasing ends, the table is met with a brief moment of silence as the three of us stare at one another before breaking out into a fit of laughter.

This had all felt right, being with them here.

Fate had led me to the one person I had least expected.

But that made our love just that more enticing.

Epilogue

Jasmine

One Year Later

I let out a groan as I move the table with a pile of heavy books towards a different part of the store. Each move started with a few tilts here and there, and now I was going insane moving it from one side to another.

"I think it's fine right in the center." Oren pitches.

I roll my eyes and sigh, turning around to meet him. I try to explain that I can't leave the table of books in the middle because it disrupts the flow of the place when people begin walking around.

"It disturbs the customers," I argue, pushing the table against the corner wall that, for some reason, felt much farther away than it should.

"I think it just disturbs you. Besides, I want the first thing for people to see when they walk in to be those fabulous books signed by the author herself, who so happens to be the owner of this bookstore," Oren says, getting in the way of me moving my table.

"Oren, move." I swat my hand on his arm and continue pushing on the table, which won't budge with him in front of it.

Oren's smile makes a brief appearance at my attempt at trying to move the table before quickly disappearing to keep up with his seriousness.

"Jasmine, I did not cheer you on through the race to have your books pushed to the back of the store. I'm an investor in this store and want them to be in the front." Oren grabs the ends of the table with all the books piled on top and lifts it, bringing it front and center.

My eyes can't help but admire the bulging veins and the flexing of his muscles as he brings it over.

Wait.

He pulled the investor card.

Snap out of it, Jasmine.

"You can't pull the investor card on me." I snap.

"I just did, and the reason I did so was because you want to throw your published books into a dark fucking corner of the room so that you don't have to feel some type of way if people choose not to buy your book." I straighten my posture, crossing my arms over my chest as he continues to see right through me.

Of course, I was afraid of people rejecting my book. At least I didn't have to see it happen if they did so at other book-stores. I didn't even want to sell it here in the first place. Oren used his investor card again, which was an idea that we had agreed on when he felt that there were some things that he should have an opinion on.

I didn't really understand at the time why he would need it, but the only two times he had used it were to reference having my book out in the open at my store, which made me fully aware of his intentions.

And like every promise, we pinky swore, and there was no breaking those.

"Jasmine, no one is going to say no to book porn. Especially a well-written one, so get behind that counter as I become your first customer of the day." I roll my eyes before stomping away towards the counter.

Oren makes his way towards the door, flipping the sign to open and walking out. He walks away from the store only to turn back a minute later and enter it again.

"Hi there," Oren greets, walking up to my counter.

"Hello," I say through my smile, trying to compose the laughter building up in my chest.

"You wouldn't happen to know of this new author who just published her debut romance novel, would you? Her name is Jasmine Monroe. I've also heard her called a divine goddess, which I completely agree with." Oren says, trailing his eyes down my body.

I lean over and grab his chin to face my eyes again before nudging my head towards my signed books that were now front and center in the store.

It had taken a couple of rejections from publishing houses until I finally got one yes. Finally, after a year, it was here in my store. And Oren was going to make my first buy special, just as he had done when he was my first buyer at the opening of the bookstore café.

It's been a little over a year since Oren and I got together, and somehow, we still manage to prioritize our friendship.

Oren takes his time picking the book, acting like a customer looking for their next buy. He then turns around, brings the book over to me, and places it on the counter.

"This is the one," Oren says, handing me the book. A bookmark is already placed within it, which I hadn't remembered adding to it. I open the book to the page where the bookmark is held, my eyes following the words written on it.

Will

You

Marry

Me?

I shut the book as a gasp escapes my lips. Looking up, I see Oren gone from my eye level and now on his knees in front of me. A beautiful golden band holding onto a pave cushion-cut diamond lies perfectly on the black velvet box. My heart skips a thousand beats. I open my mouth to respond, but the words are gone.

"Jasmine, my love, I wasn't sure how to do this. If you asked me anything about you, I'd have the answer. But I didn't know how to propose to you. I wanted it to be special, but I wasn't quite sure how to make it special. So, I thought about what you love." Oren brings out his hand for me to take. I walk around the counter to get closer. He removes the ring from the velvet cushion, places his knee on the floor, and holds the ring up to me.

"Jasmine, this store is our first product together. And it will be the first of many." Oren teases.

I can't help but let a sob of joy escape my lips as he continues his speech. "So it's only right that I get on one knee and propose to you in the first place. We started our dreams with the book that brought you closer to me. Jasmine Monroe, please don't keep me waiting any longer. Will you marry me?" Oren asks, his hand slightly shaking as he holds out the ring.

"Yes," I answered. "Of course, I will; that's not even a question."

Tears stream down my face as Oren slides the ring onto my finger and brings himself up to press his lips against mine.

"You, my love, are mine forever," Oren whispers.

"That sounds like a plan," I respond, pressing my lips to his.

Forever with Oren had always been the plan, but the ring on my finger only validated it even more.

He was my muse forever.

And I was his.

Chapter One

Present Day

At twenty-two years of age, I never saw myself in the position of having to run around my penthouse just to try and get away from my overbearing mother. I wouldn't have allowed her to come in if I knew she'd be chasing me around my home.

"Eloise, please just listen to me!" My mother pesters as she follows me down the hall.

"This helped me get pregnant when I was having a rough time, too."

I groan in mortification.

This could not be happening right now.

"Mother, I don't need any of your remedies," I shout, reaching out to the nearest door and quickly entering it and locking it before she could catch up to me.

I hear my mother's body hit the door and can't help but let

out a chuckle. It served her right to come into my home just to pressure me into having a child.

I was fortunate not to have heard anything from them when William and I had made our six-month mark in our marriage. But now that we would be making a year in a couple of weeks, their persistence to ensure I got pregnant was becoming consistent.

It was all because my marriage hadn't been enough, in their eyes. My father agreed to merge his company with Wren Technology, which guaranteed him one less company in the competition and a *son* to take over for him. Of course, my marriage had not been enough to settle the agreement. My father wanted to make sure that our company stayed within our bloodline, and that's where my uterus took part in his plan.

It's not that I didn't want children; I just didn't think this was the right time to bring in a child—not that it even mattered. To have a child, you'd need to actually partake in the activity that leads to the making of one, and William and I had only ever done it once.

And that had been a mistake.

"Eloise, honestly, stop acting like a child. This is a normal conversation to have. All you have to do is rub the oils on your—"

"Absolutely not, mother!"

A deep chuckle has me peer my head up to look over to the desk in the middle of the study.

William sat there in all his glory, laying back on his desk chair as he looked over at me in amusement. His dark hair was slicked back, and he was dressed casually in his jeans and black shirt. His beard was longer than when I had first met him. After our wedding, he had let it grow out and maintained it at that length. It made him look older, but I liked it. His blue eyes radiated from across the room. There was something about William that made you feel like he knew exactly what you were thinking.

Help me, I mouth at him, my mother's rant continuing from the other side of the door.

William lifts himself up from his chair, walking over to me. I assume he's heading towards the door to speak with my mother, so I move out of his way. But his arm shoots out and blocks my way as he corners me into the wall. I look up to face him, his eyes dragging down my body. He did it quite often; I wasn't sure if it was because he liked what he saw or hated it completely.

Regardless, I was too scared to ask.

"How long has she been pestering you about this, blondie?" His voice is strict, and I swear I can hear a bit of annoyance in it, too.

"I don't know, a couple of weeks ago," I reply.

"Eloise." I can hear the sternness in his voice as he continues to look at me. His overbearing presence makes me feel even meeker.

I had entered his study because it was the first door closest to me, and I thought he wouldn't be home today. It was Tuesday, which guaranteed that he would be in the office. But I was obviously mistaken.

"Like three months? Maybe… I'm not too sure." Actually I'm positive it's been three months but maybe if I sound confused or unsure he won't be as angry with me.

"God, blondie, why didn't you say anything before?" He groans, pinching his nose in a stressed manner.

I only give him a shrug in response, not wanting to get into any detail about how I didn't want to be more of a disruption in his life than I already was.

William had given up a lot just to satisfy our parent's wishes to marry us. Before we married, he had been engaged to Jasmine Monroe, a beautiful woman I could never compare to.

Especially not in his eyes.

"Eloise, it's going to be a year, and you still aren't pregnant. You have to fulfill your duty as his wife." My mother's commentary only has my stomach tying a tighter knot that will possibly end up with me vomiting my breakfast. Her commentary is durable as long as I'm the only person in the room having to hear it. But with said husband, who I lacked fulfilling my wifely duties with, standing right in front of me, it makes me even more anxious and embarrassed.

William lets out a curse under his breath and reaches for the door handle. He unlocks it and opens it to find my mother and her many remedies in hand.

Mom stops her, ranting as she looks up at William. He practically towers over her tiny frame, but then again, he did the same with my own, being that he was 6'4. That had been something I found out on our honeymoon. Our drunken banter led us from talking about our height and our feelings to speaking only with our bodies in the hotel room.

But it had all been a mistake, just something that happened in the spur of the moment.

"Oh, hello there, William; Eloise hadn't told me you would be here today." My mother glares over at me through the tiny space William left between him and the wall.

"It's because she didn't know; I intended to go to the

office, but all my meetings for today were canceled, so working from home today seemed fitting," William answers, his eyes practically staring into my mother's soul as the silence grows thick between them.

"Clarice, do you think I'm unable to fulfill my husbandly duties in getting my wife pregnant?" William asks, puzzling me with his question. He had never spoken to my parents like that.

"N-no." My mother stutters, realizing she's crossed a line.

"Great. I suggest you never bring that topic back up again in this house. When Eloise and I decide to have a child, we will make sure it happens. Until then, no more harassing my wife."

With that, William closes the door to the study, leaving my mother out there on her own. Hopefully, that was more than enough for her to get the hint to leave.

William turns to face me again, remaining silent before stepping toward me.

"Blondie, what did I say on our wedding day?" William murmurs.

I shrug, recalling his private vows to me.

"That you were not my parents; you are my equal. That you'd always take my side." I recall.

"Correct. So the next time something like this happens, you let me know instantly, okay?" William demands.

A short nod is all William needs to return to his desk. I make my way back to the door, but his voice stops me from leaving.

"Oh, and blondie, let the chef know what you want to eat tonight; we're having dinner."

I furrow my brows in confusion, "we have guests

coming?" I didn't know we would have people coming over tonight. Usually, William would add it to our calendar so that it wouldn't catch either of us off guard. But nothing has been put on the agenda for this week.

"No, it will be just you and me," William states, looking through the paperwork on his desk and not bothering to look up at me for one second.

We never had dinner together, not like that.

Not just us.

"I don't really eat dinner unless—" William lifts his gaze up at me, his eyes darkening at my words.

"Eloise... pick a dish for tonight at six."

"Okay," I manage to murmur as I step out back into the hall, away from my husband's intense glare.

Acknowledgments

Firstly, to my parents, Eddie and Ana, who have always encouraged me to live out my dream, supported me through every change in my life, and cheered me on. I hope I continue to make you proud.

To Jenny, I could write an essay on how much your encouragement and support have gotten me to where I am today. No one could ever top your belief in me. Thank you for supporting all of my book ideas and, most importantly, for encouraging me to pursue this one.

To Michael, Thank you for instilling your "who the hell cares?" mentality in me. It's helped me defeat my anxiety on the days I felt that I wasn't meant to be a writer.

To Lila and Katya — Ladies, I did it! I'm so happy you guys were able to be part of this journey with me, from listening to me rant about my ideas and characters to helping me make candles and stickers for my ARC packages. Thank you for your support.

To Marcela and Michell — My girls! You have no idea how much your excitement and constant check-ups pushed me to finish this book. I can always count on you guys to be in my corner, cheering me on, and I promise I'll always be in yours.

To Ashley — I hope you can say that my writing has improved since our middle school days. Crazy enough, you've always loved it and continue to want to read everything I write. I hope your love and support never fade away.

To Farhan, Thank you for being my Oren. For believing in me when I didn't believe in myself. For motivating me when I wanted to give up. Not every woman has been able to find herself an Oren, and I am so grateful to say that I found myself one. I'm for sure never giving mine up.

Lastly, to every English teacher I ever had. I finally did it! Thank you for being my introduction to the world of literature. I have fallen completely in love with it.

About the Author

Eliana Vazquez is a self-published author from Kearny, New Jersey. She graduated from the University of New Haven, where she majored in communications, her concentration being in Film and Media Production. When she's not at her desk writing you can find her enabling her coffee addiction and buying more books than she could ever read.

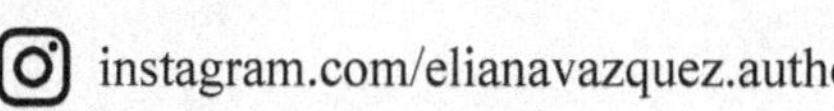
instagram.com/elianavazquez.author

tiktok.com/@elianavazquez.author

* 9 7 9 8 9 8 9 4 1 0 4 0 8 *